IT WAS DARK OUT.
THAT DID NOT HELP.

Neither did the fact that I didn't see them coming. I put up a fight, though. I dented some heads good with the weighted, oak head buster I carry when I go out. I tossed one guy through the only glass window in the street. But I just never got rolling. I had no chance to use the tricks I had stashed up my sleeves.

Somebody whapped me up side the head with a house. I think it was a house. Had to be a house. No mere man could hit me that hard. The lights went out—with me still trying to figure out who and why.

When I woke up, I was bouncing along face downward, staring at a floor sliding past inches from my nose. Four guys were carrying me, and I didn't like their looks. They weren't the brunos I'd danced with earlier. Those had been standard lowlife, out for the price of a drink. These clowns wore dirty, ragged uniforms.

That failed to cheer me up....

Deadly Quicksilver Lies

GLEN COOK

A ROC BOOK

ROC
Published by the Penguin Group
Penguin Books USA Inc., 375 Hudson Street,
New York, New York 10014, U.S.A.
Penguin Books Ltd, 27 Wrights Lane,
London W8 5TZ, England
Penguin Books Australia Ltd, Ringwood,
Victoria, Australia
Penguin Books Canada Ltd, 10 Alcorn Avenue,
Toronto, Ontario, Canada M4V 3B2
Penguin Books (N.Z.) Ltd, 182–190 Wairau Road,
Auckland 10, New Zealand

Penguin Books Ltd, Registered Offices:
Harmondsworth, Middlesex, England

First published by ROC,
an imprint of Dutton Signet,
a division of Penguin Books USA Inc.

First Printing, March 1994
10 9 8 7 6 5 4 3 2

 REGISTERED TRADEMARK—MARCA REGISTRADA

Printed in Canada

1

There ain't no justice, I guarantee absodamnlutely. There I was, comfy as could be, feet on my desk, a pint of Weider's porter in my hand, Espinosa's latest potboiler in my other hand, and Eleanor reading over my shoulder. She understood Espinosa better than I did. For once the Goddamn Parrot wasn't squawking. I sucked up that sweet silence more enthusiastically than I did the beer.

Some fool went to hammering on my door.

His pounding had an arrogant, impatient edge. Meant it would be somebody I didn't want to see. "Dean! See who that is! Tell him to go away. I'm out of town. On a secret mission for the king. Won't be back for years. And I wouldn't buy what he's selling anyway, if I *was* home."

Nobody moved. My cook-slash-housekeeper-slash-factotum was the one who was out of town. I was at the mercy of wannabe clients and the Goddamn Parrot.

Dean had gone to TemisVar. One of his herd of homely nieces was going to get married. He wanted to make sure her fool fiance didn't wake up before it was too late.

The pounding continued bruising my door. I'd just installed it, replacing one broken down by a villain who couldn't take a hint. "Damned insensitive jerk!" I muttered. Hollering and threats backed the hammering. The neighbors were going to get upset. Again.

5

Sleepy, puzzled noises came from the small front room between my office and the door. "I'll kill him if he wakes that talking chicken." I glanced at Eleanor. She offered no advice. She just hung there, baffled by Espinosa.

"Guess I better dent a head before I got to deal with another citizens' committee." Or had to put up a new door. Doors aren't only not cheap, they're hard to come by.

I dropped my feet, stretched my six feet two, got going. The Goddamn Parrot made a noise. I peeked into his room.

The little buzzard was only talking in his sleep. Excellent! He was one pretty monster. He had a yellow head, blue neck ruff, red and green body and wings. His tail feathers were long enough I could maybe someday cash in with a band of gnomes who needed decorations for their hats. But a monster he was, for sure. Somewhere sometime somebody put a curse on that foul-beaked vulture so he's got the vocabulary of a stevedore. He lives to be obnoxious.

He was a gift from my "friend" Morley Dotes. Made me wonder about the nature of friendship.

The Goddamn Parrot—dba Mr. Big—stirred. I got out of there before he took a notion to wake up.

I have a peephole in my front door. I peeped. I muttered, "Winger. Wouldn't you know?" My luck and water have plenty in common, especially always heading downhill. Winger was a natural disaster looking for a place to happen. A stubborn disaster, too. I knew she'd pound away till hunger got her. She didn't look underfed.

She wouldn't worry about what the neighbors thought, either. She noticed the opinions of others the way a mastodon noticed undergrowth in the woods.

I opened up. Winger moved forward without being invited in. I stayed put and almost got trampled. She is big and beautiful, but her candle doesn't burn too bright. "Need to talk to you, Garrett," she said. "I need some help. Business."

I should have known better. Hell. I *did* know better. But times were dull. Dean wasn't around to nag me. The Dead Man had been asleep for weeks. I had nobody but the Goddamn Parrot for company. All my friends were beset by lady friends, a trial that hadn't befallen me during any recent epoch. "All right. I know I'm gonna be sorry, but all right. I'll give you a listen. Promising nothing."

"Hows about a brew while we're jawing?" Winger shy? I don't think so. She headed for the kitchen. I took a look around outside before I shut the door. You never knew what might be tagging after Winger. She didn't have sense enough to look back. She survived on luck, not skill.

"Awk! Holy hooters! Garrett! Check them gazoombies."

Damn! What I got for not closing the door to the small front room.

The street showed me only a clutter of people and animals and dwarves and elves and a squadron of centaur immigrants. The usual.

I shut the door. I went to the small front room and closed that door, ignoring outraged allegations of neglect. "Stow it, bird. Unless you want to get neglected right into some ratman's dinner pot."

He laughed. He mocked.

He was right. I have no use for ratmen, but I wouldn't do that to them.

Then he yelled rape. I didn't worry. Winger had heard it before.

"Help yourself, why don't you?" I said when I hit the kitchen, like she hadn't helped herself already. She'd glommed the biggest mug in the house, too.

She winked. "Here's to ya, big guy." She knew exactly what she was doing but didn't have the grace to be embarrassed. "You and your sidekick in there."

"Yeah? You want a parrot?" I drew myself a mug, settled at the kitchen table.

"That crow in a clown suit? What would I do with him?" She planted herself opposite me, beyond dunes of dirty dishes.

"How about get yourself an eyepatch, get into the pirate business?"

"Don't know if I could dance with a pegleg. It ever say 'Shiver me timbers' or 'Argh, matey'?"

"What?"

"What I thought. You're trying to stick me with a substandard bird."

"Huh?"

"That's no sailor bird, Garrett. That critter is pure city. Knows more gutter talk than me."

"So teach him some sea chanties."

"Yo ho ho. Dean finally croak?" She stared at the dishes.

"He's out of town. Got a niece that's getting married. Looking for a part-time job?"

Winger had met some of Dean's nieces, all of whom brought new meaning to the word homely. She controlled her astonishment, though, and pretended to miss my hint about the dishes. "I was married once."

Oh, boy. I hoped she didn't get started.

She was still married but didn't let legal trivia encumber her. "Don't go misty on me, Winger."

"Misty? You shitting me? After that, Hell is gonna look good."

Winger is a tad unusual, case you haven't noticed. She is twenty-six, as tall as I am, and built like the proverbial masonry privy—on an epic scale. Also, she has what some guys think is an attitude problem. Just can't figure out how to stay in her place.

"You want my help," I reminded. Just a poke. My keg wasn't bottomless. I smirked. Maybe she was desperate enough to take the Goddamn Parrot off my hands.

"Uhm." She would get to the point only after she had mooched her fill. That quantity would clue me as to the state of her fortunes.

"You're looking good, Winger." Even Winger likes to hear that."Must be doing all right."

She assumed I meant her outfit. That was new and, as always, remarkable. "Where I work, they want you should dress snappy."

I kept a straight face. "Unusual" is only the most cautious, gentlest way to characterize Winger's taste. Let's say you couldn't lose her in a crowd. If she went around with the Goddamn Parrot on her shoulder, nobody would notice the bird. "That outfit *is* pretty timid. When you worked for that fat freak Lubbock . . ."

"It's the territory. These guys want you should blend in."

Again I kept my face straight. Being amused by Winger when Winger isn't amused can be hazardous to your health—especially if you're dim enough to, say, crack wise about her blending in.

"Old-timer's gone, eh? What about the ugly thing?" She meant my partner, the Dead Man, so-called because he hasn't run any footraces since somebody stuck a knife in him four hundred years ago. "Ugly thing" is apt. He isn't human. He's a Loghyr, which explains why he's still hanging around so long after he was murdered. Loghyr are slow and stubborn, especially when it comes to sloughing off the old mortal clay. They're deliberate, he would say.

"Asleep. Been weeks since he bugged me. I'm in heaven."

Winger sneered, flipped blond hair out of her face. "Likely to wake up?"

"Maybe if the house catches on fire. Got something to hide?" The Dead Man's big trick is mind reading.

"No more than usual. I was just thinking, it's been a dry spell. Way I hear, weather ain't been so hot for you, neither."

That was my pal Winger, so shy and demure. Somehow, with her, the romance and adventure were absent. "Thought you had desperate business."

"Desperate?"

"You like to tore the door down. You woke up the Goddamn Parrot with your whooping and hollering." That about-to-become-roasted squab was holding forth up front. "I figured you had killer elves slavering on your trail."

"I just wish. I told you how my luck's been. I was just trying to get your attention." She refilled her mug, did mine, headed for my office. "All right, Garrett. Business first."

She paused, listened. T.G. Parrot was on a roll. She shrugged, slipped into my office. I followed quickly. Sometimes things fall into Winger's pockets if you're not there to keep an eye on them.

I wriggled into my chair, safe behind my desk. Eleanor guarded my back. Winger scowled at the painting, then eyed my book. "Espinosa? Ain't that a little heavy for you?"

"It's a real thriller." Espinosa *was* beyond me, mostly. He tended to make a big deal out of questions that wouldn't have occurred to anybody who worked for a living.

I'd gone to visit a lady friend at the Royal Library. The book was all I got.

"Philosophy is thrilling? Like a hemorrhoid. The man should've got a hobby."

"He did. Philosophy. Since when can you read?"

"You don't need to act so surprised. I been learning. Got to do something with my ill-gotten gains, don't I? I thought maybe some learning might come in handy someday. But mostly what I've learned is studying don't make you no smarter about people."

I started to agree. I know some pretty dim academics, people who live in another world. Winger cut me off. "Enough chit-chat. Here's the gig. This old broad name of Maggie Jenn is maybe gonna come see you. I don't know what's up, but my boss is willing to pay a shitload of money to find out. This Jenn crone knows me so I can't get close to her. What I figured was, why don't I get you to let her hire you, then you let me know what she's up to and I can take that to my boss."

Vintage Winger.

"Maggie Jenn?"

"That's the name."

"Seems like it ought to ring a bell. Who is she?"

"You got me. Just some old broad off the Hill."

"The Hill?" I leaned back, just a harried man of affairs taking a moment out to relax with an old friend. "I have a case."

"What is it this time? A stray lizard?" She laughed. Her laughter sounded like geese headed north for the winter. "Meow, meow."

A few days earlier, I'd gotten stung by an old biddy who'd hired me to look for her beloved missing Moggie. Never mind the details. It's embarrassing enough just *me* knowing. "That's on the street?"

Winger swung her feet onto my desk. "All over it."

Dean was in it deep. *I* hadn't told a soul.

"Best Garrett story I heard in a while, too. Thousand marks for a cat? Come on."

"You know how some old ladies are about their cats." The cat hadn't been the problem, really. The problems started when I found a real animal that was a ringer for the imaginary, red herring beast. "Who would suspect a sweet old lady of wanting to set him up for a fall guy in a scam?"

Honk honk, har har. "I would've got suspicious when she wouldn't come to my house."

What saved me was finding that cat. I caught on when I tried to take him home. "Yeah."

The Dead Man might have saved me all the embarrassment. Had he been awake.

Part of the discomfort of the mess was knowing he'd never stop reminding me about it. "Never mind that. Since we're talking about old ladies, tell me what this Maggie Jenn is going to want."

"I figure she's gonna ask you to kill somebody."

"Say what?" That wasn't what I expected. "Hey! You know—"

2

Somebody else was trying out my front door. This somebody had a fist of stone bigger than a ham. "I have a bad feeling about this," I muttered. "Whenever platoons of people start thumping the door ..."

Winger stowed her leer. "I'll disappear."

"Don't wake the Dead Man."

"You kidding?" She pointed toward the ceiling. "I'll be up there. Find me when you're done."

I was afraid of that.

Having a no-strings, no-complications friendship can have its own complications.

The small front room had grown quiet. I paused to eavesdrop. Not one obscenity marred the precious silence. T.G. Parrot was asleep again.

I thought about making it that jungle pigeon's last nap, the beginning of the big sleep, the longest voyage, the ...

Boom boom boom.

I peeked through the peephole. By-the-numbers Garrett, that's me. Fixing to live a thousand years.

All I saw was a smallish redhead facing three-quarters away, staring at something. That little bit did all that pounding? She was stronger than she looked. I opened the door. She continued staring up the street. I leaned forward cautiously.

The neighborhood pixie teens were chucking rotten fruits off the cornices and gutters of an ugly old three-story half a block up Macunado. A band of gnomes

13

below dodged and cursed and shook their walking sticks. They were all old, clad in the usual drab gray, with whiskers. Not beards, whiskers, like you see in paintings of old-time generals and princes and merchant captains. All gnomes seem to be old and out of fashion. I've never seen a young one or a female one.

One spry little codger, chanting a colorful warsong about discount rates and yam futures, pegged a broken cobblestone hard enough to actually hit a pixie. It did a somersault off a gargoyle's head. The gnomes pranced around and waved their sticks in glee and sent up an ave to the Great Arbitrager. Then the pixie brat opened his wings and soared. His laughter was a mocking squeak.

I told the redhead, "An exercise in futility. All sound and fury. Been going on all month. Nobody's gotten hurt yet. Probably all die of shame if anybody did." Gnomes are that way. Gladly make fortunes financing wars but don't want to watch the bloodshed.

I spied a sedan chair at streetside down toward Macunado's intersection with Wizard's Reach. Beside it stood something half man and half gorilla with hands that fit the prescription for whatever it was that had tried to demolish my door. "That thing tame?"

"Mugwump? He's a sweetheart. And as human as you are." The redhead's tone suggested she might be, unwittingly, insulting friend Mugwump.

"Can I help you?" Boy, would I like to help her. Mugwump was old news.

I make a point of being nice to redheads, at least till they're not nice to me. Redhead was always my favorite color, barely edging blonde and brunette.

The woman turned to me. "Mr. Garrett?" Her voice was low, husky, sexy.

I didn't owe any money. "Guilty." Surprise, surprise. She was a good decade older than my first guess. But time had stolen nothing. She was proof on the hoof that aging produces fine wines. Second-guessing,

I put her over thirty-five but under forty. Me, I'm a tender, innocent thirty and don't usually look for them quite so ripe.

"You're staring, Mr. Garrett. I thought that was impolite."

"Huh? Oh. Yeah. Excuse me."

The Goddamn Parrot started muttering in his sleep. Something about interspecies necrophilia. That got me back to the real world. "What can I do for you, madam?" Other than the obvious, if you're looking for volunteers. Hoo.

I was amazed. Yeah, female of the species is my soft spot, my blind side, but the mature type didn't usually get me. Whatever, something about this one totally distracted me. And she knew it.

Businesslike, Garrett. Businesslike.

"Ma'am, Mr. Garrett? Am I that far past it?"

I sputtered. I stumbled around and tripped over my tongue till it was black with footprints. She finally had mercy and smiled. "Can we get in out of the weather?"

"Sure." I stepped aside, held the door. What was wrong with the weather? It couldn't have been nicer. There were barely enough clouds to keep you from falling into a sky as blue as you will ever hope to see.

She brushed past without tricks, just close because she had to. I shut my eyes. I ground my teeth. I babbled, "My office is the second door on the left. I can't offer much but beer or brandy. My man Dean is away." The woman had to be a witch. Or I was out of practice. Bad.

"Brandy would be perfect, Mr. Garrett."

Of course. Pure class. "Coming right up. Make yourself at home." I dove into the kitchen. Dig dig dig till I found some brandy. A bit of a tippler, Dean hides the stuff all over so I won't know how much he has bought. I poured from a bottle that I hoped contained good stuff. What did I know about brandy?

Beer is *my* favorite food. I zipped to the office. The seasoned redhead had set up camp in the client's chair. She frowned as she studied Eleanor. "Here you go."

"Thank you. An interesting painting. There's a lot there if you look long enough."

I glanced at my honey as I settled. She was a lovely blonde, terrified, fleeing something only hinted at in the painting's background. If you looked at that painting right, though, you could read the whole evil story. There was magic in it, though much of that had gone once I got the man who murdered Eleanor.

I told the story. My visitor was a good listener. I managed to avoid getting totally lost in my own chemistry. I observed carefully. I suggested, "You might introduce yourself before we go any further. I'm never comfortable calling a woman 'Hey You'."

Her smile softened the enamel on my teeth. "My name is Maggie Jenn. Margat Jenn, actually, but I've never been called anything but Maggie."

Ah, the monster of the prophecy. Winger's old crone. Must have lost her walker. I blurted, "Maggie doesn't sound like a redhead."

Her smile warmed up. Incredible! "Surely you're not that naive, Mr. Garrett."

"Garrett is fine. Mr. Garrett was my grandpop. No. It hasn't escaped me that some women miraculously transform overnight."

"This is just a tint, really. A little more red than my natural shade. Just vanity. One more rearguard skirmish in my war against time."

Yeah. The poor toothless hag. "Looks to me like you've got it on the run."

"You're sweet." She smiled again, turning up the heat. She leaned forward. . . .

3

Maggie Jenn caught my left hand, squeezed. "Some women enjoy being looked at that way, Garrett. Sometimes they want to look back." She tickled my palm. I stifled an urge to pant. She was working me and I didn't care. "But I'm here on business and it's important, so we'd better get to it." She took her hand back.

I was supposed to melt, going through withdrawal.

I went through withdrawal.

"I like this room, Garrett. Tells me a lot. Confirms what I've heard about you."

I waited. Clients go through this. They're desperate when they arrive. They wouldn't come to me if they weren't. But they stall around before admitting that their lives have gone out of control. Most end up telling me how they chose me. Maggie Jenn did that.

Some change their minds before they get to the point. Maggie Jenn did not.

"I didn't realize I was so well known. That's scary." Apparently my name was common coin among the ruling class, to which Maggie Jenn clearly belonged, though she had not revealed where she fit. I should avoid the flashy cases. I don't like being noticed.

"You're on everyone's list of specialists, Garrett. If you want a coach built, you go to Linden Atwood. You want unique flatware, you commission Rickman Plax and Sons. You want the best shoes, you buy Tate. You need prying and spying, you hire Garrett."

"Speaking of prying and spying."

"You want me to get to the point."

"I'm used to people circling in on their troubles."

She reflected a moment. "I see where they might. It's hard. All right. To the point. I need you to find my daughter."

"Huh?" She blindsided me. I was all tensed for her to ask me to kill somebody and all she wanted was the basic Garrett service.

"I need you to find my daughter. She's been missing for six days. I'm worried. What's the matter? You have the funniest look."

"I get like this when I think about working."

"You have that reputation. What will it take to get you out of the house?"

"More information. And the fee settled." There. I could be proud of me. I was taking command, being businesslike, handling my weakness.

So how come I was practically agreeing to take a case blind?

Actually, despite my reputation and past habit of laziness, I had been working steady, minor stuff, grabbing a few marks while I avoided the house and Dean, the Dead Man and the Goddamn Parrot. The former suffer from the delusion that it will be a better world if I work myself to death. T.G.P. just nags.

"Her name is Justina, Garrett. She's an adult, though just barely. I don't hang over her shoulder."

"An adult? What were you, ten years old? . . ."

"Flattery will get you everywhere. I was eighteen. She turned eighteen three months ago. Never mind the math."

"Hell, you're a spring chicken. Twenty-one with a few years' experience. You don't need to stop counting yet. I bet plenty of people take you for Justina's sister."

"Aren't you the sweet talker."

"Actually, I'm only being honest. I'm way too distracted to ..."

"I'll bet the girls love you, Garrett."

"Yeah. You hear them chanting in the street. You saw them climbing the walls so they can get in through a second-story window." TunFaire being TunFaire, my house has only one ground floor window, in the kitchen. Iron bars cover it.

Maggie Jenn's eyes sparkled. "I have a feeling I'm going to wish I'd met you sooner, Garrett." Those eyes promised. Maybe I was going to wish that, too.

A redhead will knock me for a loop every time.

She continued. "To the point. Again. Justina's been running with bad companions. Nothing I can put my finger on, no. Just youngsters I don't like. I got the feeling they were up to something wicked. No, I never saw anything to confirm that."

One thing you notice about parents who are looking for strayed children. They never liked anyone the kid liked. The kid is gone because he or she fell in with evil companions. Even when they strain to be nonjudgmental, there's this basic assumption that the friends are no good. If any of the friends are of another sex, boy, howdy!

"I expect you'll want to know all about her before you start, right?"

We had us a built-in assumption I'd be working for Momma Jenn. Momma Jenn was used to getting her own way. "Best way to do it. I knew a guy in my line whose whole thing was to get right inside the head of whoever he was hunting. He'd ignore everything but the character of that one guy. He'd almost become that guy. 'Course, lots of times he could've got his man quicker by looking at the big picture."

"You'll have to tell me about some of your cases. It's not a side of life I see. Must be exciting. Suppose you come to my house for an early supper? You can examine Justina's room and her things and ask your questions. Then you can decide whether or not you want the case." She smiled a smile that put her earlier efforts to shame. She was confident. I was getting roasted, toasted, manipulated, and I loved every second of it.

I said, "It happens I'm free tonight."

"Perfect." She rose, began donning flesh-colored gloves I hadn't noticed before. She considered Eleanor. Her face darkened. She shuddered. Eleanor can have that effect. "Fifth hour?" Maggie asked.

"I'll be there. But you'll have to tell me where."

Her face did darken then. Big mistake, Garrett. I was supposed to know without being told. Unfortunately, I knew so little about Maggie Jenn I didn't know that she would be irked because I didn't know who she was or where she lived.

The lady was a trooper. She carried on. She dallied only a moment before offering an address.

I got real nervous real sudden.

We were talking way up the Hill, where the richest and most powerful of the rich and powerful live, up where the altitude itself is the best indicator of wealth and might. Blue Crescent Street was in the realm of fairy tale as far as I was concerned.

Maggie Jenn was a lady with big connections, but I still could not recall why I thought I should know her name.

It would come when it was really inconvenient.

I escorted the lovely lady to my front door. The lovely lady continued to smolder and invite. Would the evening have *anything* to do with a missing daughter?

4

I stood bemused by Maggie Jenn swaying toward her litter. She knew I was watching. She made it a good show.

That killer stump Mugwump watched me watch. I didn't get the impression that he wished me well.

"You never stop foaming at the mouth, do you?"

I realized that I *had* settled down to savor every second of Maggie's departure. I tore my gaze away, turned to see which of my busybody neighbors was going to permit me to bask in the chill of her disapproval. I discovered, instead, a very attractive little brunette. She had approached from the other direction.

"Linda Lee!" This was my friend from the Royal Library, about whom I'd been thinking while holding Espinosa's book instead. "This is the nicest surprise I've had in a while." I went down to meet her. "I'm glad you changed your mind." Linda Lee, barely five feet tall, with beautiful big brown puppy eyes, was just about the cutest bit of a librarian I could imagine.

"Down, boy. This is a public place."

"Come into my parlor."

"If I do that, I'll forget all about why I came here." She plopped herself down on a step sideways. She locked her ankles together, pulled her knees up under her chin, wrapped her arms around them, and looked at me with a little girl innocence she knew would turn me into a love zombie.

It was my day to be a plaything.

I could handle it. I'd been born for that role.

Linda Lee Luther was no innocent, whatever impression you got at first glance. But she did try hard to be the icemaiden some folks thought a librarian should be. She tried but failed. Real ice wasn't in her nature. I just stood there, wearing my winningest grin, confident that she would talk herself into leaving the public eye.

"Stop that!"

"What?" I asked.

"Looking at me like that. I know what you're thinking. . . ."

"I can't help that."

"Yes, well, you're going to make me forget why I came here."

I didn't believe that for a second, but I'm a good guy. I can go along with a gag. "All right. Tell me about it."

"Huh?"

"What brought you here if not my irresistable charm?"

"I need your help. Professionally."

Why me?

I didn't believe it. Librarians don't get into fixes where they need guys like me to get them unfixed. Not cute little bits like Linda Lee Luther.

I'd begun moving toward my door. Preoccupied, Linda Lee rose and followed. I had her inside. I had the front door closed and bolted. I tried sneaking her past the open door of the small front room. The Goddamn Parrot mumbled obscenities in his sleep. Lovely Linda Lee did not take exception. I began to recall why I was so fond of this girl. I asked her, "What's got you so distracted?"

This was her big chance to come back with something clever and suggestive, an opportunity she wouldn't have wasted usually. But she just moaned, "I'm going to get fired. I just know it."

"That doesn't seem likely." Really.

"You don't understand. I lost a book, Garrett. A rare book. One that can't be replaced. It may have been stolen."

I eased into my office. Linda Lee followed me. Where was this attraction when I wanted to use it most?

"I have to get it back before they find out," Linda Lee continued. "There's no excuse for me having let this happen."

I told her, "Calm down. Take a deep breath. Hold it. Then tell me all about it, from the beginning. I'm already tied up in a job that's going to keep me busy for a while, but there's still a chance I can suggest something."

I took her by the shoulders, maneuvered her over to the client's seat. She settled.

"Tell me from the beginning," I reminded.

Aargh! The best laid plans, and so forth. Instead of spinning her sad tale of woe, she started sputtering and gesturing, original mission completely forgotten.

Uh-oh.

The Espinosa. Right there on my desk.

I hadn't quite observed all the formalities when I'd borrowed it. The library powers that be don't trust ordinary folks with books, anyway. Books might give us ideas.

I gobbled something placatory that got lost in the uproar, totally failed to steer her back to that matter of the loss that had brought her to me. "How could you do this to me, Garrett? I'm already in trouble. . . . If they miss this book too, I'm dead. How could you?"

Well, the how had been easy. It wasn't a very big book and the old veteran guarding the door had been napping. He'd had only one leg, anyway.

Words continued to vomit from my lovely Linda

Lee. An awesome performance. She got a grip on the Espinosa like it was her firstborn about to be repoed by a dwarf with a polysyllabic name.

How do you argue with panic? I didn't.

Linda Lee suddenly made a run for it. I didn't get around the desk fast enough. She squawked every step to the front door.

Wa-hoo! said the Goddamn Parrot. What a great excuse for raising hell. He went to work.

A moment later, I was watching Linda Lee scamper up Macunado, her anger so palpable eight-foot ogres scooted out of her way.

Her visit lasted so briefly I caught a last glimpse of Maggie Jenn's litter before it, too, got lost in traffic. Mugwump sent me a scowl to remember him by.

What a day. What next?

One thing seemed certain. There were no more lovelies headed my way. Sigh.

Time to take a minute to see what Eleanor thought about Maggie Jenn.

5

I settled behind my desk, stared at Eleanor. "What did you think of Maggie, darling? Should I be your basic opportunist? Go for it even if she is older than me?"

Eleanor doesn't say much but I manage by putting words in her mouth. "Yeah, I know. I went for you. A ghost." Picture that. I've been infatuated a few thousand times but hopelessly in love only twice, most recently with a woman who died when I was four. "So what's the big deal she's a few years older, eh?"

Weird things happen to me. Vampires. Dead gods trying to resurrect themselves. Killer zombies. Serial murderers who keep right on killing after you find them and send them off to the happy hunting ground. So why consider a love affair with a ghost outrageous?

"Yeah. I know. It would be cynical of me. What? Sure, she plans to use me, too. I know. But what a way to be used."

From the hall, I heard, "Yo, Garrett. I'm getting gray hairs hanging around up here."

Winger. Damn! I can't remember everything, can I? I rose slowly, still distracted. Maggie Jenn had cast a spell on me, no doubt about it. I'd almost forgotten my disappointment over Linda Lee.

I found Winger sitting on the stairs. "What are you doing, Garrett? The old broad left fifteen minutes ago." She didn't mention Linda Lee's hollering.

"I've been thinking."

"That's dangerous for a guy in your condition."

"Huh?" I didn't have a comeback. For only about the ten thousandth time in my life. The perfect response would spawn sometime as I lay tossing and turning an hour before dawn.

Winger strode to the Dead Man's door, stuck her nose in. His room takes up half the ground floor. I looked over her shoulder. All 450 pounds of him remained planted in his chair, still as death. The Loghyr's elephantlike snout dangled down a foot to his chest. Dust had begun to collect on him, but the vermin hadn't found him yet. No point cleaning until they did. Maybe Dean would come home first and save me the trouble.

Winger backed out of there, grabbed my elbow. "He's out of it." She knew because he hadn't reacted to her. He has no use for females in general and less use for Winger. Once, I threatened to boot Dean out and move her in.

"What did she say?" Winger asked as we headed upstairs. "Who's the target?"

"You don't know?"

"I don't know squat. All I know is I'm getting paid a shitpot full to find out."

Money was important to Winger. It is to all of us, in a palsy sort of way: nice to have around, fun to be with. But for Winger, it was like a patron saint.

"She wants me to find her daughter. The girl's been missing for six days."

"Say what? I'll be damned. I was sure it was going to be a hit."

"Why?"

"No special reason. I guess I added the cues up wrong. Looking for her kid? You take the job?"

"I'm thinking about it. I'm supposed to go up to her place, check out the kid's stuff, before I decide."

"But you'll take it, right? Make yourself some of that old double money?"

"An intriguing idea. Only I haven't seen single money from anybody yet."

"You sly bastard. You're thinking about topping the old broad. You're here with me and you're thinking about that. You're a regular villain."

"Winger! The woman is old enough to be my mother."

"Then you or mom is lying about their age."

"You're the one that went on about what an old hag she was."

"What's that got to do with anything? Hell. I forgive you, Garrett. Like I said, you're here. And she's not."

Arguing with Winger is like spitting into a whirlwind. Not much profit in it.

Only through a supreme effort did I get away in time to join Maggie Jenn for dinner.

6

"Ta-ta," I told the Dead Man—softly, so the God-damn Parrot wouldn't hear. "I spent the day with a beautiful blonde. In penance, I'm going to spend the evening with a gorgeous redhead."

He did not respond. He sure would have had he been awake. Winger had a special place in his heart. He had half believed my threat to marry her.

Laughing gently, still unforgiven, I tiptoed toward the front door. Before his departure, at incredible expense (to me), Dean had had a key lock installed in the new door, like I hadn't survived before he was there to slam bolts and bars into place behind me. Dean placed his trust in the wrong things. A key lock never stops anybody but the honest people. Our real protection is the Dead Man.

Loghyr have many talents, dead or alive.

I strutted away smiling at one and all, deaf to their squabbles. We were getting a lot of nonhumans in the neighborhood, mostly rough type refugees from the Cantard, never shy about expressing opinions. There was always a fuss among them.

Worse, though, were the proto-revolutionaries. Those crowded every loft and sleeping room. They overflowed the taverns, where they chattered foolishly about ever less workable dogmas. I understood what moved them. I didn't think much of the Crown, either. But I did know that none of us, them or me, was ready to try on the king's shoes.

A real revolution would make things worse. These days no two revolutionaries agree whither the Karentine state, anyway. So they would have to murder one another wholesale before ...

Revolution had been tried already, anyway, but so ineptly that hardly anybody but the secret police knew.

I ignored the hairy-faced, black-clad agents of chaos on the corners, scowling paranoiacally while they debated doctrinal trivia. The Crown was not in much danger. I have contacts in the new city police, the Guard. They say half the revolutionaries are really spies.

I waved to people. I whistled. It was a glorious day.

I was on the job, however. Though I was whistling my way to dinner with a beautiful woman, I observed my surroundings. I noticed the guy following me.

I roamed. I dawdled. I ambled. I strolled. I tried to get an estimate of the clown's intent. He wasn't very good. I pondered my options.

Turning the tables appealed to me. I could shake him, then follow him when he ran to report.

I do have enemies, sad to admit. In the course of my labors, occasionally I inconvenience some unpleasant people. Some might want to even scores.

I hate a bad loser.

My friend Morley Dotes, a professional killer who masquerades as a vegetarian gourmet, claims it's my own fault for leaving them alive behind me.

I studied my tail till I was sure I could handle him, then hurried along to keep my date with Maggie Jenn.

7

The Jenn place was a fifty-room hovel on the edge of the innermost circle of the Hill. No mere tradesman, however rich, however powerful, would reach that final ring.

Funny. Maggie Jenn had not struck me as the aristo type.

The name still nagged. I still did not recall why I ought to know it.

That part of the Hill was all stone, vertical and horizontal. No yards, no gardens, no sidewalks, no green anywhere unless on the rare third-story balcony. No brick. Red or brown brick was what the mob used to build. Forget that. Use stone that was quarried in another country and had to be barged for hundreds of miles.

I'd never been to the area so I got disoriented.

There weren't any spaces between buildings. The street was so narrow two carriages couldn't pass without climbing the sidewalks. It was cleaner than the rest of the city, but the gray stone pavements and buildings made the view seem dingy anyway. Walking that street was like walking the bottom of a dismal limestone canyon.

The Jenn address was in the middle of a featureless block. The door was more like a postern gate than an entrance to a home. Not one window faced the street, just an unbroken cliff of stone. The wall even lacked ornament, unusual for the Hill. Hill folk build to outdo their neighbors in displays of bad taste.

Some slick architect must have sold some otherwise shrewd character the notion that starkness was the way to shine. No doubt storehouses of wealth changed hands, the ascetic look being more costly than mere gingerbread.

Me, I like cheap. Gimme a herd of double-ugly gargoyles and some little boys peeing off the gutter corners.

The knocker was so discreet you almost had to hunt for it. It wasn't even brass, just some gray metal like pewter or tin. It made a restrained *tick tick* so feeble I'd have thought nobody inside could hear it.

The plain teak door opened immediately. I found myself face-to-face with a guy who looked like he got stuck with the name Ichabod by malicious parents back around the turn of the century. He looked like he had spent the numerous intervening decades living down to the image that kind of name conjures. He was long and bony and bent. His eyes were red and his hair was white and his skin was oh so pale. I muttered, "So this is what they do when they get old. Hang up their black swords and turn into butlers." He had an Adam's apple that looked like he was choking on a grapefruit. He didn't say a word, he just stood there staring like a buzzard waiting for a snack to cool.

He had the biggest bony arches over his eyes I ever saw. They were forested with white jungles.

Spooky guy.

"Dr. Death, I presume?" Dr. Death was a character in the Punch and Judy shows going around. Ichabod and the bad doctor had a lot in common, but the puppet was six feet shorter.

Some people have no sense of humor. We had us one of those here. Ichabod neither cracked a smile nor twitched one of those woodlots camped over his eyes. He did speak, though. Fair Karentine, too. "You have some cause for disturbing this household?"

"Sure." I didn't like his tone. I never like the tone of Hill servants. It's filled with the defensive snobbishness you find in the tone of a turncoat. "I wanted to see if you guys really do shrivel in the sunlight." I had the advantage in this dumb game because I was expected and he'd been given my description. And he'd recognized me.

If he hadn't recognized me, he would've slammed the door against my nose. Word would have gone out to the thugs who defend the rich and mighty from nuisances like me. A band would be hastening hither to deal me an exemplary drubbing.

Come to think of it, they could be hastening anyway, if Ichabod had a confederate with no better sense of humor. "Name's Garrett," I announced. "Maggie Jenn asked me to come for dinner."

The old spook stepped back. He never said a word, but it was plain he doubted his boss's wisdom. He didn't approve of letting my kind in the house. No telling what might have to be dragged back out of my pockets before they let me go. Or maybe I'd scratch off some fleas and leave them to colonize the rugs.

I glanced back to see how my tail was making out. Poor sod was playing hell staying inconspicuous.

"Nice door," I observed as I caught it edge-on. It was four inches thick. "Expecting a debt collector with a battering ram?" Hill people are rich enough to have those kinds of problems. Nobody would loan me enough for me to get in trouble.

"Follow me." Ichabod turned.

"That should be 'follow me, sir.'" I don't know why the guy made me antagonistic. "I'm a guest. You're a flunky." I began having second thoughts about revolutions. When I go over to the Royal Library to see Linda Lee, I poke around in the books, too. Once I read one about rebellions. Seems like the servants of

the overthrown get it worse than their masters do—
unless they are perceptive enough to be agents of the
rebels.

"Indeed."

"Ah. A comment. Lead on, Ichabod."

"The name is Zeke, sir." The sir dripped sarcasm.

"Zeke?" That was as bad as Ichabod. Almost.

"Yes, sir. Are you coming? The mistress doesn't
like to be kept waiting."

"Do lead on, then. The thousand and one gods of
TunFaire forfend that we distress Her Red-
headedness."

Zeke elected not to respond. He'd concluded that I
had an attitude problem. He was right, of course, but
for the wrong reasons. And I was a little ashamed. He
was probably a nice old man with a herd of grandkids,
forced to work into his dotage in order to support
ungrateful descendants who were the offspring of sons
killed in the Cantard.

I didn't believe that for a minute, though.

The interior of that place bore no resemblance to
the outside. It was pretty dusty now, but it had started
out as the daydream of some wharfside loser who
imagined himself a great potentate. Or a great potentate with the tastes of a wharfside loser. I'll get some
of these and a bunch of those and . . . And the only
thing missing was a troop of houris.

The place was lousy with tasteless billows of wealth.
Plush everything and way too much of it, and even
more of everything as we moved nearer the center of
the pit. Actually, we seemed to advance from zone to
zone, each another expression of bad taste.

"Whoa!" said I, unable to restrain myself. "There
it is." *It* being a mammoth's-foot cane and brolly
stand. "You don't see a lot of those."

Zeke gave me a look, read my reaction to that bit
of down-home chic. His stone face relaxed for a mo-

ment. He agreed. In that instant, we concluded a
shaky armistice.

No doubt it would survive no longer than Karenta's
armistice with Venageta, which had lasted a whole six
and a half hours.

"Sometimes we cannot relinquish our pasts, sir."

"Maggie Jenn used to be a mammoth hunter?"

The peace was over. Just like that. He hunked along
sullenly. I think that was because I'd admitted I didn't
have the faintest idea what Maggie Jenn used to be.

How come everyone thought I should know who
she was? Including me? My famous memory was
doing famously today.

Zeke ushered me into the worst room yet. "Madame will join you here." I looked around, shading
my eyes, began to wonder if Madame didn't used to
be a madam. The place was for sure done up in whore-
house modern, probably by the same nancy boys who
did the high-fly joints down in the Tenderloin.

I turned to ask a question.

Ichabod had abandoned me.

I almost squeaked for him to come back. "Oh,
Zeke! Bring me a blindfold." I didn't think I could
stand the sensory assault otherwise.

8

It got to me. I stood around like I'd just made eye contact with a medusa. I'd never seen so much red. Everything was a red of the reddest reds, overwhelmingly red. Ubiquitous gold leaf highlights only heightened the impact.

"Garrett."

Maggie Jenn. I didn't have the strength to turn. I was scared she'd be wearing scarlet and lip rouge of a shade that would make her look like a vampire at snack time.

"You alive?"

"Just stunned." I waved a hand. "This is a bit overpowering."

"Kind of sucks, don't it? But Teddy loved it, the gods know why. This place was Teddy's gift, so I keep this part the way he liked it."

I did turn then. No, she hadn't worn red. She wore a peasanty sort of thing that was mostly light brown and white lace and a silly white dairymaid's hat that set off her hair. She also wore a heavyweight smile that said she was amusing herself at my expense but I was free to join in the fun. I told her, "I'm missing something. I don't get the joke."

Her smile faded. "What do you know about me?"

"Not much. Your name. That you're the sexiest woman I've run into in an age. Various self-evident characteristics. That you live in a classy neighborhood. And that's about it."

35

She shook her head. Red curls flew around. "Notoriety isn't worth much anymore. Come on. We don't stay here. You'd go blind."

Nice to have somebody crack wise for me. Saved me the trouble of thinking them up and pissing her off.

She led me through several memorable rooms which weren't important enough to note. Then we roared out into the real world, bam! A dining room set for two. "Like a night in Elf Hill," I muttered.

She hadn't lost her hearing. "I used to feel that way. Those rooms can be intimidating. Go ahead. Plant it."

I took a chair opposite her at the end of a table long enough to seat two dozen people. "This is a love nest?"

"Smallest dining room I've got." Hint of a smile.

"You and Teddy?"

"Sigh. How fleeting infamy. Nobody remembers except the family. That's all right, though. They're bitter enough for everybody. Teddy was Teodoric, Prince of Kamark. He became Teodoric IV and lasted a whole year."

"The king?" Bells began to ring. Finally. "It's starting to come."

"Good. I won't have to put myself through a bunch of explanations."

"I don't know a lot. That all happened when I was in the Marines. In the Cantard, we didn't pay much attention to royal scandals."

"Didn't know who was king and didn't care. I've heard that one." Maggie Jenn smiled her best smile. "I bet you still don't follow royal scandals."

"They don't affect my life much."

"It wouldn't affect your work for me, either, you knowing or not knowing all the dirt."

A woman came in. Like Zeke, she was as old as original sin. She was tiny, the size of a child about to lunge into adolescence. She wore spectacles. Maggie

Jenn took good care of her help. Spectacles are *expensive*. The old woman posed, hands clasped in front of her. She neither moved nor spoke.

Maggie Jenn said, "We'll start whenever you're ready, Laurie."

The old woman inclined her head and left.

Maggie said, "I will tell you some of it, though, to soothe that famous curiosity of yours. So you do what I'm paying you to do instead of rooting around in my past."

I grunted.

Laurie and Zeke brought in a soup course. I began salivating. I'd eaten my own cooking too long.

That was the only way I missed Dean, though! You bet.

"I was the king's mistress, Garrett."

"I remember." Finally. It was the scandal of its day, a crown prince falling for a commoner so hard he set her up on the Hill. His wife had not been thrilled. Old Teddy had made no pretense of discretion. He'd been in love and didn't care if the whole world knew. A worrisome attitude in a man who might be king.

It suggested character flaws.

For sure. King Teodoric IV turned out to be an arrogant, narrow-minded, self-indulgent jerk who got himself snuffed within a year.

We aren't tolerant of royal foibles. That is, our royals and nobles aren't tolerant. Nobody else would consider assassination. It just isn't done outside the family. Even our mad dog revolutionaries never suggest offing the royals.

I said, "I do wonder, though, about this daughter."

"Not Teddy's."

I slurped my soup. It was broth and garlic somebody tossed a chicken across. I liked it. Empty bowls went away. An appetizer course appeared. I didn't say anything. Maggie might talk just to extinguish the silence.

"I've made my dumb mistakes, Garrett. My daughter was the result of a lulu."

I chomped something made of chicken liver, bacon, and a giant nutmeat. "This's good."

"I was sixteen. My father married me off to a virgin-obsessed animal who had daughters old enough to be my mother. It was good for business. Since nobody ever told me how you don't get pregnant, I got. My husband had fits. I wasn't supposed to whelp brats, I was supposed to warm his bed and tell him he was the greatest there ever was. He went buggo when I had a daughter. Another daughter. He had no sons. It was all a female plot. We were out to get him. I never had the nerve to tell him what would happen if us women really gave him what he deserved. He got a taste, though." Nasty smile. For one second, a darker Maggie shone through.

She nibbled some food and left me room to comment. I nodded and kept chomping.

"The old bastard never stopped using me, whatever he thought about me. His daughters took pity and showed me what I needed to know. They hated him more than I did. I bided my time. Then my father got killed by robbers who got twelve copper sceats and a pair of junk boots more than a year old."

"That's TunFaire."

She nodded. That *was* TunFaire.

I nudged, "Your dad died."

"So I no longer had any reason to please my husband."

"You walked."

"After I caught him sleeping and beat the living shit out of him with a poker."

"I'll take that to heart."

"Good idea." There was mischief in her eye. I decided I was going to like Maggie Jenn. Anybody who could live through what she had and have a little mischief left . . .

It was an interesting meal. I got to hear all about how she met Teddy without hearing word one about what she did between her shoeleather divorce and that first explosive encounter with the future king. I suspected she had loved Teddy as much as he'd loved her. You wouldn't keep something as ugly as those red rooms in memory of somebody you disliked.

"This place is a prison," she told me, a little misty.

"You got out to visit me." Maybe they let her out on a tease release program.

"Not that kind of prison."

I stuffed my face and let that old vacuum suck more words out of her. I don't deal well with metaphor.

"I can leave any time I want, Garrett. I've been encouraged to leave. Often. But if I do, I lose everything. It's not really mine. I just get to use it." She gestured around her. "As long as I don't abandon it."

"I see." And I did. She was a prisoner of circumstance. She had to stay. She was an unmarried woman with a child. She had known poverty and knew rich was better. Poverty was a prison, too. "I think I'm going to like you, Maggie Jenn."

She raised an eyebrow. What an endearing skill! Few of us have sufficient native talent. Only the very best people can do the eyebrow thing.

I said, "I don't like most of my clients."

"I guess likable people don't get into situations where they need somebody like you."

"Not often, that's a fact."

9

The way things started, I became convinced that a certain eventuality had been foredoomed from the moment I'd opened my front door. I'm not a first date kind of guy, but I've never strained too hard against the whims of fate. I especially don't struggle to avoid that particular fate.

Dinner ended. I was unsettled. Maggie Jenn had been doing these things with her eyes. The kind of things that cause a bishop's brain to curdle and even a saint's devotion to monasticism to go down for a third time in those limpid pools. The kind of things that send a fundamentalist reverend's imagination racing off into realms so far removed that there is no getting back without doing something stupid.

I was too distracted to tell if the front of me was soaked with drool.

There had been banter and word games during dinner. She was good. Really good. I was ready to grab a trumpet and race around blowing *Charge*!

She sat there silently, appraising me, probably trying to decide if I was medium or medium well.

I made a heroic effort to concentrate. I managed to croak, "Tell me something, Maggie Jenn? Who would be interested in your affairs?"

She said nothing but did the eyebrow trick. She was surprised. That wasn't what she'd expected me to say. She had to buy time.

"Don't try to work your wiles on me, woman. You don't get out of answering that easily."

She laughed throatily, exaggerating that huskiness she had, wriggled just to let me know she was capable of distracting me as much as she wanted. I considered distracting myself by getting up and stomping around to study some of the artwork decorating the dining chamber but discovered that rising would be uncomfortable and embarrassing. I half turned in my chair and studied the ceiling as though seeking clues amongst the fauns and cherubs.

She asked, "What do you mean about people interested in my affairs?"

I did pause to reflect before I gave away the store. "Let's back up some first. Did anybody know you were coming to see me?" Of course somebody did. Else Winger wouldn't have come to me first. But I needed Maggie's perspective.

"It wasn't a secret, if that's what you mean. I did ask around once I decided I needed a man of your sort."

Hmm. What *was* a man of my sort?

This was not an unfamiliar phenomenon. Sometimes the unfriendlies get the jump because they hear about my client asking after someone who can help. "Next step, then. Who would be bothered if you started looking for your daughter?"

"Nobody." She was getting suspicious.

"Yeah. It would seem like nobody ought to care. Unless maybe they were to give you a little support."

"You're scaring me, Garrett."

She didn't look scared. I said, "Might be a good idea to be scared. See, I knew you were coming."

"What?" She was troubled for sure now. She didn't like that at all.

"Just before you showed up, a friend who's in my racket stopped by to warn me you'd be coming." Saying Winger and I are in the same business is stretching

a point, maybe. Winger is into anything likely to put
money in Winger's purse, preferably fast and easy.
"He thought you were coming to buy a hit. That's
why he warned me." Catch that clever misdirection.
Not even a dead Loghyr often mistakes Winger for
male.

"A hit? Me?" She knew the argot. She was off bal-
ance but coming back fast.

"He was sure of it." But I wondered. Winger took
shortcuts. Big, slow, lovable, goofy, crafty, bigoted,
and lazy Winger. She was confident that anybody she
couldn't sweeten with reason she could bring around
with a good old-fashioned ass-kicking. She was just a
big old simple country girl with simple country ways—
if you accepted her the way she wanted to be taken.

I was going to have words with Winger about Maggie Jenn. If I could find her. I didn't think that would
be tough. The big goof was bound to turn up on her
own, soon. Probably before I was ready.

I said, "Then somebody followed me here."

"What? Who? Why?"

"Got me. I only mention it to show you that somebody out there is interested."

Maggie shook her head. It was a fine head. I was
starting to lose my focus again. I concentrated on de-
scribing the villain who'd followed me.

Maggie smiled wickedly. "Garrett! Don't you ever
think about anything else?"

"Lots of times." I thought about starting a little
contest in which we would see who could run the
fastest.

"Garrett!"

"You started it."

Unlike many women, she did not deny her complic-
ity. "Yeah, but . . ."

"Put yourself in my place. You're a red-blooded
young man who's suddenly alone here with you."

"Flattery will get you everywhere." She chuckled.

Ouch! This was getting painful. "You do dish up a ration of shit, don't you?"

I chuckled right back and put myself into my own place, assuming she meant to put herself into her own place and things would proceed to proceed. But after a painful pilgrimage to her side of the table all proceedings proceeded to grind to a halt. Reluctantly—it seemed—she slipped away from me. I muttered, "We can't keep on like this if you want to sell me on looking for your daughter."

"You're right. This is a business arrangement. We can't let nature get in the way."

I was willing to let nature play havoc, but I said, "Durn tootin'. I don't sell that way, anyway. I sell on logic and facts. That's me. Just-the-facts-ma'am Garrett. How about you start giving me some of those instead of using all your energy on those come-hither eyes?"

"Don't be cruel, Garrett. This is as difficult for me as it is for you."

10

So, eventually, we reached the suite belonging to Maggie's daughter Emerald. "Emerald?" I asked. "What happened to Justina?" Emerald. Wouldn't you know? Where are all the lovely Patricias and Bettys?

"I named her Justina. Emerald is what she uses. She picked it, so don't give me that look."

"What look?"

"The one that says you're shitting me. *She* picked it. She was fourteen. Everyone else went along, so I use Emerald sometimes myself."

"Right. Emerald. She insisted." Of course. That's what became of Patricia and Betty. They started calling themselves Amber and Brandi and Fawn. "But she might be going by Justina. When life gets serious, they fall back on their roots. Anything I need to know about the suite before I start digging?"

"What do you mean?"

"Am I going to find something you think needs excusing ahead of time?"

Wonder of wonders, she understood. "You might. Only I never go in there, so I don't know what it might be. Yet." She gave me a strange look. "Are you looking for a fight?"

"No." Though maybe, unconsciously, I didn't want her hanging over my shoulder. "Back to that name. Might as well go after this by the numbers, find out everything you can tell me before I start looking for things you don't know."

She gave me that look again. I *was* a bit testy. Had I developed that strong a dislike for work? Or was it because I knew she would lie and distort and whatever else it took to shape reality to her own vision? They all do, even when there's no hope they won't get found out. People. They do make you wonder.

"Justina was after my grandmother."

I understood from her tone. Never was a kid who did not resent hearing how he or she was named after some old fart they never met and couldn't care less about. My mom played that game with me and my brother. I never figured out why it meant anything to her. "Any special reason?"

"The name's been in the family forever. And Granny would have been hurt if . . ."

The usual. Never made sense to me. You sentence a kid to a lifetime of misery on account of somebody might get his feelings hurt if you don't. Three rousing oriental cheers, say I: foo-ee, foo-ee, foo-ee. Who is going to be upset the longest?

You entered Emerald's suite through a small sitting room. There you found a small writing desk with its chair, in blond wood. There was an oil lamp on the desk. There was one more chair, a storage chest with a cushion on top, and a small set of shelves. The room was squeaky clean and more spartan than it sounds. It did not look promising.

I hate it when they clean for company. "Your daughter ever take a powder before?"

Maggie hesitated. "No."

"Why did you hesitate?"

"Trying to decide. Her father kidnapped her when she was four. Some friends convinced him that a child is better off with her mother."

"Would he try something like that today?"

"Probably not. He's been dead eight years."

"Chances are he wouldn't." As a rule, the dead don't get involved in custody disputes.

"She got a boyfriend?"

"A girl from the Hill?"

"Especially a girl from the Hill. How many does she have?"

"What?"

"Look, believe it or not, it's easier for Hill girls to slip around than it is for downtown girls." I offered examples from my own cases, one of which had featured a bevy of Hill girls working the Tenderloin just for the thrills.

That stunned my Maggie Jenn. She had a blind area, an inability to believe her baby could be anything less than the absolute image of what she desired. It hadn't occurred to her that Emerald was going to break her heart. Plainly, she didn't understand that people sometimes did the wicked stuff for other than survival reasons. Whoring as an amusement was a concept too alien to encompass.

Only the classes in between don't believe in whoring.

"You didn't grow up on the Hill."

"I admit that, Garrett."

I had the suspicion that my pretty Maggie had maybe had to make ends meet to make ends meet during the hiatus between husband and crown prince. I didn't need to know about that, though. Not yet, anyway. Maybe later, if it began to look like the past had some bearing. "Plant yourself on a chair. Talk to me about Emerald while I work."

I prowled.

11

Maggie said, "To my knowledge she has no boy-friends. Our circumstances don't let us meet many people. We aren't socially acceptable. We form a class unto ourselves."

A very classy class it was, though Maggie Jenn and her kid weren't its only members. The sisterhood of mistresses is quite large. At these rarified heights, a man is expected to have a mistress. It demonstrates his manhood. Two is better than one.

"Any friends at all?"

"Not many. Girls she grew up with, maybe. Maybe somebody she studied with. At her time of life, kids are real status conscious. I doubt anybody would let her make any strong connections."

"What's she look like?"

"Me, twenty years less shopworn. And wipe that silly grin off your mug."

"I was thinking how looking for you twenty years younger would have me hunting somebody barely out of diapers."

"And don't forget that. I want my baby found, not—"

"Right. Right. Right. Any special stress between you before she disappeared?"

"What?"

"Did you have a fight? Did she stomp out yelling about how she was never coming back in ten thousand years?"

"No." Maggie chuckled. "I had a few of those with *my* mother. Probably why she didn't squawk when my father sold me. No. Not Emerald. This kid is different, Garrett. She never cared about anything enough to fight. Really, honestly, swear to whatever god, I wasn't a pushy mother. She was happy just to go along. Far as she was concerned, life is a river and she was driftwood."

"I maybe lost something in all the excitement. Or maybe I've started remembering things that never happened. I could have sworn you were going on about her having fallen in with bad companions."

Maggie chuckled. She snorted. She looked uncomfortable. She did it all fetchingly. I tried to imagine her as she might have been in Teodoric's day. I was awed by the possibilities.

She stopped wriggling. "I fibbed a little. I heard about you having a relationship with the Sisters of Doom and figured you were a sucker for a kid in trouble." The Sisters of Doom is an all-girl street gang. The girls were all abused before they fled to the street.

"It was a relationship with one Sister. Who left the street."

"I'm sorry. I overstepped."

"What?"

"It's obvious I just stomped on some tender feelings."

"Oh. Yeah. Maya was a pretty special kid. I messed up a good thing because I didn't take her serious enough. I lost a friend because I didn't listen."

"Sorry. I was just trying to find a sure hook."

"Did Emerald see anybody regularly?" Business would take me away from memories. Maya was not one of my great loves, but she was pretty special. And both Dean and the Dead Man had approved of her. There had been no separation, she just didn't come around anymore and mutual friends all hinted that she wouldn't unless I grew up a little.

That don't punch your ego up, considering it traced back to a girl just eighteen.

Emerald's writing desk had numerous cubbies and tiny drawers. I searched them as we talked. I didn't find much. Most spaces were empty.

"She does have friends but making friends doesn't come easy."

That wasn't the story as it was told a few minutes ago. I suspected Emerald had troubles that had nothing to do with social status. Chances were she was lost in her mother's shadow. "Friends are where I'll find her trail. I'll need names. I'll need to know where I can find the people who go with them."

She nodded. "Of course." I slammed a drawer, turned away from her. I had to keep my mind on business. The woman was a witch. Then I sneaked a peek. Did I really want to leave all that, to go hunting somebody who probably didn't want to be found?

Ha! Here was something. A silver pendant. "What's this?" Purely rhetorical. I knew what I had. It was an amulet consisting of a silver pentagram on a dark background with a goat's head inside the star. The real question was, what was it doing where I had found it?

Maggie took it, studied it while I watched for a reaction. I didn't see one. She said, "I wonder where that came from?"

"Emerald into the occult?"

"Not that I know of. But you can't know everything about your children."

I grunted, resumed my search. Maggie chattered like the fabled magpie, mostly about her daughter, more in the way of reminiscences than useful facts. I listened with half an ear.

I found nothing else in the desk. I moved to the shelves. The presence of several books brought home how much wealth Maggie stood to lose. Because a book takes forever to copy, it is about the most expensive toy you can give a child.

I grunted as I picked up the third book. It was a small, leather-bound, time-worn thing with a goat's head tooled into its cover. The leather was badly foxed. The pages were barely readable. It was one old book.

My first clue was that it was not written in modern Karentine.

Those damned things never are, are they? Nobody would take them seriously if any schnook could pick one up and decipher the secrets of the ages.

"Check this out." I tossed the book to Maggie. I kept one eye on her as I resumed my search.

"Curiouser and curiouser, Garrett. My baby is full of surprises."

"Yeah." Maybe. That whole visit was full of surprises. Including those tree-sized fingers pointing at witchcraft of the demonic sort.

The bedroom and its attached bath yielded more occult treasures.

Much later I asked, "Is Emerald especially neat?" Neat would not describe any teen I knew.

"Only as much as she has to be. Why?"

I didn't tell her. I had gone into full investigator mode. We crack first-line investigators never answer questions about our questions, especially if those are posed by our employers, lawmen, or anybody else who might help keep us out of the deep stink. Fact was, though, that Emerald's apartment was way too neat. Compulsively so. Or nobody lived there. My impression was of a stage set. I was wondering if it might not be exactly that, carefully primed with clues.

All right, I told me. Get busy deducting. Clues are clues to something even when they're artificial or false.

I was not that sure. What I had was some inconsistent indications of witchcraft—which did little to amaze, dismay, alarm, or otherwise excite my new employer.

Maybe I was going at this from the wrong end.

Tap on the shoulder. "Anybody in there?"

"Huh?"

"You just froze up and went away."

"Happens when I try to think and do something at the same time."

She did her eyebrow trick. I distracted her by flashing her back. I told her, "I've got enough to start. You give me that list of names. As soon as we settle the finances."

We had no problems there till I insisted on half my fee up front. "It's an inflexible rule, Maggie. On account of human fallibility. Too many people get tempted to stiff me once they've gotten what they want." But that was not the only reason I pressed.

The less a client argues the deeper his desperation.

My pretty Maggie Jenn argued way too long. Finally, she huffed, "I'll have Mugwump bring you that list as soon as I can."

I was thrilled. I really wanted to see Mugwump again. Maybe I could tip him a talking parrot.

12

I stood in the shadows down the street from Maggie's, just staying out of sight while I thought.

Like most folks, I don't get any kick out of being played for a patsy. But people do try. It's an occupational hazard. I'm used to it. I expect it. But I don't like it.

Something was going on. I was being used. None too subtly, either. Unless Maggie my sweet was a lot less worldly than I suspected, I didn't see how she could think I would buy everything.

I'd sure enjoyed the job interview, though. As far as it had gone.

The thing to do now was what she had said she didn't want me to do: investigate Maggie Jenn. For my own safety. In my line, what you don't know can get you killed as fast as what you do know. Once I could guess where I really stood, maybe I'd do something about Emerald.

I glanced at the sky. It was dark but still early. I could touch some contacts, take a few steps along the path to enlightenment. Right after I dropped Maggie's retainer off at home. Only a fool carries a load like that longer than he must. TunFaire teems with villains who can count the change in your pocket at a hundred yards.

I could imagine no explanation of recent events more convincing than what Maggie purported. Nevertheless, there was Winger. I shook my head. The cobwebs did not go away. They never do. All part of the service. All part of my naive charm.

I looked for my tail. No sign. Maybe he got tired and went home. Maybe the Hill's security thugs whispered sweet nothings in his ear, like, "Get lost pronto or you'll crawl home with two broken legs." Or maybe his job had been done once he'd found out where I was going.

I shoved off. All that thinking was giving me shin splints of the brain.

Good thing I exercise. I had oomph enough to vacate the area steps ahead of an unpleasant interview with the goon squad, who did not seem to care if I had legitimate business on the Hill. They had been summoned by Ichabod, no doubt, in a vain hope that my attitude could be improved.

I zigged and zagged and backtracked and used all my tricks. I didn't spot a tail so I went home, got rid of Maggie's retainer, drew myself a long draught, then sat down for a cold beer and a chat with Eleanor, who seemed concerned about the state of my soul.

"Yeah," I confessed, "I'm getting more flexible when it comes to taking money." I spoke in a whisper. I did not want to waken the Goddamn Parrot. I'd even tiptoed in and filled his seed tray.

If I remembered to feed him more often, he might have a higher opinion of me. Maybe.

"So what? If they're villains, they deserve to be done out of their money." She had taught me that money has no provenance. "If they aren't villains, I'll see that they get their money's worth."

More or less. Sometimes I don't exactly deliver what the client has in mind. One such case resulted in Eleanor coming to live with me.

It had taken me a while to outgrow the notion that taking a man's money meant having to go for the results he wanted. I must be getting old and judgmental.

These days, I try to give people what they deserve instead.

Which yields mixed results for sure. Even so, I get more offers than I want. But a lot of fat jobs go elsewhere because some folks have decided to avoid me. Most especially the kind who rob people with paper instead of a blade. Lawyers and slicks. I have embarrassed my share of those.

Actually, I mostly avoid working. I don't think anybody ought to work more than it takes to get by. Sure, I wish I could afford my own harem and fifty-room palace, but if I worked hard enough to get the money, I'd have to work as hard to keep it. I wouldn't get a chance to enjoy it.

After a few beers, I developed a whole new attitude. I told Eleanor, "Think I'll go down to the Joy House, hang out with the guys."

She smirked.

"It's just to pick up street talk about Maggie Jenn."

Eleanor didn't believe one word.

I had to find me a new girlfriend.

13

Morley Dotes never changes but his neighborhood can. Once upon a time, that was the worst. You weren't alert, you could get killed for the price of a bowl of soup. For reasons to do with Morley's intolerance of squabbles and his sometime role as arbitrater of underworld disputes, the neighborhood grew almost reputable and came to be called the Safety Zone. Those who worked the shadow side met and did business there, with every expectation of suffering none of the embarrassment, unpleasantness, or disappointment one faced at the hands of lone wolf socialists in other neighborhoods.

Every city needs some quiet area where business can get done.

"Waa-hoo!" shrieked the guy who came sailing out the door as I walked up to Morley's place. I ducked. That fellow touched down halfway across the street. He made a valiant effort to land running and did a laudable job till a watering trough slunk into his path. Slimy green water fountained.

Another man came out sprawled like a starfish, spinning and howling. He was one of Morley's thugs-turned-waiter.

This was backwards. The way these things go is Morley's people toss troublemakers. They don't get dribbled along the cobblestones themselves.

The howling waiter went across the street like a skipping stone. He crashed into the guy trying not to drown in the horse trough. If you ask me, putting those things around was a grave mistake. Horse troughs are sure to draw horses. TunFaire is infested by enough evils.

On hands and knees, I peeped around the edge of the door frame and discovered true pandemonium.

A behemoth of a black man, who beat my six feet two by a good three feet, and who had to slouch so he wouldn't split his noggin on the ceiling, was having himself a grand time cleaning house. He snarled and roared and tossed people and furniture. Those few men accidentally exiting through the front door were lucky. They were out of the action. Those who tried to leave under their own power got grabbed and dragged back for the fun.

The feet of the walls were littered with casualties. The big man had a fire in his eye. No mere mortal was going to quiet him down. Some very skilled mortals had tried and had found places among the fallen.

I knew the berserk. His name was Playmate. He was one of my oldest friends, a blacksmith and stable operator, a religious man who was as gentle a being as ever lived. He went out of his way to avoid stepping on bugs. I had seen him weep for a mutt run down by a carriage. Like all of us, he had done his time in the Cantard, but I was sure that even there he had offered violence to no one.

I thought about trying to talk him down. I left it at a thought. We were good friends, but Playmate had equally good friends among the fallen. Everybody loved Playmate.

And I had learned about being a hero doing my five years as a Royal Marine.

No way could Playmate have gone this mad.

Morley Dotes himself, dapper and exasperated, watched from the stair to his office. He was a darkly handsome little character, dressed way too slick for my taste. Anything he put on looked like it was baked onto him. Anything I put on looks slept-in after ten minutes.

Morley was so distressed he was wringing his hands.

Guess I'd have been upset myself if someone was busting up my place. The Joy House started as a front—Morley was an assassin and bonebreaker—but it had grown on Dotes.

A short, slim form snaked through the crowd and leapt onto Playmate's back. The big man roared and spun. He did not dislodge his rider, Morley's nephew Spud, whose mother had passed him to his uncle because she could not manage him anymore.

For a while, Spud just held on. Once he was confident of his seat, though, he let go with one hand and fumbled at his belt. Playmate kept spinning. The idea gradually got into his head: spinning and prancing and roaring would not get the weight off his back.

He stopped, got his bearings by consulting stars only he could see. He decided to run backwards and squish Spud against a wall.

Spud had his own plan, though.

Spud was set on being a hero in his uncle's eyes.

The kid wasn't stupid, he just suffered from natural elvish overconfidence.

His hand came up from his belt clutching a black cloth sack. He tried popping that over Playmate's head. Guess who did not cooperate?

That sack was a mark of the esteem in which Playmate was held. The guy was set on destroying the world, but nobody wanted to stop him badly enough to kill him. Not one soul inside the Joy House wanted to do anything but get him under control. Not your true TunFairen attitude, I guarantee. Life is the cheapest commodity of all.

Morley moved as soon as he understood what the kid was doing. He didn't run or appear to hurry, but he got there right on time, a moment after Spud did get his bag into place, a moment after Playmate

started his all-out plunge toward the nearest wall.
Morley hooked a foot behind the big man's heel.

Boom!

Playmate sprawled. Spud separated just in time to
keep from being sandwiched. He was a lucky kid. Instead of getting squashed and collecting some broken
bones, he just got coldcocked.

Not so Playmate. My old pal tried to get up. Morley
popped him a bunch of times, so fast you barely saw
him move. Playmate didn't like that. He figured
maybe he ought to take that sack off and see who was
aggravating him. Morley hit him a bunch more times,
in all those places where blows are supposed to
incapacitate.

There came a day when Playmate, buried under a
dozen people, finally stopped struggling.

14

Morley looked down at Playmate. He was breathing hard. I strode inside, chirped, "Congrats. You wore him down."

Morley checked me from glazed eyes, failed to recognize me for a moment, then wailed, "Oh, damn! You. On top of everything else."

I looked behind me to find out who was causing my best pal so much distress. I'd fix him! But the guy was too fast for me. The doorway was empty.

I put on my best hurt face. I get to practice a lot around the Joy House. Morley's guys are always riding me. Naturally, I play along.

I righted a table, selected a chair, made myself comfortable. I eyeballed Playmate. "What happened? You have to pump that guy up on weed to get him to swat flies."

Morley took several controlled breaths, picked up a chair, and joined me. "Excellent question, Garrett." Playmate wasn't doing anything now. In fact, the roars from beneath the flesh pile sounded suspiciously like snores.

Morley Dotes is a bit short for a grown man but isn't entirely human. He has dark-elf forebears. But he never lets the human in him get in his way.

Maybe the mix is responsible. He is a mass of contrasts, especially in his profession as opposed to his hobby. His health food haven has become a hangout for half the villains of TunFaire. Contrast again: the clientele is half those double-nasties and half the kind of clown you *expect* to find gnoshing tubers of uncertain provenance.

"Boy did pretty well," Morley observed, glancing at Spud. The kid's real name was Narcisio. Only his mother used that.

"Pretty good," I admitted. "More balls than brains."

"Runs in the family."

"What happened?"

Morley glowered. Instead of answering me, he shocked the house by bellowing, "Eggwhite! Get your heathen ass out here!"

I was amazed, too. Morley employs vulgarity only rarely. He fancies himself a gentleman rogue. Gentlemen rogues are slick like they're covered with lard. But a villain is a villain, and Morley is one of the worst because he gets away with everything. I should try to take him down. I don't because he's my friend.

A thug ambled out of the kitchen. He wore cook's garb but carried his professional resume scarred on his face. He was old and looked as stupid as a stump, which answered a question: what becomes of hard boys if they live long enough to get old? They become waiters. I didn't see how this goon had survived to get there, though. He looked like a guy who needed a major run of luck to get through any given day.

Maybe the gods do love the incapacitated.

Morley beckoned.

Eggwhite edged our way. His gaze kept darting toward Playmate. Playmate had begun to reappear as guys climbed off and went to set the bones of their buddies.

"Big mess, huh?" Morley said.

"Yeah, boss. Big ole mess."

"You have any idea why I would entertain the notion that you might have been at fault? Can you tell me why your face popped into mind the moment my friend asked me what happened?"

Will wonders never cease? He never called me friend before.

Eggwhite muttered, "I guess on account of I got a weakness for doing jokes."

Morley grunted. "That one of your pranks?" Playmate was sleeping like a baby now, but he was going to be hurting when he woke up. "That big ha-ha there?" Morley's tone was hard, the street leaking through. He was angry. Eggwhite was petrified.

Morley asked, "What did you do?"

"Put angelweed in his salad?" Eggwhite made it a question, like a kid caught in a lie experimenting with a new tactic.

"How much?"

Excellent question. Angelweed didn't earn its heavenly name because it will boost your mind into paradise but because it will send you off to hallelujah land if you aren't careful. Slipping it into a salad would be a clever way to dose somebody. The leaves look like spinach that's gone a little bluish.

"Half a dozen leaves." Eggwhite looked everywhere but straight at Morley.

"Half a dozen. Enough to kill most people."

"He's humongous, chief. A goddamn mountain. I thought it would take—"

"And there's the problem." Morley's voice dropped way down, to a level of softness that meant he was in a killing mood. Eggwhite started shaking. Morley continued, "I told you when I hired you I didn't want any thinking. I wanted you cutting vegetables. Get out."

"Chief, look, I can—"

"You're gone, Eggwhite. Out the door. Walking or carried. Up to you."

Eggwhite gulped. "Uh ... Yeah." He headed for the door.

I observed, "He's making off with your cook outfit."

"Let it go. I don't want to make a scene."

I gave him an encore look at my eyebrow trick.

"I hate firing people, Garrett."

I added the fish-eye to the raised eyebrow. This was the most feared hired knife in town? Was he putting me on?

He kept plugging. "I do it only because you have to if you want to be successful in business. Besides, I owe him eight days pay." Before I could comment, he eyed me directly. "What is it this time, Garrett?"

"How about a platter of that stuff with the black mushrooms, pea pods and whatnot, on the wild rice?" I dropped money onto the table.

Morley gave me my fish-eye back with interest. He gathered my coins, examined them as though he suspected they were counterfeit. "You want to eat? Here? And you're willing to pay for it?" He sank his fangs into a coin, the classic hardness test.

"I wouldn't go so far as to employ the concept of privilege, but it is an age of wonders. You've converted me. I'm born again. I'm never going to eat anything but swamp tubers, bark, and gravel ever again."

15

Morley stirred Playmate's fingers with his toe. "He's alive, but I couldn't tell you why." He came back to where I was wolfing the mushroom stuff. It contained more garlic than mushrooms. "Trying to keep the girls away?"

"I don't need garlic for that. I have natural talent."

He wasn't in the mood for banter. Guess I wouldn't have been either had my place just gotten trashed. "What are you into now, Garrett? What do you need?"

"I'm doing a missing person caper." Love that word. I told him the story, leaving out only those parts a gentleman leaves out. "I want to know whatever you know about Maggie Jenn. Felt like she was running a game on me."

"Somebody must be running a game on somebody. I don't think you saw the real Maggie Jenn."

"Huh?"

"Never mind the witty remarks. I'm thinking you must have been chosen for your ignorance."

"Thanks. How about shoving a stick in the spokes of the scheme by lighting a torch in the darkness?"

"That wouldn't be right. Not quite. You not being up on the adventures of the royals *could* be part of it, but . . ."

"All right. I don't know what you know, Morley. That's why I'm here."

"It isn't impossible that you spent the afternoon

with a king's lover, but I'd call it wildly improbable. Maggie Jenn exiled herself to the Isle of Paise after her Teddy boy died. If there was a daughter I never heard. Kind of thing that would be kept quiet, though. On the other hand, that place on the Hill sounds like the one where Teodoric stashed his doxy. Curious."

That was an understatement. "I'm lost, Morley. None of this makes sense."

"Only because you don't have the key."

"I'm missing the key, the lock, the damned door, and all the hardware. Somebody ran a game on me? I'll buy that. Happens all the time. But the woman also paid me to look for her daughter."

"How well?" Was that smile a smirk?

"Handsomely, shall we say? Enough so I'm sure she expected something in return. Even top of the Hill don't throw money away."

"Good point."

"*If* Maggie Jenn came back," I mused, "what would she do?"

"She has no reason to come back. She lives like a queen out there. She'd find nothing but trouble here." Morley eyed Playmate. "Pity you didn't get here earlier. He always kept track of the royals."

"He won't be doing anything but whine about his headache for a week."

"You in a hurry?"

I wondered. "Maybe not. No apparent jeopardy. Just a puzzle. Maggie didn't seem in any hurry, just worried."

"You buy the woman's story?"

I never take a client's story at face value. Some natural law compels them to lie part of the time. "Maybe. Some. It feels like the truth being used for something else."

"I'll put out feelers. Meantime, you ought to corner Winger."

"That occurred to me." I didn't relish trying to get

anything out of her, though. "It's not an appetizing idea."

Morley chuckled. "She's a handful. The trick is get her thinking what you want is her idea."

"Ingenious. How?"

"With great difficulty."

"I can get advice like that from my parrot and save the price of this fish food."

"Way I hear, Dean is out of town and the Dead Man is asleep. You being hard up for company, I just wanted you to feel at home. Crumbs! You try to be a pal." He grinned a diabolical dark-elf grin.

"You want to be a pal, find out about Maggie Jenn."

His grin dwindled. "Try to be a pal." He shook his head.

He would check around because he thought he owed me. And I agreed. I collect like a loanshark.

"Bed is starting to sound good," I thought aloud. "It's been a hard day."

Morley grunted. His nephew came to the table. Getting no hint that he ought to take his big ears elsewhere, he spun a chair around and straddled it. Around us, Morley's people, moving slowly and muttering about their aches and pains, put things together again. Spud asked, "How is Mr. Big, Mr. Garrett?"

I cursed.

Morley had sent me the Goddamn Parrot when he was in an Eggwhite mood. That was far enough out of character that I suspected Sarge and Puddle had a hand in developing the scam. The bird came guaranteed to have a major hatred for cats and a habit of attacking them from above. I accepted him because Dean had a habit of accumulating strays.

Spud gave me a dirty look. He was the only one in the world with any use for that foul-mouthed jungle chicken. Make that any love. The Dead Man had a use. Wherever I went, he could send Mr. Big after, nagging.

I had tried to give the beast away. There were no takers. I gave it every chance to fly away. It wouldn't escape. I was getting near taking heroic measures. "Spud, you're so worried about Mr. Big why don't you come get him? He needs a home where he's appreciated."

"No, you don't," Morley sneered. "That there is *your* bird, Garrett."

I scowled. This was a squabble I couldn't win.

Dotes showed all those pointy teeth again. "I hear some parrots live a hundred years."

"Some, maybe. In the wild." I could donate Mr. Big to a charity. Like some hungry ratman. "I'm out of here, friend."

Morley laughed.

16

It was dark out. That did not help.

Neither did the fact that I didn't see them coming. I had no chance to get ready.

I put up a fight, though. I dented some heads good with the weighted oak head-buster I carry when I go out. I tossed one guy through the only glass window in the street. But I just never got rolling. I had no chance to use the tricks I had stashed up my sleeves. Somebody whapped me up side the head with a house. I think it was a house. Had to be a house. No mere man could hit me that hard. The lights went out—with me still trying to figure out who and why.

Ordinarily, I come around slowly if I've had my conk bopped. Not so this time. One minute I was in dreamland, the next I was bouncing along face downward, wrapped in something soggy, staring at a floor sliding past inches from my nose. Four guys were carrying me. I was leaking red stuff. I couldn't recall drinking any wine. I had the worst headache anyone ever had since the dawn of time.

A fine pair of female legs strode along practically in nibbling range. I really wanted to appreciate those. In other circumstances, I would have devoted hours to those legs. But a guy does have to keep some perspective.

Things were not going well. This sort of thing was

not a normal part of my life. I tried to shove the pain away long enough to think.

Aha! They had me wrapped in a wet blanket. I didn't want to poop somebody's party, but that didn't make me happy. I roared and twisted and flopped and wriggled and bellowed. I failed to make any impression. I did get a gander at what went with the gorgeous gams. The wealth was piled on all the way to the top. I could have fallen in love. But this was not the time or place. Beside a fire, maybe on a bearskin rug, maybe just her and me and some TunFaire Gold wine. . . .

I didn't like the looks of the guys. They weren't the brunos I danced with earlier. Those had been standard lowlife, out for the price of a drink. These clowns wore dirty, ragged uniforms.

That failed to cheer me up.

They were unreasonable. They wouldn't answer questions. Nobody responded at all, except Miss Legs. She just seemed sad. I hollered and flopped some more. They kept on lugging me down a long hall.

Long hall, huh? And what was that smell?

Everybody stopped but me. I thrashed some more. I was serious about it now. I knew where I was. This was the crazy floor of the Bledsoe, the imperial charity hospital.

The empire is long gone, but its works and the imperial family linger, the latter hoping for a recall. They sustain the hospital, which serves the indigent poorly.

The cackle factory is a bad place. They stick you in there you could be gone forever. Wouldn't matter that somebody made a mistake.

"Hey! Put me down! What the hell is this? What am I doing in here? Do I look like I'm crazy?"

That was the wrong question. I had to look like a prime specimen. And the way things work, they would assume that they wouldn't have me if I didn't belong.

Man, this was the dirtiest trick anybody ever played on me.

A door crashed open. It was oak and iron and about nine inches thick. I glimpsed my destiny.

One of my guides bellowed. Somebody scuttled away. The boys tossed me through the doorway without missing the frame. I landed hard. The Legs gazed at me pityingly. The door closed before I convinced her this was all a horrible mistake.

I unwrapped myself by rolling around, stumbled over and wasted energy pounding on the door. I exercised the full range of situationally specialized vocabulary, but without the enthusiasm I might have managed had my head not hurt so much. You do these things even when you're wasting your time. The rituals must be observed.

I heard noises behind me. I spun around.

At least a dozen men stood staring at me. I checked the ward beyond them. There were lots more men back there. Plenty were wondering about the new guy. Some studied my outfit. Plainly, there had been no general clothing issued in years. Nor had anyone taken a bath during the modern era. Here was the source of the odor I'd caught in the hall. A glance told me the welcoming committee all belonged inside. It was obvious in their eyes.

I pounded and yelled some more. Service did not improve.

At least they hadn't dumped me into the violent ward. Maybe I stood a chance.

An old character who looked like he weighed about fifty pounds stumbled toward me. "How are you doing? I'm Ivy."

"I was doing great till about five minutes ago, Ivy."

"How are you doing? I'm Ivy."

"He don't say nothing else, Ace."

Right. I'm a quick study. Ivy never even looked at me. "Gotcha."

A guy about nine feet tall guffawed. "You don't pay Ivy no nevermind, boy. He's crazy."

"How are you doing? I'm Ivy."

This was the tip of the iceberg. The part that would be easy. It was sure to get weird.

After thinking a while, somebody yelled at the big guy, "You got so much room to talk, muddlebrain?"

"Yeah? What do you know? I don't belong in here. I was set up. Somebody drugged me or something. I woke up in here."

Oh, my. A fellow traveler as bad off as I. I had a lot of sympathy for him—till some grinning idiot shrieked, "Powziffle! Powziffle pheez!" Or something like that.

The big guy hunched up, stooped, made gurgling noises, and started running around the ward like a gorilla, howling. His howls would have chilled the spine of a banshee.

"How are you doing? I'm Ivy."

The big man' racket started some other guy screaming. His cries were a species I'd heard in the islands, coming from a guy caught out in no-man's land with a bad gut wound, begging for somebody to kill him. Soldiers from both sides would have done so gladly after a while. But nobody was dumb enough to go out there and let the other side snipe. So we'd all just laid low and listened, ground our teeth, and maybe thanked our personal gods it wasn't us.

I glared at that door. Maybe I could chew my way through.

Or maybe ... My pockets hadn't been cleaned. They must've been in an awful hurry to get me put away. A real bunch of screwup charlies.

Patients came to check me out—those who still had a foot in our world. Many were timid as mice. A look sent them scurrying. Others ... Some might have been there as accidentally as I, only instead they belonged in the ward for the dangerous.

I wished everybody would back off.

Any doubts I had about the irregularity of my commitment disappeared when I discovered that they hadn't cleaned my pockets. Had I been brought in legitimately, all my possessions would have been taken from me and would never have surfaced again.

I was encouraged. About a roach-weight worth.

The physical plant wasn't encouraging. The ward was a hundred feet wide, three hundred feet long, and two storys high. There were rows and rows and rows of sleeping pallets but not nearly enough to go around.

The ceiling was way up there, a good twenty feet. Windows peeked through the wall opposite the door, way high, too small for a man to get out even after he cut the bars. I supposed they passed light during the day. What little light was available now leaked through windows high on the door side wall, there so the ward could be observed by hospital staff.

"How are you doing? I'm Ivy."

"I'm doing just fine, Ivy. What say you and me bust out of this toilet?"

Ivy looked at me directly, startled, then scampered away.

"*Anybody* want to break out?"

17

My suggestion drew an underwhelming response. I gathered that half the patients could not be dragged out and the other half thought I was crazy. There? Forsooth!

The big man who had cautioned me about Ivy's lack of capacity recapacitated himself. He came over. "Ain't no way out, Slick. They was, half these guys would be long gone."

I glanced around again. The prospects seemed ever less promising. "They feed us?"

The big guy grinned that grin the old salts put on when they see a chance to teach a greenhorn. "Twice a day, you're hungry or not. Through them bars down there."

I looked. I shrugged. Them bars was hopeless. "Things are that bad I might as well get me some shut-eye before I start my serious worrying." I looked for an empty pallet. I had some thinking to do. Especially about why I found myself in such straits.

I wanted to scream as loud as any of the whacks in there with me.

"You get in line for a bed," the big guy cautioned me. "You make friends, maybe somebody will share. Otherwise, you just wait till enough guys die to leave you your own." His casual manner told me this was one of the capital laws of the ward. Amazing. You'd expect it to be *total* survival of the strongest.

"My kind of flophouse." I settled near the door.

That didn't seem to be a popular area. Plenty of elbow room there. I pretended to fall asleep.

There were no corpses in the ward and no smell of death. That suggested that staff removed the dead quickly. So, how to use that in a scam the staff hadn't seen before?

I gave the notion of a riot a look. Feeble. If I was the Bledsoe staff, I'd just let everybody starve till the fuss stopped.

"How are you doing? I'm Ivy."

My act wasn't fooling Ivy. I considered putting him out of his misery.

Which gave me an idea. A twist on the riot scheme. I went looking for the big guy. I found him seated against the far wall. I planted the reverse side of my lap on the hardwood, grunted. "I got about enough splinters."

"Send out for a chair."

A wise guy. "How come it's so quiet?"

"Maybe on account of it's the middle of the god-damn night." Eloquent verbal stylings, too.

"I mean, we only had one screamer." Not counting him. Nobody was yelling at the moment. "I heard there was lots of screamers. Mostly guys who can't handle what they remember about the Cantard."

His face darkened. "Yeah. There's some of them. They get drugged if they get too bad. Like they get each other going."

Interesting. "Know any way to set one of them off now?"

He studied me narrowly. "What you up to, Slick?" He thought there had better be a damned good reason for pulling a stunt like that.

"Up to getting out of here."

"Can't do that."

"Maybe not. But they didn't empty out my pockets before they dumped me in here. You game to try?"

He thought about that. His face grew darker.

"Yeah. Yeah! I got business out there. Yeah. You get the damned door open, I'll go."

"You figure any of these guys would help?"

"Plenty would go if the walls fell down. I don't know how many would help make them fall."

"So could you get some guy screaming as the first step?"

"Sure." He got up, strolled to the far end, messed with somebody a minute, headed back. Plenty of inmates watched him. The man he'd visited started screaming. Chills slithered all over me. He was one of the lost souls.

The big man asked, "Good enough?"

"Perfect. Now try to round up some guys willing to help out."

He went away again.

I went into my act. "Shut up down there! I'm trying to sleep."

The guy didn't stop screaming. I'd been afraid he would. I glanced at the observation windows. Someone was up there, but the racket didn't interest him. Were they that indifferent? I needed to be seen.

I yelled at the screamer. Somebody yelled back at me. I yelled at him. Some genius yelled at both of us like that would shut us up. The racket picked up. We were like a troop of monkeys. Some of the men started moving around, just shuffling numbly, without purpose.

The uproar finally caught the ear of whoever was on duty. He looked down but didn't seem concerned.

I screamed louder than the screamer, threatening mayhem if he didn't shut it up.

"How are you doing? I'm Ivy."

"Pack your trunk, Ivy. We're checking out of this cuckoo inn."

The big guy came by. "I got a dozen guys willing, Slick. You want more?"

"That's plenty. Now I need everybody back away

from the door. It's going to get nasty there when they come in." I hoped. If I hadn't been suckered too bad.

"They'll figure we're up to something, Slick. They only look dumb."

"I don't care. That won't matter. I just need the door open."

He sneered, confident I was on a fool's quest.

I screamed some more at the screamers.

There were several people at the observation windows now—including she of the glorious gams.

I chuckled, sure I was on my way out. No woman would work the Bledsoe unless she had a giant soft spot. I roared, bounded over pallets, started strangling the loudest screamer.

The big guy came by and pretended to drag me off. I gave him further instructions, then ran him off. He wasn't a bad actor.

Me, I was a master. I made it look real good. To my surprise, none of my fellow patients tried to stop me.

I only strangled my victim a little, enough to cause unconsciousness.

I galloped to the other end of the room, went to work on another screamer.

Soon there were guys flying all over the place. The majority got into the spirit. It wasn't exactly a riot, though. Real violence was almost nonexistent. But the pandemonium was not pretend.

I glimpsed the woman arguing with the men. She wanted to do something. They didn't.

Excellent.

A little goblin breed three feet tall scrunched himself into a ball near the door.

Upstairs, charity apparently overcame common sense.

I kept the show rolling. People did get hurt, but *I* wasn't in a charitable mood, to put it mildly. If I stayed a nice guy, I wasn't ever going to get out. If I didn't get out, I'd never get the chance to crack the heads of the clowns who'd put me in.

The big guy came around again. He bounced me around some. "They're coming," I told him. "And you don't have to be so enthusiastic here."

He seemed scornful. I don't know about what.

18

I glanced at the door, then cautioned the big guy, "Take it easy. We don't have to convince them now." No one was near the door but the little breed. He would be sorry he had volunteered. "How many will come?"

The big man shrugged. "Depends on how worried they are. Least eight or ten. You better watch out." He tripped me. I tripped him back. We rolled around and punched each other. He was having a great time. "They have a policy of kicking the living shit out of troublemakers."

"I kind of figured that was part of the program. Hell, I've stopped bleeding. I'm ready for anything." I wasn't looking forward to the kicking part. You lays your bets and takes your chances, but I was hoping things would go well and I would not have to deal with any boots.

You have to believe you're going to win.

I did have to win. Nobody knew where I was. It could be weeks before anybody even missed me, what with Dean out of town and the Dead Man sleeping. It might be weeks after that before anybody tracked me down. If anybody bothered to try.

I didn't have weeks. I didn't feel I could waste the time I'd spent inside already. The Dead Man might chuckle and tell me to consider it a learning experience, which is what he does when I have a bad day.

77

If I didn't break out, it was going to be the all-time bad day to start a long string of bad days.

The woman stayed at the observation window. I kept howling my head off and throwing people around and strangling other guys making noise.

The thing that got me, down deep, was that almost half the guys in the ward didn't get involved. Most of those never opened their eyes. They just laid there, indifferent.

Man, that was scary. That could be me in twenty years if I blew this.

Fear provided the inspiration I needed to keep howling and foaming at the mouth. I tried speaking in tongues. That came to me naturally. A little something for when I got too old to make it on the street. A good howl and roll man can start his own church.

The door opened.

Wonder of wonders, miracle of miracles, those dopes actually opened the door.

It swung outward. Attendants boiled inside. They knew something was up. They were ready for bear. They had clubs and small shields. They all looked about twelve feet tall. They formed in a tight knot before they started forward.

A few months earlier, in a moment of weakness brought on by engulfing an inland sea of beer, I'd bought some stuff from a third-rate wizard who'd called himself Dread but whose name was really Milton. You don't never trust the skills of a wizard named Milton—as I'd learned to my sorrow on trying to use one of his charms. His stuff came with a warranty, but he wasn't around to make good on it.

In my pockets were several tiny bottles, the last of my purchase. According to Dread, they constituted the ideal means of dealing with unfriendly crowds. I didn't know, never having tested them. I wasn't sure I even recalled Dread's instructions. It was real drunk out that night.

I told me I had another good reason for wanting out. I had to find old Milt and register a consumer complaint.

As I recalled, all I had to do was throw a bottle against a hard surface, then stand back.

I did the throwing part. My bottle missed all the boys and bounced off the wall. It skittered back into the midst of the attendants. Guys walked all over it, but it didn't break.

My guardian angel was on the job. Cursing him, I tried again.

The second bottle broke. Gray mist boiled off the wall. It reached the attendants. They started cussing. Cussing turned to howling fast.

Meantime, my little breed volunteer slithered into the doorway so it couldn't be closed. His job was going to get nasty if the staff got determined.

The attendants in the ward lost all interest in quieting people down. They were too busy scratching and rubbing and yelling.

Maybe Dread wasn't a complete fraud.

I inhaled a bushel of clean air and charged. I was ashamed of me for pulling such a dirty trick. Almost. I wouldn't take it back. If I spent much time hanging out with Ivy and the boys, I'd end up singing in the same choir.

The mist didn't bother me much. I did start itching a little. Since I had a major headache and an acre of bruises, an itch seemed pretty trivial.

Somebody was hollering in the corridor. They'd left somebody to cover the door. He was aggravated at my breed doorstop.

Who wasn't doing so good. The mist tended to settle. He'd gotten more than the attendants had.

Nonetheless, he fulfilled his mission.

I smashed into the door so hard I feared I'd dislocated my shoulder. Oh, damn, did that hurt! And that damned door only gave barely enough to let me skip over the whining breed.

"Surprise!" I popped the guard outside. A whole herd of patients stampeded out behind me. Those that didn't have scores to settle with particular attendants still inside.

Naturally, luck would have another squad of staffers arriving just then. I did my banshee routine and charged. Boy, was I going to have a sore throat when all the hollering was over.

These attendants were bigger and meaner than the first bunch. There were eight of them. That put the odds in my favor because I was mad enough to whip a whole battalion. "Nothing personal, guys." Then I recognized two of the clowns who had carried me in the wet blanket. "Like hell!"

I didn't get a lot of help at first. Surprise did for a couple of attendants, but then the others got going. They played a game using me for a shuttlecock. My companions had been beaten too often. They held back till my nine-foot buddy jumped in.

"Oomph!" I said, breaking some guy's knuckles with my forehead. "Took you long enough."

It turned into a real brawl. Fists and feet and bodies flew. I skinned my knuckles to the elbow pounding handy chins and jaws. I got my own chin and jaw liberally pasted. My nose avoided rearrangement.

All that thumping was just the thing for a headache.

I had opportunities to be thankful that I have good teeth as I sank them into people who didn't have my continued good health foremost in mind.

When the fur stopped flying and the dust settled, me and the big guy were the only ones standing. And I needed the help of a wall.

I stumbled to the door at the end of the hall, beyond the vanquished attendants. It was locked. It looked every bit as massive as the door to the ward. Well, all that work for nothing. I exchanged glances with the big guy. He grinned, said, "I told you." He wiped blood off his face, grinned some more. "They going to have a time cleaning this one up, though. We got most of the night staff in here."

"Fine. We're a step closer. Let's drag these guys into the ward." Maybe we could use them as hostages.

All of a sudden, we had plenty of helpers. Guys turned brave, thumped heads soundly whenever an attendant threatened to wake up.

I checked the end of the hall I hadn't checked before. Another locked oaken vault door. Of course. "I guess this just isn't my day." It had had its moments earlier, but the downs were starting to outweigh the ups. "Anybody want to guess how long it'll be before they come after us again?"

The big guy shrugged. Now that the active part was over he seemed to be losing interest.

I produced two tiny folding knives that hadn't been taken, reflected that this incident was going to generate strident calls for an investigation of how blades and sorcerous gook and whatnot had gotten to the inmates. Like there'd ever been a doubt that any inmate who could flash the cash couldn't buy any damned thing he wanted.

An investigation might mean hope. If it was serious, it would require my testimony. That would mean the pointing of fingers at the kind of people who'd take bribes for falsely imprisoning heroes like me. Ugh! They'd be villains who'd be aware of the distress my testimony could cause their careers. Surely they'd take steps to assure a paucity of witnesses likely to testify.

I gave the big guy a knife. "Carve me some kindling out of anything wooden. If we get a decent fire going, we can burn our way through those doors."

He grinned but without the wild eagerness he'd shown before. He was winding down.

The notion of arson did excite some of the others.

We all got to work ripping the stuffing out of pallets and whittling on the ward door.

Then I suffered another brainstorm, way late, unlike the hero of an adventure story. I claim genius only because nobody else thought of the obvious first. The adventure boys would have planned it from the start. It's one of their old tricks.

The Bledsoe staff wore uniforms, scruffy though those were.

I got my fires burning at both ends of the hall. Ivy tended them. His vocabulary didn't improve, but he became more animated. He liked fires. He even paid attention when I said, "Use plenty of horsehair. We want plenty of smoke." The horsehair came out of the pallets.

Ivy grinned from ear to ear. He was one fulfilled lunatic.

The people outside would *have* to make a move. They couldn't wait us out once we had fires burning. Fires had to be fought.

I had to have a guy follow Ivy and make sure his fires didn't grow too fast. Already they seemed likely to burn through the floor before they ate through the doors.

Once the smoke was thick enough, I picked an attendant my size and started trading clothes. He got the best of the deal.

My companions caught on. Soon they were squabbling over the available uniforms. I made sure Ivy and the big guy got theirs. I wanted one for the little breed who'd body-blocked the ward door, but he'd have gotten lost in a shirt.

Interesting that I had so many supporters now that it looked like I had prospects.

The smoke almost got too thick before somebody outside decided action had to be taken *now*.

19

They brought almost every warm body they had left. They burst through both doors at once, behind thrown buckets of water. They concentrated on the fires to begin, taking what lumps they must until those were extinguished, then they started whipping on anybody in arm's reach. When they got into the ward, they started hauling fallen comrades away.

It was real exciting for a while. The issue was definitely in doubt.

The smoke got to me more than I expected. After they dragged me out and I decided it was time I made a run for it, I found that my legs were saying no way.

"Don't. You aren't ready yet."

I didn't look up and give myself away. Around me, impelled by the cunning of madness, my buddies did the same. What a team!

There were better than twelve men scattered along the hallway, many from the ward. The rest had gone down in the current invasion.

The speaker was a woman, the owner of the legs. She added, "Get the smoke out before you do anything."

I coughed and made noises and kept my face hidden. She moved on, evidently to tend someone else who was stirring. A female doctor? How about that? I never heard of such a thing, but why not?

I scooted back till my spine found a wall, raised myself up against that, lifted my head to scope out an

escape route. I kept seeing two of things when I could
see through the water in my eyes. I got my feet under
me again and practiced standing up till I could do it
with no hands.

My chosen escape route did not become overgrown
while I was catching my breath. I shoved off the wall
and started staggering. There was a stairwell door
straight ahead, out in the remote distance, on the far
horizon, about twenty feet away. All kinds of racket
came from behind it, as though thunder-lizards were
mating in the stairwell. I didn't pay the racket any
mind. I didn't have any mind left over. What I had
was busy thinking "out."

I was chugging right along, hardly ever falling down,
when she of the glorious gams intercepted me. "What
are you trying to do? I told you . . . Oh!"

I grinned my winningest grin. "Oh-oh."

"Oh, my god!"

"Hey, no. I'm just a regular guy."

Maybe she had trouble hearing over the racket from
the stairwell. Or maybe she had trouble hearing over
the uproar from the hall and ward. She sure didn't get
my message. She whooped and hollered like she
thought she was going to get carried off by a lunatic
or something.

I grabbed a wrist, mostly to keep from falling down.
I noticed that she was blond and recalled that that
was one of my favorites but I didn't have oomph
enough to let her know. The bleeding had stopped a
long time ago, but my head wasn't much better. The
smoke hadn't done me any good, either.

I hacked out, "Pipe down! We're going for a walk,
sister. I don't want anybody should get hurt, but that
ain't my top priority. You get the drift? You keep on
wailing. . . ."

She shut up. Blue eyes big and beautiful, she
bobbed her head.

"I'll cut you loose at the front door. Maybe. If

you're good and I don't get no more trouble." Snappy rhetoric, Garrett. Your roots are showing.

I was getting the edge on the smoke, though. I was ready to bet myself she would be good. A figure like that, it burned. No. Forget fire. Fire means smoke. I just swallowed enough smoke to last forever.

I leaned on the lady like she was my sweetie. "I need your help." Rotten to the heart, I am. But this would be our only date.

She nodded again.

Then she tripped me, the naughty girl.

And *then* my friend Winger blasted through that stairwell door, flinging battered orderlies ahead of her. "Goddamn, Garrett! I bust in here fixing to save your ass and what do I find? You trying to bop some bimbo in front of the whole damned world." She grabbed my collar, hoisted me away from my latest daydream, who had gone down when I had. Winger set me on my feet, then proceeded to whip the pudding out of a burly, hirsute attendant who meant to object to the irregularity of the way she was checking me out. Between punches she grunted, "You got to get your priorities straight, Garrett."

No point mentioning who tripped who. You don't explain to Winger. She creates her own realities.

While she was amusing herself with the hairy orderly, I asked the lady doctor, "What's a nice girl like you doing in a place like this?"

She wouldn't answer even after I apologized for playing so rough.

"For heaven's sake, Garrett, give it a rest," Winger snapped. "And come on."

I went along because she grabbed hold and took off. I grabbed the blonde as we went past. Down those stairs we went, stepping over the occasional moaning attendant. Winger had come through like a natural disaster. I bubbled, "I do hope I haven't been too much trouble. Unfortunately, I can't hang around just because somebody out there wants me in here instead of stomping on his toes." I put on my grim face. "When I catch up with him, I'll make sure he gives you a big donation. Big enough to cover damages."

Winger rolled her eyes. She didn't slow down and she didn't let go.

The lady of the legs said, "You're serious, aren't you?"

Winger grumbled, "As serious as he can get when he's in rut."

My new friend and I ignored her. I said, "That's right. I find things for people. Just this morning, a lady from the Hill asked me to find her daughter. I'd barely started looking when a band of ruffians set upon me. Next thing I knew, I was coming to and there you were and I thought I'd died and gone to one of those afterlives where they have angels, only my head hurt too much."

"I risked life and limb for this," Winger muttered. "Your head is about to hurt a whole lot more."

The lady doc looked at me like she really wanted to believe. She said, "He does spread it thick, doesn't he?"

"With a manure rake," Winger growled, reverting to uncultured country ways. You can take the girl out of the sticks, and so forth.

I said, "You ever feel the need to get in touch, just go up Macunado Street. When you get to Wizard's Reach, start asking around for where the Dead Man stays."

The lady offered a weak smile. "I might do that. I just might. Just to see what happens."

"Fireworks. For sure."

Winger suggested, "Save yourself for marriage, honey. If there's anything left."

The lady's smile vanished.

You can't win them all. You especially can't when you have friends intent on throwing the game.

We'd reached the street in front of the Bledsoe. I tried to sprint off into the night at a fast shamble. I figured I ought to make tracks before some avenging orderly appeared.

After I'd gone a few steps, Winger observed, "That was the most disgusting display I've seen yet, Garrett. Don't you ever stop?"

"We have to get out of here." I glanced over my shoulder at the Bledsoe. A glimpse of the place nearly panicked me. That had been close. "We got to disappear before they send somebody after us."

"You think they're not going to know where to look? You all but gave that bimbo your address."

"Hey! You're talking about the love of my life. She won't give me away." I didn't let her see my crossed fingers.

Winger shifted ground. "Why would they bother, anyway? Really?"

At this point, they probably wouldn't. Anything they did now was likely to draw more attention than they could stand.

I shrugged. That's always a useful, noncommital device.

20

I waited till we had a good head start, just in case the hospital gang did decide to come after me. Then I grabbed Winger's hand in a comealong grip.

"Hey! What the hell you doing, Garrett?"

"You and me are going to sit here on these steps like young lovers and you're going to whisper sweet nothings about what the hell is going on. Got it?"

"No."

I added some muscle to the hold.

"Ouch! Ain't that just like a man? No gratitude. Save his ass and—"

"Looked to me like I was doing an adequate job of saving it on my own. Sit."

Winger sat, but she kept grumbling. I didn't let go. I wouldn't get any answers if I did.

"Tell me about it, Winger."

"About what?" She can turn into the dumbest country girl that ever lived.

"I know you. Don't waste stupid on me. Tell me about Maggie Jenn and her missing daughter and how come as soon as I take this job I get jumped, cold-cocked, and shoved into the cackle factory in such a big hurry the fools don't bother to empty my pockets? All the time I'm in there, I'm wondering how this could happen to me when only my pal Winger knows what I'm doing. And now I'm wondering how my pal Winger knew I needed help getting sprung from the Bledsoe. Stuff like that."

"Oh. That." She thought a while, making something up.

"Come on, Winger. Give truth a try. Just for the novelty."

She offered me a Winger-sized dirty look. "I was working for this pansy name of Grange Cleaver. . . ."

"Grange Cleaver? What kind of name is that? Come on. Tell me there ain't nobody named Grange Cleaver."

"Who's going to tell this? You or me? You want to sit there and listen to the echo of your lips clacking, that's all right with me. Only don't expect me to hang around listening, too. I know how corny you get when you're up on your high horse."

"Me? Corny?"

"Like some holy joe Revanchist roll in the aisles preacher."

"You wound me."

"I'd like to, sometimes."

"Promises, promises. You were working for a character with a name even a dwarf wouldn't tolerate."

"Yeah. His mom and dad were probably named Trevor and Nigel." She gave me another dirty look, thought about getting stubborn. "I was working for him, you like his name or not. He had me watching Maggie Jenn. Because he expected her to try to kill him, he said."

"Why?"

"He didn't say. I didn't ask. The kind of mood he was in most times, it didn't seem like a bright idea to nag."

"Not even a guess?"

"What's with you, Garrett? I get three marks a day if I mind my own business and do my job. I maybe get kneecapped if I don't."

Thus did we head for an argument about moral responsibility. We'd had it about fifty times before. The way Winger saw it, if you covered your own ass you were doing your part.

She was trying to divert me.

"Guess it don't matter, Winger. Go on. Explain how you ended up here."

"That's easy. I'm a big dummy. I figured you for a pal. Somebody what didn't deserve that raw a deal."

"How come I feel like there are some details shy here? You think you could put a little flesh on those bones?"

"You can be a real pain in the butt, Garrett. Know what I mean?"

"I've heard that rumor." I waited. I did not relax my grip on her hand.

"All right. All right. So I was working for this Cleaver. Mostly on watching the Jenn bimbo, but on other stuff sometimes, too. It was like regular work, Garrett. Top pay and always something needed doing. Tonight I figured out why. Cleaver was putting me out front. People watched me while him and his nancy boys pulled stunts in the shadows."

I grunted but provided no sympathy. I can't find much of that for somebody who won't learn. Winger had gotten herself used before. She was big and good-looking and a woman, and because she was a woman hardly anyone took her seriously. This Grange Cleaver probably just thought she was a handy freak, though he was a freak himself.

"I know, Garrett. I know. You heard this one before. Probably you'll hear it again. Sometimes it works out profitable."

Meaning she took advantage of those who used her, playing dumb country girl while she pocketed their silver candlesticks.

I gave her a shot at my famous raised eyebrow.

"I know. I know. But I got to get by while I build my reputation."

"I suppose." Getting a nasty rep was an obsession with her.

"Thanks for the passionate support. At least I caught on before it was too late to get out."

"Did you?"

"Get out? Damned right I did. See, this Cleaver told me, yeah, Winger, that's a great idea, putting somebody next to Maggie Jenn. Somebody else on account of she'd recognize me. But when I told him it was you I got to cover it, he got a face looked like he was about to have a shit hemorrhage. You'd a thought one of his buddies sneaked up and showed him he loved him by surprise. He got me out so fast I got suspicious. I sneaked around to where I could listen in on him."

I suspected Winger had done plenty of eavesdropping. "I've never heard of Cleaver. How come he's shook up about me?"

She spat. "How the hell should I know? You do got your rep as a super straight-arrow simp. Maybe that done it."

"Think so?" Winger was after an angle all the time. "So you wised up. Hard to believe. Usually it takes—"

"I ain't as dumb as you think, Garrett." She refused to provide proof, though. "What Cleaver was up to, he called in this bunch of street brunos. Not his regular butt buddies, just some muscle. He told them he had this big problem name of you and asked could they solve it for him? How about they sent you off to the Bledsoe? The brunos said sure and laughed and joked about how they done it before with some guys Cleaver didn't like. He's got people on the inside on the pad. He's connected to the hospital somehow. Probably through that blond baggage you was drooling on when I was trying to get you out of there."

"Yeah. Probably." But I didn't believe that and neither did she.

"Anyways, it took me a while to get away without nobody noticing. I came straight to the hospital."

I could imagine why it had taken her so long to slip away. Once she decided to quit Cleaver, she would want to collect everything valuable she could carry. Then she'd have to take that wherever she kept her stuff. Then she might have tested the waters to see if she couldn't carry off another load before she finally got around to me.

She knew I wasn't going anywhere.

The big rat.

"So you came whooping to the rescue only to find out that, through my own cunning, I had proceeded to effect my own release."

"You was doing all right," she conceded, "but you wouldn't never of gotten out of there if I hadn't whipped up on all them guys what would've gotten in your way downstairs."

Whatever else, Winger was a woman. I granted her the last word.

"You can let go the hand now," she said. "There ain't nothing left to squeeze out'n me."

"That a fact?" Then how come the country was coming on stronger all the time? She was putting on her camouflage. "And just when I was thinking it might be useful to learn how Maggie Jenn knows you. Just when I was getting curious about your pal Grange Cleaver. Since I've never heard of the guy, it'd probably save me a lot of time if you were to clue me where he lives, is he human or whatever, is he connected with the Outfit or anybody, stuff like that. Details. I'm a detail kind of guy, Winger."

Winger is your basic jump on the wagon and head out without checking to see if the mules are hitched up kind of woman, never long on scoping out plans or worrying about consequences. Neither past nor future mean much to her. That isn't because she's stupid or foolish, it's because that's the way she's made.

"You're a royal pain in the ass kind of guy, Garrett."

"That too. Hear it all the time. Especially from you. You're going to give me a complex."

"Not you. You got to be sensitive to get a complex. You're sensitive like a stinky old boot. Grange Cleaver, now he's a sensitive kind of guy." She grinned.

"You ever going to tell me something? Or you just going to sit there smirking like a toad on a cowpie?"

She snickered. "I told you, Garrett, Grange Cleaver is the kind of guy wears earrings."

"Plenty of guys are the kind of guys who wear earrings. That don't make them poofs. They might be fierce pirates."

"Yeah? He's also the kind of guy wears wigs and makeup and likes to dress up in girl clothes. I heard him brag about how he used to work the Tenderloin without the johns ever knowing how unique an experience they'd had."

"It happens." In the Tenderloin, in TunFaire, everything happens. I didn't consider this big news, though Cleaver did seem careless with his secrets. You get too public you can end up with more trouble than you can handle. Asking for trouble is plain dumb.

"He human?" I asked.

"Yeah."

"And don't hide his quirks?"

"Not around home. I never saw him go out in the street and run after little boys. Why?"

"He don't sound careful enough. You got any idea what a poof goes through in the army? Hell like you wouldn't believe. Bottom line is, any of them that don't hide it damned good don't last. The Cantard is no place to belong to an unpopular minority."

"I don't think Grange was in the service, Garrett."

"You're on a first-name basis?"

"He has everybody call him Grange."

"Real democratic kind of guy, eh?"

"Yeah."

"Right. So. He's human and male, he had to be in some service, Winger. They don't allow exceptions."

"Maybe he was a dodger."

"They never give up hunting those guys." They don't. Not ever. There is no privilege when it comes to conscription. Say that for our masters. No favoritism is shown there. In fact, in that regard *they* pay more than their share of the price. They do lead from the front.

Notice how Winger got me off on a tangent? I did. She had dropped out on this Cleaver princess but did not want to give up any information about him. That meant she still saw an angle.

Winger always sees an angle.

"Let's get back to the high road. What's between Cleaver and Maggie Jenn? If he's a shrieking faggot, why is he interested at all?"

"I think she's his sister."

"Say what?"

"Or maybe his cousin. Anyway, they're related somehow. And she's got something he wants. Something he figures is his."

"So she's going to kill him?" This was getting weirder by the minute.

I hate family wars. They're the worst kind. They put you out in no-man's land all alone without a map. Whatever you do turns out wrong. "What's he after, Winger?"

"I don't know." Now she was getting long suffering, the way people do when small children ask too many questions. "I just worked for the guy. I didn't sleep with him. I wasn't his social secretary. I wasn't his partner. I didn't keep his diary for him. I just took his money and did what he said. Then I came out to save your butt on account of I kind of felt responsible for getting you into a jam."

"You *were* responsible. You were running a game

on me. I don't know what it was because you've kept it to yourself. Chances are you're still running a game on me, you being you."

I was a little tired of Winger, which was another of her talents. She could exasperate you till you ran her off, leaving you thinking it was your idea that she was gone; leaving you feeling guilty for doing her that way.

"So what're you gonna do?" she asked. I had let go of her hand.

"I figure I'll suck up a few beers, then I'll get me some sleep. After I get me out of this clown costume and delouse myself."

"Want some company?"

That's my friend Winger.

"Not tonight. I just want to sleep."

"All right. You want to be that way." She got gone before I could react to the smug smile she left floating behind her. Before I fully realized that she was going without having told me anything useful, like where the hell I could find friendly Grange Cleaver.

21

"I just want to get some sleep." Usually famous last words for me when I'm working. I'd get three hours of shuteye the rest of the month.

The gods were toying with me—nobody messed with me at all. So naturally I kept waking up to listen for pounding at the door. Somewhere up there, or down there, or out there, an otherwise useless godlet was earning his reputation by tormenting me in ingenious ways. If he keeps on, he may get promoted to director of heavenly sewers.

So I failed to rest well despite the opportunity. I wakened cranky and stomped around cussing Dean for being out of town. There was no one else I could make miserable.

The true breadth and depth of my genius didn't occur to me till I was well along toward whipping up a truly awful breakfast of griddle cakes. I had forgotten to ask Winger about the guy who had followed me to Maggie Jenn's place.

Someone tapped on the front door. What the hell? It was a civilized hour, almost.

The knock was so discreet I almost missed it. I grumbled some, flipped a flapjack, and headed up front.

I was astounded when I peeped through the peephole. I threw the door open to let the radiance of that blond beauty shine on me. "Didn't expect to see you again, Doc." I examined the street behind the lovely, in case she headed up a platoon of Bledsoe guys who couldn't take a joke. I didn't see anybody, but that meant squat. Macunado Street was so crowded you could have hidden the entire hospital staff out there.

"You invited me." She looked like she had come directly from work, like maybe she'd pulled a double shift cleaning up. "You were panting over the idea." She had a sarcastic tone to counterweight a blistering smile. "Your big friend dunk you in icewater?"

"I just didn't expect to see you again. Look, I'm sorry about that mess. I just get wild when somebody pulls a dirty trick like dumping me in the cackle factory."

Her lips pruned up. "Can't you use a less contemptuous term?"

"Sorry. I'll try." I encouraged myself by recalling a thing or three people have said about my profession, most of it unflattering.

She relaxed. "The dirty trick is why I'm here. What is that smell?"

I whirled. Tendrils of smoke slithered from the kitchen. I shrieked and bounded down the hall. Our lady of the marvelous legs followed at a dignified pace.

I scooped blackened griddle cakes into the sink. They sent up smoke signals denouncing my skills as a chef. Hell, I was so bad I might be able to get on in Morley's kitchen. They had an opening. "I can use these to patch the roof," I grumbled.

"Too brittle."

"Everybody's a comedian. You had breakfast?"

"No. But . . ."

"Grab an apron, kid. Give me a hand. A little food will do us both good. What you want to know, anyway?"

She grabbed an apron. Amazing gal. "I didn't like the way you were talking last night. I decided to check it out. There was no record of your commitment, though when I joined the orderlies carrying you they assured me that you had been brought in by the Guard and the records were in order."

I made rude noises, started flapping a new generation of flapjacks.

"That was easy to check. A ranking Guard officer is an old friend of my family. Colonel Westman Block."

I squeaked three or four times before I managed to ask, "*Colonel* Block? They made a *colonel* out of him?"

"Wes speaks highly of you, too, Mr. Garrett."

"I'll bet."

"He told me you were *not* sent to the Bledsoe by his people—though he wished he'd thought of it."

"That's Block. Playful as a hogshead of cobras."

"He did speak well of you professionally. But he warned me to remain wary in other respects." She could get a laugh into her voice, too.

"You going to want bacon?"

"You just starting it now? You're supposed to start the bacon first. It takes longer."

"I cook one thing at a time. That way I only burn one thing at a time."

"A daring approach."

"Holds down expenses."

We cooked together and ate together and I spent a lot of time appreciating the scenery. The lady didn't seem to mind.

We were cleaning up when she said, "I won't tolerate this sort of thing. I won't tolerate the corruption that allows it to happen."

I stepped back, checked her out with different eyes. "You just start working there? You'd have to look hard to find a place more corrupt than the Bledsoe."

"Yes. I'm new. And I'm finding out how rotten the place is. Every day it's something. This is the worst yet. You might've spent your whole life wrongfully imprisoned."

"Yeah. And I wasn't the only one in there. You an

idealist and reformer?" TunFaire is infested with those lately.

"You don't need to make me sound like a halfwit."

"Sorry. Most wannabe utopians are, reality-wise. They come from well-to-do families and haven't the vaguest notion what life is like for people who *have* to depend on a Bledsoe. They can't imagine what life is like for the kind of people who work in a Bledsoe. For them taking bribes and selling donated supplies are perks of the job. They wouldn't understand you if you bitched about it—unless they figured you were trying to increase the override you take off the top."

She gave me a disgusted look. "Somebody suggested that yesterday."

"There you go. I bet you blew up. And didn't get through. And now everybody in the place thinks you're crazy. Maybe the better-placed guys in the bigger money are wondering if you're dangerous crazy. They worry about these new Guards kicking ass and taking names. It takes a while to corrupt reformers."

She settled with a fresh cup of tea, honey and mint in it. She eyed me, then mused, "West says you can be trusted."

"Nice of him to say. Wish I could say the same."

She frowned. "Point is, I'm dangerous already. A few days ago, several thousand marks worth of medical supplies vanished. Right away I filled two orderly slots with men I knew personally. Men I can trust."

"I see." In view of her Guard connection, I guessed they were Block's men. He had a character named Relway working for him, running his secret police force. Relway was *nasty*.

If Relway became interested in the Bledsoe, heads would roll and asses get kicked. Relway doesn't let bureaucratic roadblocks and legal technicalities get in his way. He gets in there and rights those wrongs.

I suggested, "You be careful. They think you brought in spies, they could forget their manners."

She sipped tea, studied me, which made me uncomfortable. Not that I object to having a beautiful woman check me out. I was born to be a sex object. But this beautiful woman had something less thrilling in mind. "I'm not as naive as you think, Garrett."

"Good. That'll save you a lot of pain."

"You have any idea who signed you in?"

"No. I was asleep. But I hear the prince who paid for it goes by the name Grange Cleaver."

"Cleaver? Grange Cleaver?"

"You know him?"

"He's a hospital trustee. Appointed through the imperial household." She studied me some more. "I told you I'm not as naive as you might think. That does include understanding that I might be in danger."

Could be was not how I would put it. "So?"

"So maybe I should get somebody to stick close by till the dust settles."

"Sounds like a good idea."

"You game?"

I was game, but not for that. "You want a bodyguard?"

"Wes says you won't sell out."

"Maybe not. But there's a problem."

"What?" She sounded irked.

"I don't do bodyguard work. Sorry. And I have a client already. Wouldn't do to let that obligation slide, much as part of me wants to. Also, your staff is going to harbor grudges. I wouldn't dare hang out around there."

She looked like she was getting mad. "Then what would you suggest?" She didn't try to change my mind. My feelings were hurt. Maybe she could have talked herself into something.

She was too damned businesslike.

Maggie Jenn would have tried to talk me into something.

"Friend of mine, Saucerhead Tharpe, could do the

job. Or several other guys I know. Trouble is the best guys all look like what they are." Then my muse inspired me. "My friend from last night will be looking for work."

My guest brightened, her mind darting past all the obvious caveats that would have obtained had Winger been male. "Can she do the job?"

"Better than I could. She doesn't have a conscience."

"She trustworthy?"

"Don't put her in temptation's way. The family silver might accidentally fall into her pockets. But she can get a job done."

"She tough?"

"She eats hedgehogs for breakfast. Without peeling them first. Don't get into a tough contest with her. She don't know when to quit."

She smiled. "I understand the impulse. When you step outside tradition, there's a temptation to show the boys you can do everything they can do better. All right. Sounds good. I'll talk to her. How do I get in touch?"

Finding Winger isn't easy. She wants it that way. There are people she'd rather not have sneaking up.

I explained what worked for me. She thanked me for breakfast, advice, and help, and headed for the front door. I was overwhelmed still. She was ready to let herself out before I got myself together. "Hey! Wait up. You didn't introduce yourself."

She smirked. "Chastity, Garrett. Chastity Blaine." She laughed at my goofy look, slipped out, and closed the door behind her.

22

By daylight, the Joy House is dull. Lately Morley has been open continuously, driven by some bizarre civic impulse that wants weeds and grass clippings made available to all. I was concerned. The place might start attracting horses.

I invited myself up to the bar. "Cook me up a rare steak, Sarge. And let Morley know I'm here."

Sarge grunted, scratched his crotch, hitched his pants, thought about it before he did anything—which was mainly to wonder aloud why I thought Morley Dotes gave one rat's ass whether I was infesting the Joy House or stinking up the place in Hell, where I belonged.

"You ought to open a charm school for young ladies of superior breeding, Sarge."

"Fugginay. Ain't dat da troot?"

I settled at a table. My steak arrived before Morley did. It was a thick, rare, prime center cut. Of eggplant. I forced part of it down by holding my breath and closing my eyes. If I didn't have to smell it or see it, it wasn't too bad.

Sarge's buddy Puddle trundled out of the kitchen, half a foot of hairy bare belly hanging out from under his shirt. He paused to blow his nose on his apron. He had him some kind of key on a rope around his neck. I asked, "What the hell are you supposed to be? One that got away? They didn't tie the noose tight enough?"

"I'm da wine stewart aroun' here, Garrett." My worst fears were confirmed—not only by ear but by nose. Puddle's breath told me he diligently tested his vintages. "Morley says we got to attrack a better class a' custom."

Time was you could have done that by dragging in a dozen derelicts. "You're just the guy who can do it, Puddle."

"Fugginay. Ain't dat da troot?"

These guys had the same rhetoric teacher.

"You want some wine, Garrett? To go wit' what you're havin' dere we got us a perky little fortunata petite what's maybe not as subtle as a Nambo Arsenal but—"

"Puddle!"

"Yeah?"

"It's spoiled grape juice. If they call it wine, it's spoiled grape juice. I don't care if you call it coy or brujo or whatever. Talk that wine snob talk till dooms-day, that don't change the main fact. Hell, go look at the stuff while it's changing into brassy brunette or whatever. It's got mold and shit growing on it. What it is, really, is how you get alcohol that winos and ratmen can afford."

Puddle winked and whispered, "I'm wit' you. The gods meant real men to drink dat stuff dey wouldn't of invented beer."

"What you do, you get Morley to serve beer by telling him it's cream of barley soup?"

Morley arrived during this exchange. He observed, "Wine is how the smart restauranteur fleeces the kind of man who walks around with his nose in the air."

I asked, "How come you want that kind of guy cluttering up your dance floor?"

"Cash flow." Morley planted himself in the chair opposite me. "Plain, simple, raw money. If you want it, you have to find ways to pry it loose from those who have it. Our current clientele doesn't have it.

Often. But I've noted that we've begun to attract adventurers. So I've started positioning us to become *the* in place."

"Why?"

He looked at me funny.

"Don't let me throw you with the trick questions, Morley. If they get too tough for you, holler."

"Look around. There's your answer."

I looked. I saw Puddle and Sarge and a few local "characters" using the place to get out of the weather. "Not real appetizing." I meant Puddle and Sarge.

"It's that old devil Time, Garrett. We're all a pound heavier and a step slower. It's time to think about facing realities."

"Puddle and Sarge, maybe." Morley didn't have an ounce of fat on him. I did my famous eyebrow trick, one of my more endearing skills.

He read that right. "A guy can get a step slow between the ears, too. He can lose that lean and hungry way of thinking." He eyed me as though I, of all people, should know that.

"Or he can start thinking like a cow because he doesn't eat anything but cattle fodder." I laid a pointed stare on the corpse of my eggplant filet. It had failed to live up to even my low expectations.

Morley grinned. "We're breaking in a new cook."

"On me?"

"Who better? Right, Puddle? No way we can disappoint Garrett. He was disappointed when he walked in the door. He'll bitch and gripe whatever we serve him."

I grumped, "You could poison me."

"If it would improve your disposition."

"There's an idea!" Puddle enthused. "Hows come I never thought a' that one?"

"Because you've never had a thought. If one got loose in that abandoned tenement of a head, it'd never find its way out," I muttered, but Puddle caught on anyhow.

"Yo! Sarge! We got any of dat rat poison left? Tell Wiggins to bring dis guy Garrett a special chef's surprise dessert."

I made noises to let them know what I thought of this level of humor and told Morley, "I need the benefit of your wisdom."

"You going to cry on my shoulder about one of your bimbos?"

"There's a thought. I never tried that. Maybe by way of a little sympathetic magic . . ."

"Don't expect sympathy from me."

"What I want to do is listen to you, not have you listen to me."

"This has to do with your Maggie Jenn thing?"

"Yes. The name Grange Cleaver mean anything?"

Morley glanced at Puddle. A shadow crossed his features. Puddle exchanged glances with Sarge. Then everybody faked indifference. Morley asked, "You saying the Rainmaker is back?"

"Rainmaker?"

"The only Grange Cleaver I know was called the Rainmaker. He was a fence. Big time. Where did you come onto the name?"

"Winger. She said she was working for him."

"That woman isn't your most reliable witness."

"You're telling me. But she did have an interesting story about how this guy was using her to keep tabs on Maggie Jenn. She said she thought Cleaver was Maggie's brother. Or some sort of close relation."

Again Morley tossed a glance at Puddle, then looked thoughtful. "I've never heard that one." He chuckled. There was no humor in the sound. "It can't be true, but it would explain a lot if it was. Maybe even including why *she* is back in town."

"You changing your position?"

"Huh?"

"You said she was in exile. What're you going on about, anyway?"

"All right. Grange Cleaver, alias the Rainmaker, was a very famous fence years ago."

"How can you be a famous fence? Seems to me you could be one or the other but not both."

"Famous among those who use the services of fences, wholesale or retail, supplier or end user. The Rainmaker operated on the swank. There were rumors he choreographed several big jobs himself, that he had a connection who got him the inside information he needed. He hit several Hill places. There weren't many guards back then. His raids were one reason the Hill folk set up their goon squads."

"This all connects with Maggie Jenn?"

"Maybe. It just occurred to me that the Rainmaker's heyday coincided with Maggie Jenn's famous affair. Specifically, with those months when Theodoric was dragging her around in public, not giving one good goddamn what anyone said."

"You have to admit nobody would've figured her for a spotter."

"Exactly. Her social crimes were reason enough to hate her."

"All of which is interesting but, as far as I can see, doesn't have anything to do with the job I'm getting paid to do." Though I might be wrong. Cleaver hadn't drafted me into the crackdome brigade because my colors clashed when I dressed. I was a threat somehow. "You still say Maggie Jenn doesn't have a daughter?"

"I said I didn't know about one. I still don't. But now I have a notion there's a lot I don't know about Maggie Jenn."

"Heard anything off the street?"

"Too soon, Garrett. It's a big town. And if the Rainmaker is in it, people who remember him might not talk."

"Yeah." A big town. And somewhere in it, a missing girl.

Somewhere in TunFaire there are scores of missing girls. More vanish every day. This just happened to be a girl who had someone willing to look for her.

I started toward the street.

"Garrett."

I stopped. I knew that tone. The real Morley was about to speak from behind all the masks. "What?"

"You be careful about the Rainmaker. He's as crazy as they come. Dangerous crazy."

I leaned against the door frame and did some ruminating. "I've got some real funny people in this one, Morley."

"How so?"

"They all have two faces. The Maggie Jenn I know and the one Winger told me about aren't much like the woman you describe. The Grange Cleaver Winger worked for and the one you describe aren't anything like the Grange Cleaver I heard about from another source. That Cleaver is one of the directors of the Bledsoe. He's connected with the imperial family."

"That's another new one on me. But so what?"

Yeah. So what? It occurred to me that Chastity's troubles with theft and corruption might stem from the very top.

For some reason, I just can't get used to the thinking it takes to encompass that kind of villainy. It doesn't seem reasonable to steal from the poor and the helpless, though I'm sure Morley could paste on his puzzled frown and make it all clear: you steal from the poor and helpless because they can't fight back. Because nobody gives a damn. But you do have to do one hell of a lot of stealing in order to make much money.

That's why most thieves prefer wealthier victims.

23

I decided my best course was to go home and settle in with a beer or five while I figured out how to do my job. Grange Cleaver was a side issue. Maybe I'd put time in on him after I found the missing daughter. I owed the clown. But Emerald came first.

Speaking of debts, by now his people inside the Bledsoe should have reported my brilliant, dashing escape. It might behoove me to keep a close watch on my behind.

You work yourself into the right frame of mind, it's sure something will happen. I was all primed to turn paranoid. Naturally, fate just had to set me off.

"How are you doing? I'm Ivy."

I squeaked and jumped up there where the pigeons fly. I could have clicked my heels and turned a somersault on the way down but was too busy making funny noises. I landed. And there, by the gods, was my old prison pal Ivy.

And not just Ivy. Behind Ivy, grinning merrily, was that big bozo who'd helped me with my breakout.

"You guys made it, eh? That's great." I tried easing around them. That didn't work. "How many others managed? Any idea?" I was just being sociable. You do that with unpredictable and potentially dangerous people. Hell, you should do that with anybody you don't know. You should be rude only to friends you're sure won't slice you into cold cuts. That's what manners are for.

The grinning fool grinned even wider. "Most every-body scooted, Garrett. The whole ward, I think."

"How did that happen?" I'd thought the staff were gaining control when I ran out.

"Some of us guys that had uniforms on decided to go get some paybacks after we got the smoke out of our lungs. And then a bunch of the guys still inside went berserk."

"Lucky for us they weren't crazy before." But they were crazy now and on the loose. I tried easing away again. The big guy had a knack for staying in my way.

I hadn't overlooked the fact that he knew my name even though I hadn't introduced myself. "How did you guys come to be here?" Here being Macunado Street less than two blocks from my house. A coincidence that monstrous could occur only every third leap year. It wasn't leap year.

The big guy got red. He confessed, "We was sneaking around trying to find a way out and we heard you talking to Doc Chaz. So we're on the street all this time, we don't know where to go or what to do. I ast Ivy and he don't got no suggestions."

Ivy's face brightened at the mention. He introduced himself, in case he'd forgotten his manners, then went back to studying the street. He seemed more perplexed than frightened, but I didn't think it would be long till he was ready to go back inside. I suspected that would be true for a lot of men.

"So you came looking for me."

The big guy nodded like a shy kid. "Seemed like you was a guy would know what to do."

I cussed myself silently for being the kind of fool I am. "All right. I got you into this, I'm kind of responsible. Come on. I'll get you fed, put you up tonight, maybe help you make arrangements."

Yeah. I know. Chances were good they would smell like long-dead fish before I got them out. But I did have a card up my sleeve. The Dead Man isn't handicapped by manners or an overdeveloped sense of social obligation. Guests don't overstay his welcome.

I wondered if it wasn't maybe time to start nudging him. I could use a little advice.

I let my guests into my house. The big guy was as nervous as a kid in unfamiliar territory. Ivy was as curious as a cat. Naturally, the Goddamn Parrot started raising hell in the small front room. Ivy invited himself in there while I tried to solve a problem by asking the big guy, "Do you have a name? I don't know what to call you."

Mr. Big cussed Ivy for not bringing him food.

I was beginning to miss Dean for yet another reason. He had dealt with that foul feathered fiend before he left. I still wasn't used to it.

It went into its act. "Help! Rape! Save me! Oh, please, mister, don't make me do that again." It managed to sound like a preadolescent girl. The only parrot in captivity smart enough to remember more than four words, and some wit had taught it that. I just knew if the neighbors ever heard the beast I'd never convince the lynch mob that a parrot had done the squawking. The bird would not say boo till I was swinging high.

Meantime, the big fellow stood around wearing a thoughtful look, trying to remember his name. His wits seemed to turn through seasons. Must have been summertime when he helped me at the Bledsoe. Now it was late autumn or early winter. I was glad I didn't have to deal with him all the time. I could go crazy myself.

Powziffle.

Ivy closed the door to the small front room. The Goddamn Parrot went right on screeching. Ivy grinned from ear to ear. I had a feeling I knew what was going to become of that bird. He could become the companion of a tortured fellow who needed a friend desperately.

The tortured fellow roamed on down the hall while his sidekick continued to ruminate the big question.

"Hey! Yeah!" His face brightened. "Slither." Brighter still. "Yeah! That's it. Slither." His grin dwarfed Ivy's.

"Slither?" What the hell kind of name was that? A nickname for sure, though he didn't look like a Slither to me.

Ivy had his face shoved into my office. He froze. Eventually he let out a little squeak of dismay, the first break in his six-word pattern. From the direction he was facing, I guessed he'd gotten a look at Eleanor. That painting had plenty to say to anyone with the open eyes of madness.

Slither preened, proud that he had recalled his name.

I said, "You guys come back to the kitchen. We'll have us a beer and a snack." I suspected that they hadn't eaten since their flight from the hospital. Freedom does have its disadvantages.

Slither nodded and flashed his grin. Ivy ignored me. He crossed the hall to the Dead Man's room, went inside, and got himself a shock even more horrible than the terror in the shadows behind Eleanor. The Dead Man isn't furry, little, or cuddly. He can't win instant love through cute.

I pried Ivy out of there and got him into the kitchen. We settled down to a snack of cold roast beef, pickles, cheese, mustard with verve enough to water your eyes, and adequate quantities of beer. I did more sipping than eating. Once Slither and Ivy slowed enough so they took time to breathe as well as eat, I asked, "You guys able to do anything?"

"Huh?" That was Slither. Ivy was sucking up another mug of beer, his fifth. He'd begun to look brighter, more human. I'd begun to suspect the nature of his madness. He was a wino.

"What did you do before they put you in that place?"

Slither started another five-fall match with his memory.

I wondered how well he'd done before his venture inside.

Ivy drained his mug and headed for the cold well. I caught his wrist. It didn't take much to set him down. "Don't let's overdo, Ivy."

He stared at his plate a minute, then lifted a sliver of meat to his lips. He chewed slowly for a long time. After he swallowed he startled me by saying, "You can't forget to eat, Garrett. That's the thing you've got to hang onto. You can't forget to eat."

I stared at him. Slither stared at him. Slither howled, "I'll be damned! I'll be double dog damned, Garrett! He talked. What did we do? I never heard him talk before."

The event seemed to give Slither's intellect a kick in the slats, too. He started chattering at Ivy, trying to draw him out. Ivy didn't want to be drawn. He stared at his plate and picked at his food. He looked up only once, to toss a longing glance toward the cold well. The object of his affection, my keg, lay there all alone.

"Well?"

Slither looked at me. "Huh?"

"I asked what you did on the outside, before you went in."

"How come you want to know?" The fires of genius never burned real hot here.

I had to move before he faded again. "I want to know because if I know what you can do maybe I can find somebody who'll pay you to do it." There is no shortage of work in TunFaire, honest or otherwise, what with all our young men spending five years in the Cantard and a lot of them never coming home.

"Mostly I done bodyguarding. I was pretty good

when I started, but I figure I picked up something when I was down south. I started kind of fading out sometimes. I started making mistakes sometimes. I screwed up on a real good job I got on account of my size mostly, so I took another one that wasn't quite as good and I screwed up on that one, too, so I took another job and all the time the fading got worse and worse. I started not remembering anything sometimes. Nothing. Except I kept getting the feeling that I was doing things that weren't right. Maybe really wicked things, only whatever I was doing I wasn't getting caught by nobody because I always woke up at home. Sometimes I had bruises and stuff, though. And then I was right in the right place at the right time and landed me a real sweet job. I don't know what happened or how. One day I wake up, I'm there where you found me and I don't know how long I been there or what I done to get myself put inside."

I'd seen him during one blackout. Powziffle. Maybe that one had been mild and harmless. Maybe he went berserk sometimes.

But then he'd have been in the violent ward. Wouldn't he?

"What did you do in the army?" I asked.

"Nothing, man. I wasn't no friggin' ground-pounder."

I knew that tone and that look and that fire in the eye. "You were a Marine?"

"Absofugginlutely. First Battalion. Fleet Marines."

I was impressed. That meant something to a Marine. Slither had been one of the elite of the elite. So how come ten years later he set up housekeeping in the charity bughouse? The man had to be tougher than rawhide.

On the other hand, how many tough guys fall apart with a nudge in the right way at the right time?

Slither asked, "What about you?"

"Force recon."

"Hey! All right!" He reached out to slap my hand, a silly habit left over from the Corps.

They told us when we went in we'd never stop being Marines.

"If you can keep your head together, I could maybe use you on the job I'm doing."

He frowned. "What kind of work you do? Besides bust places up like you was trying to turn the whole world into a barroom brawl?"

I explained. I explained again. He didn't get it till I told him, "It's kind of like being a mercenary—only I just find things or figure things out for people who can't handle their problems themselves."

He still frowned but got the basic idea. His trouble was that he couldn't grasp *why* I'd galavant around like I was some kind of white knight.

So I put that into terms he could understand. "Most of my clients are loaded. When things go my way, I can soak them for a bundle."

Even Ivy brightened at that. But he kept looking at my cold well like it was the gate to heaven.

I got up, dug out a bottle of wine that had been around since the dawn of time, plopped it down in front of Ivy. I drew more beer for Slither and me. I settled. Ivy went to work on his bottle. After he finished a long pull, I asked, "How about you, Ivy? What did you do in the war?"

He tried. He really did. But his tongue got tangled. Gibberish came out. I suggested he take another long drink and relax. He did. That worked. Sort of.

"So?" I urged, gently, in the back of my mind beginning to hear guilt nag because I was getting soaked with a pair of fruitcakes when I ought to be hunting a missing daughter. "What did you do down there?"

"La-la-long ra-range re-re-recon. Ra-ranger stuff."

"Excellent!" Slither murmured. Civilians wouldn't understand.

I nodded encouragement and tried to cover my surprise. Ivy didn't look the type. But a lot of guys don't. And it's often guys who make the elite outfits who're good enough to survive. They know how to take care of themselves.

"Pretty grim?" I asked.

Ivy nodded. Any other answer would have been a lie. The fighting had been tough, vicious, endless, and unavoidable. Mercy had been an unknown. The war seems won now, years after our hours in the ranks, but fighting continues on a reduced scale as Karenta's soldiers pursue diehard Venageti and try to stifle the guttering republic created by Glory Mooncalled.

"Dumb question," Slither observed.

"I know. But once in a while, I run into somebody who insists he liked it down there."

"He was rear echelon, then. Or a liar. Or crazy. The ones that can't live no other way just stay in."

"You're mostly right."

In a thin voice, Ivy said, "Th-there's sp-space for them na-now we ga-got out."

I agreed with him, too.

"Tell us more about what you do," Slither said. "What you working on now that got somebody so pissed they shoved you into the Bledsoe?"

"I'm not sure anymore." I saw no reason not to so I shared most of the details. Till I mentioned Grange Cleaver.

"Wait a minute. Whoa. Hang on. Cleaver? Like in the Rainmaker, Cleaver?"

"He's called that sometimes. Why?"

"That last job I had. The plush one. I was running errands for that faggot asshole."

"And?" I suffered a little twinge.

"And I don't remember what the hell I was doing before I woke up in the bughouse, but I'm damned well sure it was the Rainmaker what put me there. Maybe on account of I bucked him."

"This is interesting. How come you're so sure?" It wasn't that long since he couldn't remember his name.

"Account of now we're talking about it, I remember two times I helped carry guys in there myself. Guys what the Rainmaker didn't figure was worth killing but what he had a hard-on for anyway, one reason or another. He'd say anybody crazy enough to give him grief belonged in the bughouse."

I held up a hand. "Whoa!" Once he got rolling he was a rattlemouth. "I have a feeling I need to talk to Mr. Cleaver."

Slither got pale. I guess the idea didn't have a universal appeal.

24

My conscience insisted I do something to fulfill my compact with Maggie Jenn. What? Well, her daughter's backtrail had been strewn with mystical whatnots, supposed surprises to mom, indicators that Emerald was into that old black magic.

The juju stuff had been so plentiful and obvious that you had to wonder about a plant. Then you had to wonder who and why (guess I should have been digging into that), and then you had to wonder if the obviousness of the evidence argued against its having been planted. Could anybody be dumb enough to think someone would buy it?

Well, sure. A lot of TunFaire's villains aren't long on brains.

I decided I'd follow the road signs, genuine or false. If they were false, whoever planted them could tell me something.

I couldn't discount the witchcraft angle. My fellow subjects will buy anything if the guy doing the selling is a good enough showman. We have a thousand cults here. Plenty lean toward the dark side. Plenty go in for witchcraft and demon worship. Sometimes bored little rich girls amuse themselves by dabbling.

Maybe I should have inquired after the state of Emerald's virtue. That had not seemed important at the time. From her mother's account, she was in good health and otherwise normal. There was no apparent reason for her to suffer virginity at her age. Most adolescents cure that before they get rid of their acne.

If you want information about something, it always helps if you corner an expert. Sure, the street is a great source of news, but out there sometimes you have to separate raindrops from the downpour. That's maybe a lot of needless sorting if you know somebody who stays on a first-name basis with all the interesting raindrops.

People had called her Handsome for as long as I can remember, for no reason I know. Though mostly human, she had enough dwarf blood to give her a very long life. She'd been a cranky old woman when I was a kid. I was sure time had not improved her temper.

Her shop was a hole in the wall in my old neighborhood. It lay down an alley so dark and noisome even homeless ratmen would have avoided it had it not led past Handsome's place.

The alley was worse than I remembered. The trash was deeper, the slime was slipperier, the smell was stronger. The reason was simple. Every day things do get worse than they've ever been before. TunFaire is falling apart. It's sinking into its own offal. And nobody cares.

Well, some do. But not enough. Scores of factions front as many corrective prescriptions, but each group prefers to concentrate on purging heretics and infidels from the ranks, which is easier than improving the state of the city.

I should complain? Chaos is good for business. If only I could recognize lawlessness as a boon.

No wonder my friends don't understand me. *I* don't understand me.

There *were* ratmen sheltering in that alley, which was so insignificant it didn't merit a name. I stepped over one and his wine bottle bedmate to get to Handsome's door.

A bell jangled as I entered. The alleyway had been

dark. Handsome's hole was darker. I closed the door gently, waited for my eyes to adapt. I didn't move fast, didn't breathe deeply for fear I would knock something down.

I remembered it as that kind of place.

"Gods be damned! It's that Garrett brat. I thought we got shut of you years ago. Sent you off to the war."

"Nice to see you again, too, Handsome." Whoops! Big mistake there. She hated that name. But she was in a forgiving mood, apparently. She didn't react. "You're looking good. Thank you for caring. I did my five. I came home."

"Sure you didn't dodge? Garrett men don't never come home."

Gave me a twinge there. Neither my brother nor my father, nor my father's father, had come home. Seemed like a natural law: your name was Garrett, you got the glorious privilege of dying for crown and kingdom. "I beat the odds, Tilly." Handsome's real name was Tilly Nooks. "Guess that old law of averages finally caught up with the Venageti."

"Or maybe you're smarter than the run of Garrett men."

I'd heard similar sentiments expressed before. Tilly spoke more forcefully than most. She carried a grudge. My Grandfather Garrett, who went long before my time, jilted her for a younger woman.

That bitterness never kept her from treating us kids like we were her own grandchildren. Even now I can feel her switch striping my tail.

Handsome entered the shop through a doorway blocked by hanging strings of beads. She carried a lamp that had shed no light on the other side. The lamp was for me. Her dwarvish eyes had no trouble with the gloom.

"You haven't changed a bit, Tilly." And that was true. She was just as I remembered.

"Don't feed me that bullshit. I look like I been rode hard and put away wet about a thousand times."

That was true, too.

She looked like a woman who'd survived seventy very hard years. Her hair was white and thin. Her scalp shone through even in that light. Her skin hung loose, as though she'd halved her weight in a week. It was pale though mottled by liver spots large and small. She moved slowly but with determination. It hurt her to walk, but she wouldn't surrender to her frailties. I recalled those making up the bulk of her conversation. She complained continuously but wouldn't slow down. She was wide in the hips and her flesh drooped badly everywhere. Had I been asked to guess, I would've said she'd borne a dozen kids from the shape she was in, only I'd never seen or heard of any offspring.

She peered at me intently, trying to smile. She had only a few teeth left. But her eyes glittered. The mind behind them was as sharp as ever. Her smile turned cynical and weary. "So, to what do we owe the honor, after all these years?" Maybe she wasn't going to catch me up on her lumbago.

The rest of "we" was the scroungiest calico cat that ever lived. Like Handsome, she was ancient. She, too, had been old and scroungy and worn out all those long years ago. She looked at me like she remembered me, too.

You can't lie to Handsome. She always knows if you do. I learned that before I was six. "Business."

"I heard the kind of business you're in."

"You sound like you disapprove."

"The way you go at it, it's a fool's game. You're not going to get you no happiness out of it."

"You could be right."

"Sit a spell." Groaning, she dropped into a lotus position. That she could had amazed me as a kid. It amazed me now. "What's your business here?" The cat set up camp in her lap. I tried to remember the beast's name, couldn't, and hoped the question wouldn't come up.

"Witch business, maybe. I'm looking for a missing girl. The only clue I have is that I found witchcraft type stuff in her rooms."

Handsome grunted. She didn't ask why that brought me to her. She was a major supplier of witchy stuff; chicken lips and toad hair and frog teeth. "She left it behind?"

"Apparently." Handsome provided the very best raw materials, but I've never understood how. She never left home to acquire stock and I never heard of anybody who wholesaled that stuff. Rumor says Handsome is rich despite the way she lives. Makes sense to me. She's supplied the witch trade for generations. She's got to have chests full of money somewhere.

"Don't strike me as the kind of thing a witch would do."

"Didn't me, either." Occasionally a bunch of baddies will ignore the lessons of history and try to rob Handsome. None succeed. Failure tends to be painful. Handsome must be a pretty potent witch herself.

She's never said she's a witch. She's never claimed special powers. The fakes do that. The fact that she's grown old swimming with sharks says all that needs saying.

I told her my story. I left nothing out because I didn't see any point. She was a good listener.

"The Rainmaker is in it?" Her whole face pruned into a frown. "I don't like that."

"Oh?" I waited.

"We haven't seen him for a while. He was bad news back when."

"Oh?" Handsome liked to talk. Given silences to fill, she might cough up something especially useful. Or she might take the opportunity to catch me up on her illnesses and infirmities. "People keep telling me he's bad, but it's like they're embarrassed to say how. It's hard to get scared once you've spent five years nose to nose with Venageta's best and more than that butting heads with people like Chodo Contague." Chodo used to be the kingpin of crime in TunFaire.

"A Chodo uses torture and murder and the threat of violence like tools. The Rainmaker hurts people on account of he enjoys it. My guess is he's anxious not to get noticed. Otherwise he wouldn't stuff people into the Bledsoe. We'd find pieces of them all over town." She went on to paint the portrait of a sadist, yet another view of Cleaver.

I was starting to have misgivings about meeting the guy. But I had to do it, if only to explain that not liking a guy isn't any reason to shove him into the cackle factory.

Handsome rattled on, passing along fact, fancy, rumor, and speculation. She knew an awful lot about Cleaver—in the old days. She could tell me nothing about him now.

"All right," I finally put in, stopping that flood. "What about witchcraft cults today? The kind of black magic stuff that would appeal to bored kids? Any of that going around?"

Handsome didn't say anything for a long time. I wondered if I'd overstepped somehow. Then she said, "There could be."

"Could be?" I couldn't picture her not knowing everything about such things. "I don't get it."

"I don't got a monopoly on witchcraft supplies. They's other sellers around. None to match me for quality or inventory, but they's others. Been new people coming into the trade lately. Mostly they go after the nonhuman market. The folks you want to talk to is Wixon and White. They don't ask questions the way I would and their slant is toward your rich crowd."

"I love it when you talk dirty."

"What? Don't you jump to no conclusions about

folks on account of where you find them, boy. They's geniuses in the Bustee and fools on the Hill."

"I don't see what you're saying."

"You always was dense."

"I'd rather people said things straight out. That way there's no confusion."

"All right. I don't know anything about anything like what you're hunting, but I got me a strong suspicion that they's a whole passel of rich folks getting used by some real nasty demon worshippers. Wixon and White is where you start. They'll sell anything to anybody what's got the money."

"That's all I wanted. A place to start. You remember Maggie Jenn?"

"I recollect the scandal."

"What kind of woman was she? Could she have been connected to the Rainmaker?"

"What kind of woman? You think we was friends?"

"I think you have an opinion." If she didn't, it would be a first.

"They was a thousand stories. I think maybe they was some truth in all of them. Yes, she was connected. Bothered that Teodoric considerable. One time he threatened to have the Rainmaker killed. Worried the Rainmaker enough that he got out of town. I heard Teodoric was plotting to hunt him down when he got killed hisself."

"Any connection?"

"Coincidence. Every king makes him a crop of enemies. The Rainmaker staying away after Teodoric died says he had other reasons to go. There was talk he got the wise guys mad. I wonder what brought him back?"

She mentioned wise guys. It could have to do with Chodo's semi-retirement. Already several ambitious men had tried to take advantage, but Chodo's daughter played the game as hard as her father. She would cast a cold eye on the Rainmaker if he made a wrong move.

And on the law side we had us the new Guard, who would love to lay hands on a famous villain—if one could be found who didn't have connections. The Rainmaker might do.

I inched toward the exit. "Wixon and White?" I was afraid she'd do the old give us a kiss.

"That's what I said. You come around more than once every twelve years, you hear?"

"I will," I promised, with all the good intentions I always have when I make that promise.

She didn't believe me. It was getting so I was beginning to doubt myself.

25

I've done some dumb things in my time—for example, forgetting to ask Handsome where Wixon and White hung their shingle. I remembered after I was three blocks away. I hustled back—and got what I deserved.

Her shop wasn't there anymore. The alley wasn't there. I was boggled. You hear about that stuff, but you don't expect it.

After that disappointment, I just strolled to the nearest place where I knew somebody and asked if they'd ever heard of Wixon and White. It's a fact. Somebody you know will at least know somebody who knows the person or place you want.

That's the way I got to it. A bartender I knew, name of Shrimp, had heard of Wixon and White from a client. So Shrimp and I shared a few beers on me, then I started hiking. The Wixon and White establishment lay way out in the West End.

They were closed. Nobody answered my knock. The place was a rental. Wixon and White were so highly priced and cocksure they didn't live on the premises.

That part of the West End is pure upscale. The shops all serve those who have money they don't know what to do with. Not my kind of people. Not any kind of people I can understand, buyers or sellers.

I kept an eye out for armed patrols. Those had to be around, else the shops would all be boardups. I wondered if the Outfit wasn't involved. Some of the shops had glass windows. That meant real heavyweight protection.

Wixon and White looked like a place that would serve upper-crust dabblers in black magic, at embarrassing prices. Wixon or White, whoever did the buying, probably acquired inventory from Handsome, tripled her retail, then tripled it again. Then they'd probably jack up the price on particularly thick-witted customers. The people who shopped the area would be the kind who got off on telling friends how much they paid for things.

Feeling my prejudices coalesce into an urge to break glass, I got me out of there.

I had nothing to do and no inclination to go home to a house where all I'd have for company would be a psychotic parrot and a couple of bark-at-the-moon boys. I hoped that foul-mouthed squab was starving to death.

I asked myself why I didn't stop in and see how Playmate was doing. He might have regained consciousness by now.

26

Damn! Playmate looked none the worse for wear. I snapped, "What the hell are you? Twins?"

"Garrett!" He swept out of the shadows of his stable, arms spread wide. He'd been using a pitchfork to do what you do a lot of if you operate a stable. He didn't seem stiff or sore. He swept me up in a hug. He's never stopped being demonstrative when I come around, though it's been a long time since I saved his business.

"Easy, man. I'm breakable. Unlike some I could name." The tenderness wasn't gone from my ambush bruises.

"You heard about my mishap?"

"Heard? I was there. I'm surprised you can walk, what they had to do to bring you down."

"I am a little sore. But somebody's got to care for the beasties."

"So send for the boys from the tannery." Me and horses don't get along. Nobody takes me seriously, but I know for a fact that the whole species is out to get me. The moment nobody is looking, the moment I have my back turned, those damned oatburners start moving in.

"Garrett! What a cruel thing to say."

"You think the best of everybody." They've got Playmate fooled. They stood right there in their stalls sneering and measuring me for a shroud while he defended them. He actually loves the monsters. He thinks I'm just ribbing him, making jokes in bad taste.

Somebody he'll learn. When it's too late.

I asked, "Got a lot of work to do?"

He indicated the manure pile. "You have to haul the hay in and the fertilizer out. They don't take days off."

"Make that pressing work. You have time for a few beers? On your old buddy? That pile won't go anywhere."

"Not if I don't move it." He frowned. "On you? Must be an awful big favor."

"What?"

"Must be some giant favor you want. You never offered to buy me a beer before."

I sighed. "Wrong." This was a battle I'd been fighting for years. All my friends insist I never come around unless I want something. Wasn't all that long since I'd bought Playmate dinner and all the beer he could drink, so he'd introduce me to a man who made coaches. "But I'm not going to fight." I'd show him. "You coming?"

The trouble with a guy Playmate's size is, he can't just drink *a* beer. One beer is a drop in the necessary stream. The man decides to get seriously ripped you have to send for the beer wagons.

He picked the place. It was a small, dark, shabby one roomer furnished in Early Thrownaway. Everyone there knew Playmate. They just had to come say hello. It was a long time before we could talk—and that got interrupted every time another body arrived.

Meantime, we ate. And drank. On me. Ouch, said my purse.

Hole in the wall though that place was, it served a fine dark ale supposedly brewed on the premises. And someone in the kitchen had a more than nodding acquaintance with the art of cookery. I devoured slice after slice of a roast that would have embarrassed Dean's best effort.

The prices were reasonable, too—for those not trying to support a one-man regiment in the habit of eating only when someone else was buying. I asked, "How come this place isn't swamped with customers?"

Playmate awarded me one of his righteous, thoughtful looks. "Prejudice, Garrett."

"Uh-hum?" It was testing time again. Playmate, who wanted to be a priest once, has to keep checking to make sure I stay more good guy than bad.

Forewarned, sure he was going to zing me by telling me the place was run by ratmen—whom I dislike more than I dislike horses, with, admittedly, weaker cause—I was pleasantly surprised when he told me, "It's run by centaurs. A refugee family from the Cantard."

"Where else?" Through a heroic effort I kept a straight face. "I can see how they might have trouble building a clientele." Centaurs aren't beloved. They'd long served Karenta's forces as auxiliaries in the Cantard. But when the mercenary Glory Mooncalled defected and proclaimed the Cantard an independent republic, every centaur tribe joined him. Chances were this family had fought Karenta till recently. When things fell apart down there, where did they run? Straight to the cities of Karenta, whose soldiers they'd been killing.

I don't understand why they're welcomed. Sure, there's room in the economy, what with all the young men gone for soldiers. But all those young men are going to be coming home. Venageta has been driven from the Cantard. Glory Mooncalled has been crushed. Sort of.

Centaurs. Bloody hell.

I kept my thoughts to myself, shifted subjects, told Playmate what I was doing for Maggie Jenn. I didn't overlook such embarrassing adventures as my unexpected visit to the Bledsoe. Playmate wasn't Winger. He wouldn't spread it all over town. He smiled gently and forebore the opportunity to score a remark on the state of my mental health. That's why I love the guy. None of my other friends could have resisted.

He asked, "What do you need from me?"

"Need? Nothing."

"You come, brought me out here, fed me, and filled me up with beer, Garrett. You got to want something."

"That stuff used to be funny, Playmate. About a thousand years ago. Ragging me for the fun, I can go along with that. For a while. But it's gotten real old. I wish you guys would find a new song to sing."

"You mean that?"

Butter wouldn't have melted in my mouth. "Damned straight." I was getting what I needed already, an uncritical ear and a break from loneliness.

"You just don't realize," he muttered. Louder, "In that case, maybe I can help."

"Huh?"

"I know a little something about the witchcraft scene. I have clients who belong to that world."

I was surprised. His religion, a self-defined offshoot of Orthodoxy, doesn't hold much truck with witches. Which doesn't make a lot of sense when you think about how big sorcery and demonism are in this burg. But I have a suspicion that religion isn't supposed to make sense. If it did, there'd be no buyers.

This was Playmate showing off his tolerance again.

"All right. I'll take you up on it. There any new covens around?"

"Of course. In a city this size, there are always covens forming and falling apart. Human nature, being what it is, there are always egos getting bruised and—"

"I understand. You heard of any in particular? Any that have been recruiting young women?"

"No."

"Damn! So, that's that. Well, then, tell me about Maggie Jenn. Morley tells me you've got the skinny on the royals."

"Tell me what you already know."

I highlighted.

He told me, "There isn't much I can add. She did have a daughter. I thought the girl died but evidently not. Nobody's proved it, but Maggie probably was a pricy pro before Teodoric took her up. Under a different name, of course. Morley was wrong about her being in exile. She does spend most of her time on the Isle of Paise, but that's preference. She spends a month each year in the Hill place. If she doesn't use it, she loses it. She does keep her head down when she's in town. She doesn't want her enemies to get too unhappy."

I nodded, understanding. I signaled for more of that excellent house brew. I had enough inside me already that sounds had buzzes around their edges, but that superman Playmate hadn't yet stumbled over his tongue.

"Grange Cleaver," I said. "The Rainmaker. What about him?"

"Been a while since I've heard of him. Curious that he's back in town."

"Maybe. I think it has something to do with Maggie Jenn."

"You be careful of him, Garrett. He's crazy. Blood crazy. They called him the Rainmaker because he left so many weeping widows around. He was big into torture."

"Just your average, everyday psycho next door. What was between him and Maggie Jenn?"

"I can't swear. From the little I've heard, he could've been her pimp."

"Her pimp?" I tried it out. "Her pimp." That had a feel to it, all right.

I dropped some money in front of Playmate, for the house. "Enjoy. I'm going to go put my thinking cap on."

Playmate divested himself of various remarks of the sort that have become fashionable among my acquaintances. I ignored him.

That last piece of news put a whole different weight on everything. Unless I was guessing way wrong.

It could happen.

27

Once bitten, twice shy? How often have I gotten nipped because I don't have the sense to get out of this racket? Often enough that I no longer wander around without tools to defend myself. Often enough that I stay alert once somebody starts getting physical.

Despite a few ales too many, I spied the ambush on Macunado—mainly because the night traffic was missing. The denizens of my fair city can smell trouble at a thousand yards, like small game when a troll is prowling the woods.

So it was as rowdy as a desert ruin around my place. It was so quiet I had trouble picking out the ambushers.

I finally caught the stir of a shadow in a breezeway across Macunado. There was no way to sneak up from where I was, so I retreated, took a long way.

All of a sudden I felt cheerful, the prospect of cracking heads making me high. That wasn't my way. The case was getting to me—if it *was* a case. I wasn't convinced.

I came at the guy from behind, singing a ratman working song. Far as I know it's the only working song they have, so few of them actually hold jobs. . . . Between the fake accent and fake drunken singing, my man was way off guard. He cussed me instead of getting set for trouble.

I staggered up and popped him between the eyes with my headthumper. He said "Gleep!" and stumbled backward, his knees watery. I grabbed his shirt, pushed him down onto his knees, slipped behind him, and laid the length of my stick under his chin. "All right, bruno, I lean back sudden and you find out what it'll be like the day you hang." I gave a little jerk to make my point. Also to keep him from getting too much air. He wouldn't be interested in much else if I kept him on short rations. "Get the point?"

He got the point. He grunted cooperatively—after I'd cut him off for a while.

"Excellent. Now here's the part where you tell me who sent you and how many buddies you have and where they're hanging out."

Give the guy credit. He was loyal to his pals. You don't see a lot of that in street thugs. He made me take him to the brink of the big sleep before he gave in. That was right after I whispered, "I've always found that the best way to run a bluff is don't be bluffing. You don't help me out here I'll just hunt me down another guy."

I was bluffing.

He made noises indicating that I'd smooth-talked him into cooperating. I eased off on the stick. "Maybe you better talk on the exhale. Or I might get edgy. You guys messing with me last night got my dander up."

Wham! I quick thumped him for thinking about what he was thinking of trying. "So who sent you?" I went back to choking him.

"Cleafer," he gasped. "Guy named Cleafer."

"Surprise, surprise," I muttered. "He happen to say why?"

Grunt and choke. Meant no, and who gave a damn why anyway? This Cleafer was paying real money.

"How may pals you got with you?"

Seven. Seven? "I'm flattered. This Cleafer must have a high opinion of me." I have a high opinion of me, but my enemies don't usually agree.

My man made sounds indicating he couldn't have agreed less. I took that to mean that he was recovering too fast. I popped him again.

I get less nice as I get older.

We chewed the fat till I knew where his buddies were hiding and I understood their grand strategy, which was to round me up and drag me off to their boss's hideout. Friendly Grange Cleaver, pre-owned property salesman, wanted to have a chat.

"Yeah. I like that idea. We'll do that. Only maybe we won't stick too close to the original scheme."

I popped the guy again, hard enough to put him to sleep. He was going to have a headache worse than the one his gang had given me.

Funny. I didn't feel bad about that.

So I went around pounding the stuffings out of guys till thumping heads no longer made me feel better. I wondered what folks on the shadow side would say when word got around. After the usual exaggerations, it might start worrying the kind of people who get in my way.

Nobody would believe it, probably. Everybody thinks I use Morley Dotes for all my heavy work.

I rounded up the smallest thug, a bit of a guy so tiny he had to be a breed. I slung him over my shoulder and headed for the Joy House.

Sometimes you can use a helping hand.

28

Morley tousled the little fellow's hair. "He's mad, Garrett. This is one you'd better not leave behind." We were in Morley's office upstairs at the Joy House. The veggie killers were rioting downstairs.

"And after I decided to give him a break. Any of those guys related to you, Stubby? Your lover or something?"

The little breed glared.

"I like this guy." Morley frowned at Spud, who was sizing the prisoner up for some painful burns.

"What?" the kid demanded.

"He's still officially a guest."

"Sure. And if I was here with a guy who'd just offed my whole gang but me I think I'd be a little more disturbed. Look at that fool. He's already sizing us up for some pain when it's him that's in the shit."

"Narcisio! Language!"

"He's got a point, Morley," I said. "The clown ought to be more scared."

"He's going to be, Garrett. It's just that he's from out of town."

I agreed. "How can you tell?" I wanted to see if his thinking paralleled mine.

"Because he isn't scared. Look, now he's got an idea who has him. He's starting to tense up. They didn't tell him anything when they gave him the job. They just put money in his pocket and told him to help with a snatch."

"I do believe you're right." I tried out a ferocious smile, like the guys from the violent ward would wear if they were sent out to play.

Morley was right. The little guy had heard of Morley Dotes even if he hadn't heard of me. He squeaked. Maybe Winger was right about reputation's tool value.

"I do believe he has a notion to deal," Morley observed.

"So," I said. "You want to be lucky number seven, the one who got away, or just another stiff?"

"Lucky seven sounds great to me."

"Look at that. He kept his sense of humor, Morley. I think that's great. All right, Lucky, what was the plan?" I told Morley, "Be a shame to let it go to waste."

Morley flashed a humorless grin. "Best thinking you've done in years." He was ready to go. I'd been surprised by how quickly he'd agreed to help. I recalled the glances between him and Sarge and Puddle. Was there old business between them and the Rainmaker?

I worry when Morley gets agreeable. I always end up getting jobbed.

"How much are you ready to spend, Garrett?"

I considered my agreement with Maggie Jenn, then the size of my advance. "Not much. You have something in mind?"

"Recall the Rainmaker's reputation. We could use some specialists to calm him down if he gets excited."

"Specialists?" Here comes a sales pitch. "Like who?"

"The Roze triplets." Naturally. Perennially underemployed relatives.

Specialists I wouldn't call them, but those guys *could* calm people down. Doris and Marsha were about sixteen feet tall and could lay out a mammoth with one punch. Part giant, part troll, the only way to beat them was to booby-trap their resolve with barrels of beer. They'd drop anything to get drunk.

The third triplet was an obnoxious little geek barely Morley's size good for nothing but translating for his brothers.

"No, Morley. This is a freak show already. I just want to talk to the guy, find out why he's messing with me."

Morley stared at Lucky. "Garrett, Garrett, just when I thought you were developing sense. You don't talk to the Rainmaker. All he understands is raw power. Either you can kick his ass or he can kick yours. Unless he's changed his spots in a big way."

I grimaced.

"What?"

"My budget is pretty tight."

"Big news, big news."

"Hey!"

"There you go getting cheap again, Garrett. You want to save money? Don't bug the Rainmaker. Just lock your door and snuggle up to your moneybags and hope he can't think of a way to get to you. After tonight, he'll be trying for real."

I knew that. Cleaver sounded like he was all ego and no restraint. All the reason he needed I'd already provided.

What a dummy, Garrett. Your troubles are all your own fault. You should try a little harder to get along.

I mused, "How did he know I was out of the Bledsoe?"

Morley and Spud perked up, smelling a tale not yet told. I had to yield enough sordid details to get them off my back. Which was way more than I wanted anyone to know, really. "I get any razzing back off the street I'm going to know where to lay the blame."

"Yes." Morley gave me his nasty smile. "Winger." That smile turned diabolical. He saw he'd guessed right. I hadn't thought about who knew the story already.

What Winger knew could spread from river to wall in a night. She liked to hang out with the guys, get drunk and swap tall tales. The story would grow into a monster before she was done with it.

I said, "You *really* feel like we need the Rozes, get the Rozes."

"You gave me a better idea."

"Well?"

"Use those clowns you have stashed at your place. Make them earn their keep. You said the big one owes Cleaver anyway."

"That's an idea. Lucky, what direction are we going to head?"

Morley added, "Keeping in mind that I'll be a lot deadlier a lot quicker than Cleaver if Garrett is disappointed."

"West." The little fellow's croak contained undertones of frightened whine. I didn't blame him. He was in the proverbial between of the rock and the hard place.

"West is good," I said. "West means we can drop by my place on the way."

I assumed Lucky's buddies would have cleared off.

Morley and his bunch looked unexcited by this opportunity. They're villains, though, and no villain in his right mind got within mind reading range of the Dead Man. However strong my assurances that he was asleep.

"His bark is worse than his bite," I said.

"Right," Sarge sneered. Puddle and Morley backed him up. Spud took that as his cue to ape his elders. I gave up.

29

I found Ivy in the small front room arguing with the Goddamn Parrot. The Goddamn Parrot was making more sense. Beer and brandy odors were potent. Which had drunk more? Who knows? The Goddamn Parrot would suck it up as long as you let him.

Ivy seemed determined to clean me out before he got kicked out. I told him, "You'd better ease up or there won't be anything left for breakfast."

Ivy looked distressed. You could see him struggling to light a fire under the pot of his thoughts. I doubted he'd get them simmering. He did seem to grasp the notion that my alcohol reserves were finite.

"Where's Slither?" The big guy was nowhere in sight. There was a racket from upstairs, but nothing human could be making that.

I could see through the open kitchen doorway. The view set me to talking to myself. Friend Slither was trying to do to my larder what Ivy was doing to my drinking supply.

So much for good deeds.

They start preaching at you when you're barely old enough to walk. But what the hell happens when you *do* try to help your fellow man? You get it up the poop chute every time. Without grease.

Where do the preachers get their crazy ideas? How many cheeks do *they* have to turn? How come they aren't hobbling around with bandages on their butts?

"Where's Slither?" I demanded again.

Ivy answered with a slow shrug. I don't think he understood anything but my tone. He started trying to explain Orthodox transcircumstantiation to the Goddamn Parrot. The Goddamn Parrot made remarks with which I agreed.

I commenced a quest for Slither. Snores from above seemed worth investigation.

Slither was sprawled across Dean's bed, on his back, his snores like the bellows of mating thunder-lizards. Awe held me immobile. The man couldn't be human. He had to be a demigod. He was producing an orchestra of snores, humming and roaring and snorting and sputtering. He seemed capable of combining every known species of snore. All in the same breath.

When I could move again I went to my own room. I hate to disturb an artist at work. I shut my door, went to the window, checked Morley and his crew and the ever astonishing traffic on Macunado. Where could all those creatures be going? What drove them to be out at this hour? Was just my neighborhood in a ferment? I couldn't recall seeing as much traffic anywhere else—though the whole city seemed crowded these days.

I could hear Slither's every snore. I'd hear every snore plainly for however long he remained in my house.

So much for doing good deeds.

Morely gave the boys a glance and said nothing. He did shake his head. Even I now wondered if they hadn't made it all up about their service. Especially Ivy. He had the Goddamned Parrot on his shoulder. It mixed its finest gutter observations with declarations of, "Awrrgh, matey! We be ferocious pirates." That naturally drew a lot of attention. Just the thing you want when you're out to sneak up on a guy calls himself the Rainmaker.

My prisoner indicated a brick and stone monstrosity he insisted was the Rainmaker's headquarters. Dotes opined, "You get what you pay for, Garrett." His glance speared Ivy and Slither. "You didn't pay for the Roze brothers."

"Don't remind me." Slither was awake but might as well have been snoring. It was winter at his house. Ivy was still trying to argue with the Goddamn Parrot. The feathered devil figured he'd sorted Ivy out already and had turned to reminiscing about his sailing days.

Morley tossed a glance sideways, checking to see how near Spud was. He flexed his fingers like he suffered the same temptations I did. "Go ahead," I said.

He scowled. "Can't. But I'll figure a way."

I said, "The course of our relationship has shown me a few things about dear Mr. Big." More cunning than usual, having foreseen the possibility that the Goddamn Parrot might become a liability, I'd brought a little flask of brandy I'd dug out of a cache Ivy hadn't found.

Morley snickered. So, he knew. I said, "We need to keep Ivy away long enough to get the bird snockered."

"He was a scout, send him scouting. Along with Spud."

"You sneak." I looked at Cleaver's place. "What did they do to the guy who designed that place?" The building had been a small factory once. Undoubtedly manned by the blind. It was *ugly*. I was amazed that so much ugliness could be committed with simple construction materials.

"Probably burned him at the stake because they couldn't think of a punishment nasty enough to fit the crime." Dotes chuckled. He was going to have some fun with me playing high-nose elf.

His tastes in art and architecture naturally weren't human. For all I knew, the lunatic who designed that factory was one of his forebears.

I expressed that opinion and added, "It may be on the elvish list of historic structures."

Morley scowled. He wasn't pleased. He grabbed Spud and Ivy and told them to go check the place out. "And leave the bird here. It doesn't have sense enough to keep its beak shut."

Off they went. The rest of us got out of sight and listened to Cleaver's man bitch because I hadn't cut him loose yet. "I'm busy, man," I told him. "I'm feeding my parrot." The Goddamn Parrot was sucking up the brandy. "I'll cut you loose as soon as I know you didn't job us." I didn't think he had. Nobody sane would pick such an ugly hideout. Cleaver did sound like he had the kind of ego that would appreciate the place.

Ivy and Spud scurried back. The kid said, "The place is occupied. I didn't ask names, though. The guys I did see looked antisocial enough to be the sort Mr. Garrett wants to find."

I didn't *want* to find anybody. "You been giving him lessons?"

"It's in the blood. Needs to work on his diction and grammar, though."

"Definitely. Smartass ought to know how to talk good."

"Can I go now?" the prisoner asked.

Spud demanded, "What happened to Mr. Big? Hey! He's drunk. Uncle Morley, did you? . . ."

"No, Lucky," I said. "I still don't know you didn't job us. Suppose you just led us to a place where some hard boys hang out?"

Morley opined, "That monstrosity is the kind a fence would use. Plenty of storage. Probably an owner who hasn't been seen in years. No traceable connection to anyone if you looked for one. You going to do it?"

I considered my help. Neither Ivy nor Slither incited

confidence. "Looks like we're as ready as we're gonna get. Any tactical suggestions?"

"Straight through the front door might work."

"Wise ass. Slither, Ivy, come on." I trotted toward that monument to ugliness. My strange assistants toddled after, bewildered but loyal. Morley told Sarge to stick with us, just in case. He came himself. So Spud and Puddle volunteered, too. Spud was protesting, "Mr. Garrett, you shouldn't give Mr. Big alcohol."

What I always wanted to do: storm a fortress at the head of a pack of killer elves, fugitives from an insane asylum, and a drunken parrot.

The Goddamn Parrot was muttering something about its imperiled virtue but in Drunkenese so fluent even a tipsy ratman would have had trouble following him.

Spud said, "Uncle Morley, did you? . . ."

"Be quiet."

I looked at that jungle chicken and grinned like a dwarf just awarded an army weapons contract.

30

The place was ugly, but it was no fortress. We found an unguarded side door. I cracked the crude stopper and invited us in. Dean should've been there to see how much good locks do.

"Dark in here," Ivy said. What did he expect?

He sounded troubled, like somebody wasn't playing fair.

"Crackbrain's got one sharp eye on him," Sarge sneered. "Goddamn Rainmaker can't fool him for a secont."

"That's enough," Morley snapped. He peered around. Elves really can see in the dark, almost as good as dwarves.

"What you see?" I whispered. We all whispered. Seemed the sensible thing to do.

"What you would expect."

What kind of answer was that? What I'd expect was filth and squatters and a lot of upset on account of the style of our entrance. But only the rats seemed disturbed—and they were so confident they just went through the motions.

According to Spud, the natives resided on the other side of the building. And so they did. Mostly.

We were sneaking along a hallway illuminated by one halfhearted candle, me thinking what a cheap-skate the Rainmaker had to be, when some sleepy-eyed goof ruined everything.

He stepped out of a room just ahead, both hands

harrowing hair already well-harvested by time. He woke up fast, generated one man-sized squeal before I bopped him with my second-best headthumper. He squealed even louder. I had to pop him four times before he laid down.

"That tears it," Slither muttered. It was hard to hear him because of the racket being raised by people I couldn't see wanting to know what the hell was going on.

"Never mind the opinion survey. You know this place?"

"Never seen it before."

"Thought you said . . ."

"Never was here. That I remember."

The hall hung a right. I stayed with it. I met a native coming the other way. He had a stick, too. His eyes got big. So did mine. I swung first. He ducked, showed me some heel, whooped and hollered.

"You could have moved a little faster there, Garrett," Morley suggested. The racket ahead grew louder. Morley was concerned.

The fugitive blew through a doorway. I was only two steps behind, but when I got there the door was closed and locked. I flung one granite shoulder against it. It gave about a thousandth of an inch.

"You do it." Morley indicated Slither. "Stop whimpering, Garrett."

"I dislocated everything but my ankle bones."

Slither knocked on the door with his very large feet, smashing away numerous times before he risked his own tender shoulder.

The door exploded like stage furniture. Guess you have to have the knack.

We'd reached the warehouse area. Only a few lamps burned there. Definitely a cheapskate, the Rainmaker. Looked like the place was being used as a barracks. People flew around like startled mice, headed for other exits. Only the guys from the hall looked like fighters.

Curious.

Amidst the howl and chaos I glimpsed a familiar gargoyle, my old pal Ichabod. Excuse me. My old pal Zeke. Zeke did a fast fade. I went after him. We needed to have a talk. My pretty Maggie Jenn had troubles enough without her butler being hooked up with the Rainmaker.

I didn't find a trace. He vanished like the spook he resembled.

We searched the dump. We found no sign of Grange Cleaver. We caught only three people—the guy from the hall who I'd bopped, plus an old couple who hadn't reached their walkers in time to grab a head start.

The old woman was about a week younger than Handsome. Her husband and the thug showed little inclination to talk, but she chattered like she was so full of words they ripped out of her like gas after an unfriendly meal.

"Whoa, granny, whoa!" She'd lost me in some kind of twin track complaint that blamed her lumbago on the incredible ingratitude of her willfully neglectful children. "That's unfortunate. It really is. But what I need to know is where is Grange Cleaver?"

"You might try to be more diplomatic," Morley suggested. Like he had the patience of a saint when he was after something.

"I was diplomatic the first three times. I did my part. Now I'm not in the mood for diplomacy, I'm in the mood for busting heads."

I didn't do it good enough. Nobody was impressed until Spud let his young mouth run too long and the bad folks figured out that they were in the hands of the infamous Morley Dotes. Then, even the hard boy developed a mild case of cooperation fever.

Yep, maybe Winger was right.

Fat lot of good that all did. Granny Yak-Yak had the definitive answer and the definitive answer was: "He just went out, him and his boys. He never said where, but I figure he was gonna check on some guys he sent out a long time ago. He paid them and they never reported back." She laid a hard look on pal Lucky.

Lucky looked a tad frayed. The old folks understood whose information had brought us to uglyville. He was growing concerned about his boss's temper.

Morley spun him around. "Cleaver brought you from out of town. He do that with a lot of men, Lucky?"

Lucky gave us the daggers glare. We were leaving him no exit. "Yeah." Sullenly. He thought we were cheating on our end of the deal. Maybe we were. Tough.

"Why?"

"I guess on account of he couldn't find anybody here what was willing to work for him. 'Specially after they found out who he was when he was here before. Way I hear it, he made him some enemies back then what nobody wants to piss off."

I gave Morley a look. Some people might consider him major bad news, but he wasn't big enough bad news that his displeasure would intimidate thugs working for somebody he didn't like. I didn't think. "Chodo," I said. Call it intuition.

Morley nodded. "There was a little brother who died badly. Chodo was way down the ladder then. He couldn't get the go-ahead. But he didn't forget."

Not once in his life had Chodo Contague let a debt go unpaid. "But ..."

"You and I know. No one else does."

He and I knew that Chodo had become a vegetable after suffering a stroke. These days, his daughter was the power in the outfit. She only pretended to take instructions from her father.

"Crask and Sadler." Those two knew, too.

Morley inclined his head slightly. "They might explain a few things."

Crask and Sadler had been Chodo's chief bone-breakers before they turned on him, caused his stroke, tried to take over. They disappeared after Chodo's daughter outmaneuvered them.

Coincidentally, there'd always been some doubt about their commitment to masculinity, despite the fact that they were two human mountains on the hoof.

I described them. Lucky's discomfort made it obvious he had met the boys. I shot Morley a look. "I don't need any more complications."

Morley prodded Lucky. Lucky admitted, "You won't see them guys around here. Grange, he's got a straight look to him back home. Didn't want them guys turning up in his public life. Figured they'd be lightning rods for trouble around here. So he gave them jobs in Suddleton."

Where, I had no doubt, they spent their spare time scheming revenge on me. "Morley, you get the feeling pal Lucky is holding out? He knows an awful lot about the Rainmaker's business."

"I noticed that."

Lucky protested. "I just heard his regular guys gossiping. You know how it is, guys sitting around, killing time drinking."

"Sure. Tell me, Lucky, where you going to run when we cut you loose?"

Lucky checked the old folks, shrugged. He was scared. They weren't, though the old woman had chattered. I wondered if they were something special to the Rainmaker.

I was about to ask about Zeke when Morley remarked, "We've spent enough time here, Garrett. Help could be on its way."

Yes, indeed. It could be.

31

"You just walk along with us, answer a couple more questions," I told Lucky and the old folks, "and we'll be done." I gestured, a comealong. "There was a guy named Zeke ..."

The Goddamn Parrot did the only worthwhile thing I ever saw him do. He flailed out of the darkness shrieking, "Save me! Oh, save me, mister." His tone suggested he wasn't just being obnoxious.

He wasn't.

There were eight of them. Wasn't hardly fair to them, even considering they were all big, experienced villains. Sarge and Puddle pounded our captives, then vaulted the leftovers and began twisting limbs. There was something evilly fascinating about them at work. It was kind of like watching a snake swallow a toad.

I didn't have time to be fascinated. I was up to my crotch in crocodiles. I held them off till help arrived.

Morley and Spud flew around like they were part of some absurd combat ballet. Mr. Big flapped and squawked. He made more racket than a herd of pea-fowl. His vocabulary achieved new lows. Puddle, Sarge, Slither, Ivy, and Cleaver's thugs tried to help him expand that but had nothing to teach him.

Four brunos took quick dives.

I've heard people that've never been there claim it's impossible to lay somebody out with your fists. That's true for your average drunken amateur who gets into it with his brother-in-law at the corner tavern but not so for the unrestrained violence of professionals.

Puddle developed a bloody nose. Spud managed to get kicked in the funny bone. He leaned against a wall clutching his elbow, face pale, language vile. Such a look Morley gave him.

"Kill them, damnit! Kill them all!" The girlish voice slashed through the mayhem. "Stop playing with them and kill them!"

I spotted a short guy screaming from what he thought was a safe distance. Cleaver? The Rainmaker himself?

Morley spotted him. Cleaver's brunos were coming to the conclusion that it was not a bright idea to piss off guys who could handle them so easily. They didn't follow orders. Morley grinned and headed for the Rainmaker.

I was on my way already.

The Rainmaker, however, did not care to join the party.

That little bastard could run!

Naturally, our whole crowd dropped everything and lumbered after us, with predictable results. The Rainmaker vanished down the same rabbithole that had swallowed Zeke. His people grabbed up each others' parts and headed for the exits. Suddenly, we had us nothing but one big empty building and one hysterical parrot. And, according to Morley, "The Guard's on its way."

"You could be right." These days, people actually called for official help. These days, the police forces sometimes actually responded.

Morley snapped, "Narcisio, catch that faggot pigeon and shut it up." Mr. Big was no joke right then.

I checked to see if all our people could leave under their own power. No major injuries. Workable legs were available. It was brains that were in short supply.

Slither and Ivy helped round up the GDP. Mr. Big

made it easy. He flew into a wall full speed, cold-cocked himself.

Pity he didn't break his neck.

I considered wringing it and blaming it on the bird's own erratic piloting, but Spud kept too close an eye on the beast.

As we hustled into the street, I asked Slither, "That short guy was Cleaver, wasn't it? The shrimp with the girl voice?"

Morley seemed intensely interested in Slither's reply. Could it be he'd never seen Cleaver before?

"Yeah. That was him. That hunk a shit. I'da caught the little turd I'da turned him into a capon. Put me in the bughouse. I'da used my bare hands. Twisted 'em off. I'da fixed him." But he was shaking. He was pale. He was sweating. Rock-throwing range was as close to Grange Cleaver as he wanted to get.

Cleaver must be some swell guy.

I checked Ivy. Ivy didn't have an opinion. Ivy was all wrapped up in his feathery buddy.

Morley opined, "Cleaver is going to turn scarce now."

"Think so?"

"His being in town is no secret now, Garrett. A lot of people who don't like him will hear. And he'll have a good idea how many enemies he has once he gets together with Lucky."

"Think he'll leave town?"

"No. But he would if he had the sense the gods gave a goose. You going to have another chat with Winger?"

Guess who was hiding in the shadows outside when we came thundering out. "You saw her, eh?"

"I saw her."

We cleared the area before the Guard arrived. Safely away, I checked our surroundings more carefully. No more sign of my oversize blond friend. Maybe she wasn't interested anymore.

"You need to get her to talk, Garrett."

"I know. I know. But I want to let her come in when she's ready." I wondered why Winger wasn't off looking out for Chastity Blaine.

Morley made no mention so I supposed he'd missed the other watcher, the character who'd followed me to Maggie Jenn's place.

I was confused. Nothing made sense.

It wasn't going to get any better.

"Don't wait too long," Morley told me. "Two tries in two nights means the Rainmaker is serious."

"Seriously disturbed." Cleaver's enmity made the least sense of all. "Yeah. With that thought in mind, I'm going home and get some shut-eye."

Spud had the Goddamn Parrot. He kept whispering to the fancy pants little drunk. I tried to ease away before anyone noticed. Morley grinned and shook his head. "No, you don't. Narcisio."

My luck stays stuck in the same old rut.

32

Slither surprised me. He was a decent cook, which I learned when I stumbled down for breakfast, after having been rousted out by Ivy, who must have caught something Dean had left behind.

"You have to loosen up, Ivy," I grumbled as I toddled into the kitchen. "This isn't the service. We don't have to haul out before the goddamn crack of noon."

"My daddy always told me a man's got no call lying in bed after the birds start singing."

Inertia more than self-restraint kept me from expressing my opinion of that perverted delusion.

One songbird was wide awake up front, rendering chorus after chorus of such old standards as, "There was a young lady from . . ." I wondered if Dean still had some of that rat poison that looked like seed cakes. The rats were too smart to eat it, but that bird . . .

"You're working on a job, aren't you?" Slither was *still* vague about what I do.

"The mission," Ivy mumbled. "Old first rule, Garrett. Even a jarhead ought to know. Got to follow through on the mission."

"Watch that jarhead stuff, Army. All right. All right." Good old attitudes from the bad old days. But was the mission more likely to be advanced at sunrise than at high noon? Excuse me for entertaining doubts.

I wondered if they had noticed the changes in Tun-

Faire. Probably not. Neither was in close touch with the world outside his skull.

I surrendered. "I guess we can hit Wixon and White."

At the moment, the occult shop was my only angle. Mugwump had not yet materialized with the promised list of contacts.

Slither's cooking would have appalled Dean and sent Morley into convulsions. He fried half a slab of bacon while baking drop biscuits. He split the biscuits and soaked them in bacon grease, then sprinkled them with sugar. Poor people food. Soldier food. Food that was darned tasty when it was hot.

33

It had rained during the night. The morning air was cool. The breeze was fresh. The streets were clean. The sky was clear. The sun was bright. It was one of those days when it was too easy to relax, too easy to forget that a brighter sun means darker shadows.

Fortunately, even the shadows were relaxing. Not a one belched a villain bent on mischief. The whole town was in a rare humor. Hell, I heard singing from the Bustee.

It wouldn't last. Before sundown, the wicked would be slashing throats again.

We did develop a following, including the inept creature who had followed me to Maggie Jenn's place and a guy with an earring who was maybe a ferocious pirate, but I doubted that.

Even Ivy noticed the clumsy guy.

"Let them tag along," I said. "They'll go cross-eyed. What I do is excruciating to watch. Not to mention tough on the feet."

"Be like being back in the Corps," Slither observed.

Ivy had the Goddamned Parrot with him. That obscene buzzard had a great time. "Holy hookers, check them melons. Oh. Look it there. Come here, honey. I'll show you ..." We were lucky his diction was sloppy.

The streets were crowded. Everybody wanted a lungful of rain-scrubbed air before TunFaire returned to normal. The old and weak would be falling over left and right. All that fresh air would be poisonous.

Before we reached the West End, I spotted another tail. This guy was a first-string pro. I made him by accident, my good luck and his bad. I didn't know him. That troubled me. I thought I knew the top players.

It was quite a parade.

34

Wixon and White were open. I told Ivy, "You stay out here. You're the lookout." I went inside. Slither followed me. I wished I was as bad as I tried to look.

Both Wixon and White were on board, but no other crew or passengers were. "Bless me," I murmured, pleased to have something go my way. And, "Bless me again. More fierce pirates."

The guys eyeballed us and took just an instant to decide we weren't the sort of customers they hoped to attract. Neither mislaid his manners, though. Neither failed to notice that between us Slither and I outnumbered them by two hundred pounds.

"How might we help you?" one asked. He made me think of a begging chipmunk. He had a slight overbite and the obligatory lisp. He held his soft little hands folded before his chest.

"Robin! . . ."

"Penny, you just hush. Sir?"

I said, "I'm looking for somebody."

"Aren't we all?" Big smile. A corsair comedian.

Penny thought it was funny. Penny tittered.

Slither scowled. Garrett scowled. The boys got real quiet. Robin looked past us, toward the street, as though he hoped the answer to his dilemma might show up out there.

"I'm looking for a girl. A specific girl. Eighteen. Red hair. So tall. Freckles, probably. Put together so nice even fierce pirates might take a second look and maybe shed a tear about choices made. Probably going by either Justina or Emerald Jenn."

The guys stared. My magic touch had turned them into halfwits.

Outside, Ivy told a dowager type that the shop was closed, only for a little while. She tried to disagree. The Goddamn Parrot took exception and began screeching crude propositions.

I moved around the shop, fingering whatever looked expensive. The boys had a lot of square feet and plenty of bizarre furnishings. "That description ring any bells?" I couldn't read their reaction. Its schooled neutrality gave nothing away.

Penny sneered, "Should it?" I could tell him from Robin only by the size of his mustache. Otherwise, they could have passed as twins. A strong strain of narcissism united these wild and woolly buccaneers.

"I think it's likely." I described the black magic stuff I'd found in Emerald's rooms. My descriptions were faultless. The Dead Man taught me well. Those studied neutral faces betrayed teensy cracks.

Penny for sure knew what I was talking about. Robin probably did. Robin was a better faker.

"Excellent. You guys know the items. Presumably, you provided them. So tell me to who." I picked up a gorgeous dagger of ruby glass. Some true artist had spent months shaping and carving and polishing it. It was one beautiful, diabolic ceremonial masterpiece.

"I wouldn't tell you even if . . . Stop that!"

The dagger almost slipped from my fingers.

"What? You were going to say even if you knew what I was talking about? But you would tell me, Penny. You'd tell me anything. I'm not nice. My friend isn't as nice as I am." I flipped the dagger, barely caught it. The boys shuddered. They couldn't take their eyes off that blade. It had to be worth a fortune. "Boys, I'm that guy in your nightmares. I'm the guy behind the mask. The guy who'd use a priceless glass ceremonial dagger to play mumbletypeg on a tem-

pered oak floor. The guy who'll vandalize you into
bankruptcy. Unless you talk to me.''

I put the dagger down, collected a book. At first
glance it seemed old and ordinary, shy any occult sym-
bols. No big thing, I thought, till the boys started
squeaking answers to questions I hadn't asked.

They babbled about the man who'd bought the stuff
I'd described. Puzzled, I examined the book. And still
saw nothing special.

Why had it loosened their tongues so?

Its title was *The Raging Blades*. That made it the
central volume of the semi-fictional saga trilogy *No
Ravens Went Hungry*. *The Raging Blades* was pre-
ceded by *The Steel-Game* and followed by *The Battle-
Storm*. The whole related the glamorized story of an
historical character named Eagle, who plundered and
murdered his way across two continents and three seas
nearly a millenium ago. By today's standards, the man
was a total villain. Friend or foe, everyone eventually
regretted knowing him. By the standards of his own
time, he'd been a great hero simply because he'd lived
a long time and prospered. Even today, they say, kids in
Busivad province want to grow up to be another Eagle.

I asked, ''Might this be an early copy?'' Early copies
are scarce.

The boys redoubled their babble. What was this?
They were ready to confess to murder.

''Let me check this. You say a man with red hair,
some gray, green eyes, freckles, short. Definitely
male?'' Nods left me with one theory deader than an
earthworm in the noonday sun. Not even these rowdy
reever types would mistake Maggie Jenn for a man.
''Around forty, not eighteen?'' That fit no one I'd encountered so far, unless maybe that nasty runt in the
warehouse. ''And you don't have any idea who he
was?'' I hadn't caught the colors of Cleaver's hair and
eyes. ''You know anything about him?''

''No.''

"We don't know anything."

Eyes stayed stuck to that book while their owners tried to pretend everything was cool.

"He paid cash? He came in, looked around, picked out what he wanted, paid without quibbling about inflated prices? And when he left, he carried his purchases himself?"

"Yes."

"A peasant, indeed." Smiling, I put the book down. "You see? You can be a help when you want. You just need to take an interest." Both men sighed when I stepped away from their treasure. I asked, "You don't recall anything that would connect all that junk together?" It had seemed of a sort to me when I'd seen it, but what did I know about demon stuff? Mostly, I don't want to know.

I got headshakes.

"Everything had its silver star with a goat's head inside."

Penny insisted, "That's generic demon worship stuff. Our stock is mass-produced by dwarves. We buy it in bulk. It's junk with almost no intrinsic or occult value. It isn't fake, but it doesn't have any power, either." He waved a hand. I stepped to a display box filled with medallions like the one I'd found in Justina's suite.

"You know the girl I described?"

Headshakes again. Amazing.

"And you're sure you don't know the man who bought the stuff?"

More of that old shaka-shaka.

"You have no idea where I might find this guy?"

They were going to make themselves dizzy.

"I might as well go, then." I beckoned to Slither.

Wixon and White ran for their lives for their back room. I don't know what they thought I meant to do next. Nothing pleasant. They slammed the door. It was a stout one. We heard a heavy bar slam into place. Slither grinned as he followed me outside.

35

Slither glanced back. "How come you didn't push them harder? You seen how they sweated, 'specially when you was messing with that book."

"Sometimes I take the indirect approach. Ivy, wait right here. Whistle if anybody comes snooping." Right here was the end of a breezeway that led to the skinny alley behind Wixon and White.

The shop had no back window. Surprise, surprise. Even in the best parts of town there are few windows at ground level. You tempt fate as seldom as possible.

The place did have a rear door, though. And that wasn't much more secure than a window. I wondered what the boys did that they needed a sneak-out door. Was that how they handled customer complaints?

That back door led to the room whither the boys had fled. It did little to muffle their argument.

". . . could you have been thinking of, leaving it lay out like that?"

"I forgot it. All right?"

"You forgot it. You forgot it. I don't believe this."

"He didn't think anything about it. You saw that. All he cared about is where the Jenn chit is."

"Then why couldn't you tell him and get him out? He has to be suspicious, the way you were . . ."

"I didn't tell him because I don't know, love. She hasn't been seen since her mother came to town."

Well, well, well.

"Stop worrying about the damned book. A thug like that can't read his own stupid name."

Slither said, "Garrett ..."

I waved him off, listened as hard as I could. I had to fill in here and there, from context, to get everything.

Me and the occult corsairs were going to have another talk.

"Garrett!"

"Wait a minute!"

An unfamiliar voice observed, "You guys better be ratmen trash hogs in disguise because if you ain't ..."

"Which one you want I should eat first, Garrett?"

"... if you ain't, you're gonna be going outa here *on* a trash wagon." This sweet-talker was the spokesman for five thugs in slapdash butternut costume. I assumed that was the uniform of the neighborhood watch. I did mention how peaceful and confident the area seemed? Getting old and slow. I'd forgotten that, then I'd failed to stay alert.

They'd come from the direction Ivy wasn't covering.

I heard no more conversation behind the alley door. Naturally.

"Which one first?" Slither asked again. He was hot to go and sure he could handle them all. They weren't big guys and they all had bellies that hung over their belts. They had mean little pig eyes. Slither's growling got the boss pig thinking. He got a look like he thought maybe Slither could follow through.

Didn't seem like the best time to get into a fight. I still had a bottle of Miracle Milt's Doc Dread magic getaway juice. Last one. I whistled so Ivy would know something was up, then slammed the bottle into the bricks at the toes of the guardians of order.

I was lucky. The bottle broke.

A nasty dark stain spread like something alive. And nothing else happened. The brunos didn't twitch. They understood that something was *supposed* to happen. They didn't want to get it started.

I grabbed Slither's arm. "Time to take a hike."

A thin feather of mist curled up off the bricks. Well, better late than never. Only it leaned toward me, the one guy moving.

Slither said, "Aw, Garrett. Do I have to? Can't I just bust up one or two?"

"Go right ahead. But you're on your own. I'm leaving." The streamer of mist reached farther toward me.

I exercised my philosophy of discretion swiftly and with great enthusiasm. I grabbed Ivy as I flew out of the breezeway. That startled the Goddamn Parrot into one of his more memorable sermons.

Slither must have had an epiphany because he was stomping on my heels.

36

The Wixon and White street door was locked. The CLOSED sign stood in the window, supported by drawn shades. I had a feeling the boys wouldn't answer if I knocked.

I said, "We'll check back after those characters start thinking we've forgotten them. Right now, we'll find the weather friendlier in another part of town." I could see several butternut outfits. They weren't easily overlooked since all normal traffic had deserted the street. Way it goes in TunFaire.

We moved out as fast as Ivy would travel with that idiot bird. The butternut brunos were content to let us take our trouble elsewhere.

After a while, I asked, "Slither, you know why I like working alone?"

"Huh? No. How come?"

"On account of when I'm working alone, there's nobody around to call me by name in front of people I don't want to know. Not even one time, let alone four."

He thought about that and eventually concluded that I was peeved. "Say! That was pretty dumb, wasn't it?"

"Yes." Why shield the man's feelings? That kind of mistake can be fatal.

On the other hand, the butternuts had no reason to keep after me. They had run me off before my pockets filled with doodads they doubtless felt only they had the right to pilfer. They could beat their chests and tell the merchants association they were mighty hunters and protectors.

I couldn't see the swashbucklers pursuing the matter. All they cared about was that book. I growled, "Shut up, you mutant pigeon."

I wondered about the book. I'd read all three volumes of *No Ravens Went Hungry,* waiting around at the library. What set the story in motion was a dynastic squabble among mobs of people who were all related somehow. The prize was an almost nominal kingship over a loose association of barbarian clans. Not one person in the whole saga was the sort you'd ask into your home. This hero, this thug Eagle, murdered more than forty people during his life.

No Ravens Went Hungry was based on actual events that marinated in the oral tradition a few centuries before being recorded.

I hadn't enjoyed it, partly because no likable people were involved, but more because the author had felt a duty to name every player's antecedants and cousins and offspring and, likewise, those of everyone they ever murdered or married. After a while, it got hard to keep track of all the Thoras, Thoralfs, Thorolfs, Thorolds, Thords, Thordises, Thorids, Thorirs, Thorins, Thorarins, Thorgirs, Thorgyers, Thorgils, Thorbalds, Thorvalds, Thorfinns, and Thorsteins, not to mention the numerous Odds and Eiriks and Haralds—any one of whom could change his name any time the notion hit him.

"What now?" Slither asked, prodding me out of my thoughts.

Ivy looked over his shoulder, expectant. He seemed more disappointed than Slither about having missed a brawl. But he did stifle the Goddamn Parrot whenever that stupid harlequin hen started propositioning passersby.

"I'm going to go home, get me something to eat. That's what now."

"What good will that do?"

"It'll keep me from getting hungry." And it would set me up to get shut of him and Ivy and the parade that stretched out behind us.

I had plans.

37

I let Slither and Ivy make lunch. I retreated to my office to commune with Eleanor. Eleanor didn't help me relax. My restlessness wouldn't go away. Curious, I crossed the hall. The Dead Man appeared to be soundly asleep, but I wondered. I'd suffered similar restlessnesses before.

I didn't feel up to dealing with him, so I gobbled some food, fed the boys a quick, plausible lie about ducking out for just a minute, hit the cobblestones. I lost the people watching me by using the density of the crowds. The streets were busier than usual. There were refugees everywhere. In consequence, every street corner boasted its howling mad bigot who wanted to run them all out. Or worse.

I sensed another crisis in the wind.

Sure I was running free, I headed for the Hill.

I strode up to Maggie's door as bold as if I'd been summoned. I used that discrete knocker, over and over. Nobody responded.

Was I surprised? Not really.

I studied that grim, featureless facade. It remained grim and featureless. And uninviting.

I wandered the neighborhood for a while and wasn't challenged. I didn't stick with it long enough to press my luck.

I was halfway to Morley's place when I realized that I was no longer without a tail. The inept guy was on

me again. Say what? Maybe he had something going
after all.

I walked into the Joy House. There sat my two best
pals, Morley Dotes and Saucerhead Tharpe, making
goo-goo eyes at my favorite fantasy. "Chastity! What's
a nice girl like you doing in a place like this?"

Morley gave me a look at his darkest scowl, the one
he reserves not for victims but for guys who venture
to hint that they might possibly think the Joy House
is less than the epitome of epicurean paradises.

Saucerhead grinned. He is one great huge goof. I
love him in a brotherly way. I noticed he was missing
another tooth.

Chastity said, "I was checking up on you."

"Don't believe anything these guys tell you. Especially Morley. Can't tell the truth when a lie will do.
Just ask his wife or any of his seventeen demented
children."

Morley showed me a bunch of pointy teeth. He
looked pleased. Saucerhead's grin got bigger. He had
teeth like yellow and green spades.

I figured it was time to check my shoes, see what
I'd stepped in because my feet were whizzing past
pretty close to my mouth.

Unlikely as it seemed, folks had been saying nice
things. I sat down. "Puddle! I need some apple juice.
Shoeleather leaves a bad taste in your mouth."

Dotes and Tharpe kept smirking. Spud brought me
my drink, like to dumped it all over me. The kid
couldn't keep his eyes off the lady doctor. I couldn't
fault his taste. She sure looked good.

I told her, "You didn't answer my question."

"Why I'm here? Mr. Tharpe suggested we eat here
before we go to the hospital."

"We? The Bledsoe?" Mr. Tharpe hated the Bledsoe
with a blind passion. Mr. Tharpe was poor. Mr.
Tharpe had been born in the Bledsoe and had been

forced to rely upon its medical care all his life, excepting during his years in military service, when he had discovered what real doctoring could be. I could not imagine Saucerhead going near the place voluntarily.

A lot of people will suffer almost anything before letting themselves be committed to the Bledsoe. Many see it as the last gate to death.

"I'm bodyguarding her," Saucerhead told me.

"What? I thought . . ."

"I saw your friend." Chastity smiled. My best pals snickered.

"My friend? I'm beginning to wonder. She didn't want the job?"

"Sent her on to me," Tharpe told me.

That deserved some thought.

Morley asked, "Where are your buddies, Garrett?"

"Home minding the Goddamn Parrot. Slow roasting it, I hope. Why?"

"There's a story going around about the three of you trying to rob some nancys out in the West End."

I frowned. Strange that should be out already. "I was trying to get a line on Emerald. I never pushed that hard." I told the story.

Morley soon developed a deep frown. He let me talk, but when I finished he asked, "You're sure it was an old copy of one of the volumes of *No Ravens Went Hungry*?"

"It was *The Raging Blades*. You know something I don't?"

"Do you know the story?"

"I read the book."

"That doesn't surprise me." He grinned. He recalled my troubles with Linda Lee. "Since you've read it, you know what happens at the end. Eagle is in his eighties, still hale except that he's going blind. The women start pushing him around, probably getting even for the way he always treated them. He gets pissed off, grabs a couple of slaves, takes the treasure he's stolen over the past seventy years, and heads for the boondocks. A few days later, he comes home alone and empty-handed and never says a word about what happened to the slaves or the treasure."

"So?"

"So Eagle's treasure is one of the big prizes treasure hunters yak up when they get together. One of their myths says the earliest version of *No Ravens Went Hungry* contains all the clues you need to find it. The copyists supposedly actually found the treasure, after they produced maybe five copies of each volume, but they murdered each other before they dug it up." Morley touched the highlights of a tale of greed and double-dealing worthy of Eagle himself.

Tell the truth, Morley's story sounded like one of those worth the paper it was written on. If he hadn't had a certain familiar gleam in his eye, I would have ignored everything he said. But that gleam was there. I knew his gold sniffer had been excited. He believed. He was thinking of paying Wixon and White a visit that had nothing to do with mine.

"The second volume?" I asked, hoping to cool him down. "Why that one? It wasn't until the end of the third that Eagle buried the treasure."

Morley shrugged, smiled. Poor dumb Garrett couldn't see the obvious. Chastity gave us a funny look. She knew something was going on but wasn't sure what it was. Morley said, "You could be right," which I assume he said to confuse everybody.

He knew something he didn't want to tell. Like everyone lately. I shrugged and said, "I'm going to visit Maggie's house. Want to come along?" His gold sniffer would respond to that, too.

He said, "Why not?"

Saucerhead got it, too. He gave me a dubious look but asked no questions. No need letting Chastity in on everything. Especially since she had friends in the Guard.

She knew we were closing her out. She didn't like it, but she had a strong notion she wouldn't want to know anyway.

I asked her, "You familiar with Grange Cleaver? He ever hang out at the Bledsoe?"

"I've seen him. More lately than in the past. He seems to be living in the city, now. He's Board. Board are in and out all the time. The rest of us only pay attention if they start throwing their weight around."

"I see. What's he do there?"

"I don't know. I'm a ward physician. I don't fly that high."

Morley was ready to go. He asked, "What's he look like these days? He used to play around with disguises. Only his closest friends knew what he looked like."

Perplexed, Chastity said, "How would a disguise do him any good? There aren't many men that short."

"He wasn't always a man," Morley told her. "He could be a dwarf if he wanted."

"Or an elf?" I suggested.

"Never was an elf that ugly, Garrett!" Morley snapped. "Not that lived long enough to get out of diapers."

I thought about the prince at the warehouse. Effeminate but not ugly. Just an unlucky gal fate stuck with the wrong plumbing. "Could you describe him, Chastity? I mean, besides as short."

She did her best.

"Good enough for me. That's the guy, Morley."

Morley grunted irritably. Chastity looked perplexed again. "I'll explain later," I promised. I wondered what it was between Dotes and the Rainmaker.

Morley did have his share of feuds. I stayed out of them. And I figured it was just as well I didn't know their details. I hoped he would explain if I needed to know.

I would keep my eyes open, though. He'd been known to wait a bit too long in the past.

"You going or not?" he grumped.

"I'll catch up with you later," I told Chastity.

"Promises, promises."

Saucerhead gave me a look that told me, yes, he would look out for her. I wouldn't suggest it because it was a big sore spot with him. Once upon a time, I asked him to guard a woman and he didn't come through. She died. He slaughtered a whole herd of villains and came within an inch of death himself, but all he saw was that he'd failed. There was no talking him out of thinking that.

Chastity was as safe as it was possible for her to be.

38

"Hey, Garrett! How about you do away with the goofy grin and the glassy eyes long enough to let me in on the plan?"

"Jealous." I wrestled with the grin, got the best of it. "We're going to take what I call the Dotes Approach." We were nearing the Hill. Soon we would be on patrolled streets. I had to get my grin under control, stop daydreaming about remarkable blondes. The thugs up there had no patience with happy outsiders.

"The Dotes Approach? Dare I ask?"

"You ought to know. You invented it. Straight ahead and damn the witnesses—we'll just bust in."

"One time. During a thunderstorm in the middle of the night. Talk about exaggeration."

I didn't grace his protest with a reply. I told him, "There's an alleyway runs behind those places. Used for deliveries and by the ratmen who haul the trash away."

"Haul the trash away?"

"A novel concept, I admit. But it's true. This alley is cleaner than the street out front. I never saw anything like it."

"Almost unpatriotic, what?"

"Un-Karentine, certainly. High weirdness."

"A conspiracy."

He was needling me, probably because I was running the inside track with Chastity.

"That thing about a wife and kids wasn't playing fair." He glanced back casually.

"Sure it was. You're just sore because you didn't try the gag first. They still back there?"

"Stipulated. Maybe. She *is* worth a trick or two. They're still there. A whole parade of potential witnesses. This one is a first-class lady, Garrett. Don't mess up the way you did with Tinnie and Maya." Before I could object, he added, "You do attract it, don't you?"

"What?"

"You said it. High weirdness."

"I can't argue with that. Though this one is only weird because it doesn't make sense, not because I've got guys walking through the sky or refusing to stop committing murder just because we've killed and cremated them. I haven't seen any shapechangers and nobody is going around biting anybody's neck."

"There is an occult angle of some kind."

"I think it was planted by Cleaver. I think Cleaver has the girl. The occult crap is to throw Maggie off the trail."

"You going ahead anyway?"

I'd been considering. "For now. For them back there. Might be interesting to see who does what once they figure out what we're doing." We were on the Hill now, strutting like we were honest. Act like you belong, who notices you? Even on the Hill there's plenty of legitimate traffic. The local guardians didn't dare roust everybody. I remarked, "Someday these clowns will recall their training and set up checkpoints and start issuing passes."

Morley snorted. "Never happen." He didn't think much of the Hill brunos. "People who live here won't tolerate the inconvenience."

"Probably right." That's the problem with public safety. It is so damned inconvenient.

"You counting on those people back there being as

crooked as you are? That would be as bad a bet as counting on everyone to be honest."

"Crooked?" I protested, but I knew what he meant.

"You know what I mean. One might be secret police." The secret police were a new problem for Tun-Faire's underworld. Always flexible, though, Morley seemed to be having no trouble adapting.

"Might be." But I didn't believe that and doubted that he did. The Guard were less shy than these people. Even Relway's spies.

Morley did have to say, "Winger could have that kind of connection."

Damn! "Yeah. If there's a profit in it." I wondered. Could Winger turn up the closest thing she had to a friend, just for money? Scary. I couldn't answer that one.

I said, "You gave me some advice one time: never get involved with a woman crazier than I am."

"And I was right. Wasn't I?"

"Yeah. Oh, yeah."

We turned into the alley that passed behind Maggie Jenn's place. Luck had given us clear sailing so far. Not one patrol even came into sight. We were as good as ghosts in the official eye.

"Be careful with Winger, Garrett. She is crazier than you." He stared down that improbably clean alleyway. "Though not by much. It isn't closed off. Anyone could walk in here." He sneered, unable to believe the arrogant confidence that showed. *Nobody* lives so high on the Hill that they're immune. Even the great witches and wizards, the stormwardens and firelords, who set counts and dukes to shaking in their boots, get ripped off.

"I'll worry about Winger later. Right now we need to do a B and E before our fans show. Up there." I indicated a wrought iron balcony that existed as a drop point for garbage. The ratmen ran their waste wagons in underneath and household staff dumped away. Similar balconies ornamented the rough stone-work all along the alley.

"Except for the clean, they didn't do much to put on the dog back here, did they?" Morley asked.

"You want they should've done fancy masonry for the likes of us?"

Sneering, Morley darted forward, found handholds in the rough stonework, scrambled up, did a job on the flimsy door, then hung over the rail to help me up. The balcony creaked ominously. I flailed my way aboard. An instant later, Morley and I were inside. We peeked out an archer's slit of a window, looking for witnesses. It was a minute before any of our tails entered the alley.

Morley chuckled.

I sighed. "Only Winger."

"Where does she get those clothes?"

"If I knew, I'd strangle the seamstresses. That stuff has got to be against divine law if nothing else."

"We're inside. What do we look for?"

"Hell, I don't know. Anything. Things keep happening that don't make sense, since I'm only supposed to be looking for a missing girl. I shouldn't be up to my mammaries in maneating pirates. I'm pretty sure that finding Emerald isn't the main reason Maggie hired me."

"Huh?"

"You recall I got into this because Winger wanted me to keep tabs on Maggie. She thought Maggie wanted me to waste somebody."

"And now you're thinking maybe Winger was right, that the whole point might have been to get you butting heads with the Rainmaker."

"Could be. I thought I might find a clue here."

"So let's dig. Before Winger figures out what happened and walks through the wall."

"Absolutely. But first let's see who else takes a chance on the alley."

The whole parade passed by before it was over. Morley got a good look at them.

"That one," I said. "That's the pro."

"I see it. I *smell* it. He's a major player."

"Who is he?"

"That's the rub." Morley looked worried. "I don't know him."

I worried, too. I could figure Winger was working for Winger and anybody else she could get to pay her. The fierce pirate had to be on Cleaver's payroll. But what about this slick pro?

They did seem to be aware of one another.

Their sneakery caught some squinty eyes. Guard thugs began to appear. Even Winger cleared out rather than tempt those clowns too much.

"Quit your snickering and get to work," Morley advised. "The guys with the squashed noses won't hang around forever."

We started right there in that very room.

39

We had been whispering. Soon I wondered why. We found no trace of Maggie or her marvelous staff.

I thought it but Morley voiced it first. "People don't live here, Garrett. They haven't for years." Not one room that I hadn't visited earlier wasn't in mothballs and choked with dust. I kept hacking and honking.

"Yeah. It's a stage set they used to play out a drama for me."

"Make a guess. Why?"

"That's what I'm here to find out, if Winger wasn't right the first time."

Over and over, all we found was more of the same old dusty rooms filled with covered furniture.

"Some nice antiques here," Morley noted. He pretended indifference, but I sensed his disappointment. He could find no wealth that was easily portable. He *was* trying to think of ways to get the furniture out.

In time, because we had time to look, we did find an upper-story bedroom that had seen use but which I hadn't visited before. Morley opined, "This was occupied by a woman with no compulsion to clean up after herself."

And nobody to clean up for her, apparently. Remnants of old meals provided spawning grounds for blue fur.

Morley said, "My guess is this stuff dates from before your visit. Let's check this room carefully."

I grunted. What genius.

A minute later: "Garrett."

"Uhm?"

"Check this out."

"This" was a shocker. "This" was a woman's wig. "This" was a wild shock of tangly red hair so much like Maggie Jenn's that, in an instant, I was mug to ugly mug with a horrible suspicion.

"What's that?" Morley asked.

"What?"

"That noise. Like somebody goosed you with a hot poker."

"I tried to picture Maggie without hair." I lifted that wig like it was an enemy's severed head.

"Out with it. Out with it."

"Know what's the matter? Here's a hint. You take a wig like this wig and grab the Rainmaker and stuff his head into said wig, you'd have a dead ringer for the little sweetheart who hired me to find her kid— assuming you dressed her girlie style. A dead ringer for a sweetheart who all but point-blank invited me up here for . . ."

Morley grinned. Then he snickered. Then he burst out laughing. "Oh! Oh! That would have made the Garrett story to top all Garrett stories. People would have forgotten the old lady and the cat like *this*." He snapped his fingers. He started grinning again. "I'll bet you Winger knew. I'll just bet she did. At least she suspected. Maybe that's what she wanted to find out. Send in Garrett. He has a way with redheads. He'll go for it if you drop one in his lap." He was breaking up now, the little shit. "Oh, Garrett, she just rose way up in my estimation. That's a slicking *I* wouldn't have thought of."

"You have a tendency to think too complicated," I protested. "Winger don't think that way." I went on, arguing, I don't know with whom. My voice rose and rose as I imagined the myriad piratical horrors that might have befallen me simply because of my connois-

sieur's appreciation of the opposite sex. Just because
Maggie Jenn, who had heated me to a rolling boil,
might have been wearing a wig.

I glared at that wig. The fury of my gaze changed
nothing. It remained a perfect match for Maggie's
hair.

"You get it?" Morley asked, like it hadn't been my
idea in the first place. "Grange Cleaver put on a wig
and fooled you one thousand percent." His leer set
my cheeks ablaze.

"Maybe he did. Maybe he didn't. Let's say he did.
Just for now, let's say he's the Maggie Jenn who hired
me. Let's ignore the fact that that makes things make
even less sense than before. Cleaver wouldn't aim a
dagger at himself. So let's look for the bottom line.
Let's figure out what my employer really wanted, whoever he, she, or it was."

"Don't be so touchy, Garrett." He kept fighting the
giggles.

"The question, Morley. The question. I got paid a
nice advance. Why?"

"You could always assume you were supposed to
do what you were hired to do. Find the girl. When
you think about this mess, Maggie Jenn not really
being Maggie Jenn makes sense."

"Huh?"

"Look. If she was Cleaver in disguise, then there'd
be no conflicts in what us old experts told you about
the woman."

"I saw that when you waved that damned wig in
my face. The real Maggie Jenn is probably on her
island with her feet up and not a suspicion that her
old pal Grange Cleaver is blackening her reputation
by pretending ..."

"You have to wonder how much he did that in the
old days. When she was involved with the crown
prince."

"Not around the prince, he wouldn't have. The

prince definitely preferred girls and wasn't patient with girls who played hard to get. He knew the real Maggie Jenn."

"But a fake Maggie could have gone around looking at places that interested the Rainmaker."

"Somebody told me Cleaver might be her brother. Maybe they were twins."

"He was his sister's pimp?"

"Like that'd be the first time a guy ever sold his sister?"

"You're right. I lost it for a second. Wishful thinking. Thought I'd outgrown that. Shouldn't ever forget what slime humans can be."

"We've still got rooms to search." I didn't want to get into the subject of necessity—though Morley would have to slither down there under a snake's belly to hold an opinion of my species lower than I do.

Necessity I understand. Necessity I won't condemn. The despicable are those who sell their sisters and daughters and wives because that saves them having to work. "Bear with me, Morley."

"I do, Garrett. And with all your kind. Like it or not, you're the present and future of the world. The rest of us are going to have to find what niches we can. Otherwise, time will pass us by."

"Bravo!" I clapped. "You've got the vision. Get yourself appointed to the city board of aldermen."

"I'm not human enough. And I wouldn't have time."

I boggled for an instant. My facetious remark had been heard seriously. Interesting. Morley Dotes, bone-breaker and lifetaker, your alderman and mine?

Actually, that could be an idea whose time had arrived. The Goddamned Parrot could do as well as the crooks and incompetents and senile halfwits running things now.

TunFaire is a human city in the human kingdom of Karenta. This is established by numerous treaties. It means human rule prevails except in such ways as may be modified by treaty in particular regards or areas. TunFaire is also an "open city," meaning any race with a treaty can come and go freely, essentially with the same rights and privileges as Karentine subjects. And, in theory, the same obligations.

In practice, all races come and go, treaty or no, and a lot of nonhumans evade their civil obligations. Centaurs are the outstanding example. All treaties with centaurs perished when the tribes went over to Glory Mooncalled. Legally, they're enemy aliens. But they've been flooding into city and kingdom as Mooncalled's republic fades and nobody except extremists seems to object.

Guest workers and resident nonhumans make up half of TunFaire's population. With the war winding down and ever more folks realizing that society is headed for dramatic changes a lot of resentment is building.

Shouldn't be long before the nonhuman question becomes a central fact of politics. It is now for splinters like the Call. You won't find any euphemism or circumlocution in the message of the Call. Their strategy is kill nonhumans till the survivors flee.

Gods, I didn't want this mess of mine to lead me into the snakepit of racial politics. Lords Above or Below, render me outside politics of any stink.

Morley and I pressed on. We searched high and low, right and left, north, south, east, and west. We placed special emphasis on the suite supposedly belonging to Justine Jenn. Morley opined, "Nobody lived here, Garrett. It was stage-dressed."

I agreed.

"Think there's anything else to find?" he asked.

"I doubt it. Want to try the basement?"

"Do you?"

"I remember the last time we did a basement. I'm more inclined to go shopping."

"Wixon and White. The hens' teeth salesmen. They actually knew the girl?"

"A girl," I grumped, identities being so shifty lately.

"Good point. But it's a start. Mind if I tag along? I haven't been out that way for a while."

"Gee. I'm psychic." I'd just known he would want to go. "Wasn't for those buccaneers, I'd have serious doubts that the girl exists."

"A girl. Like you said. What say let's don't just hit the street?"

"Good thinking." We checked for observers. Winger and a ferocious pirate type were holding down the alley, pretending they couldn't see each other. "Nice to see folks get along."

"Makes the world run smoother. Crack that view slit up front and check the genius out there."

The front face of the house wasn't as featureless as it had looked from the street. I peeked.

The pro had decided we would walk out the front door like we lived there. Which he'd have done himself. He had done and admirable job of fading into the background. Nobody looking for him was going to miss him, though.

There was no sign of the inept guy. Curious.

Chuckling, Morley asked, "How long will they wait if they don't know we're not in here anymore?"

"How?"

"The rooftops."

I chuckled right back. "Sounds like an experiment worth making. Let's do it."

"We could even sic the brunos on them after we're clear."

"No, no. That's too much. I don't want to spend the rest of my life watching over my shoulder for some of Winger's paybacks."

"Good point. Let's go."

We went. It was easy. The roofs were all flat. The only hitch we encountered was getting down.

40

We tried three downspouts. None would support me. "Need some home repairs in these parts," I grumbled. "People ought to show some pride. Ought to keep up their property."

"Or we could start a weight loss program at the Garrett dump." Morley, the little weasel, could have gone down any of the spouts.

Worse, last try we had caught the eyes of some prematurely cynical kids who'd jumped to the conclusion we were up to no good. Just because we were running around on the roofs. We could have been roofers shopping for work.

No more fun. The patrol would be along soon.

Morley bent over the edge, tried another downspout. A herd of preadolescents watched from the street. I made faces, but they didn't scare. Morley said, "This will have to do."

I shook it myself. Not that I didn't trust him. He was right. It would have to do. It *was* more solid.

Still . . .

"We have to get down now, Garrett."

"I'm not worried about getting down. What concerns me is how many pieces of me there're going to be after I get there."

Morley went over the side, abandoning me to my fate. I gave him a head start, then followed, my weight taken by different supports. I had descended about eight feet when furious elvish cursing broke out below

me. For a second, I thought I had stepped on his
fingers.

"What?" I demanded.

"I'm hung up."

I leaned out so I could see. Sure enough. His shirt
was out and tangled in one of the supports that an-
chored the downspout to the building. He tried to
climb a little to get loose. For reasons known only to
the gods who engineer these things that only made
things worse. I heard cloth tear. Morley started cursing
all over again. He let go with one hand and tried to
work his shirt loose.

It would not yield. But he was being awfully
damned delicate about it.

Down below, some kid came up with the notion
that it would be fun to throw rocks at us. First shot
he got Morley on the knuckles of the hand he was
using to hang on.

Only thing that saved him was that his shirt was
hung up.

The gods give and the gods take away.

Morley's shirt tore a little more.

Morley's temper ripped. He invented new curses.

"Cut it loose!" I yelled.

"It's a new shirt. First time I ever wore it." He
continued fighting with it.

Stones peppered the wall. A racket from up the
street gave warning of the patrol. "You'd better do
something. In a couple of minutes, you're going to
have people throwing more than rocks at you."

"*I* am?"

"You am. I'm going to climb down over you and
leave you hanging."

He started to say something testy, but a small stone
hit him in the back of the head.

Blur of steel. Pretty cloth flying. Morley down that
spout like a squirrel as kids shrieked and scattered. I
caught up while he was trying to decide which kid to

run down. "Let's go." The patrol were damn near in spear-chucking range.

Morley looked like he'd rather stay and fight. He wanted to hurt somebody. He rubbed the back of his head and got set.

"Come *on!*" I commenced the old high-speed heel and toe work.

Morley opted not to take on the world alone.

41

Even Morley was puffing before we shook the pursuit. Staggering, I gasped, "It was torn already. And you've got another shirt. I've seen it."

He didn't respond. He was holding a wake for his apparel, though you could hardly tell there was a problem if he stayed tucked in.

I croaked, "Those guys've been working out." My legs were rubber.

"Good thing you started before they did." He wasn't puffing nearly enough to suit me. I don't know how he stays in shape. I've seldom seen him do anything more strenuous than chase women.

Maybe he just lucked out when he picked his ancestors.

"How about we take five?" We could afford it. I needed it. Before I puked up my toenails.

We had ended up dodging into one of those small sin sinks that cling to the skirts of the Hill and cater to and prey upon the idle rich. Nobody would help trace us there. Patrol folks weren't welcome.

Morley and I planted our posteriors on a stoop where traffic seemed limited. Once I had sucked in enough air to rekindle my sense of humor, we began fantasizing scenarios wherein Winger did Winger sorts of things to find out what we were up to inside Maggie's house—only with her suffering my kind of luck instead of her own.

You would have thought we were eleven again. We ended up with the giggles.

"Oh, damn!" I couldn't stop laughing, despite the bad news. "Look who just showed up."

The clumsy guy almost tripped over us before he realized that he had found us. His eyes got big. His face went pale. He gulped air. I gasped, "This clown has got to be psychic."

"Want to grab him?"

The suspicion that we might try occurred to him first. He went high-stepping around a corner before we finished swatting the dust off the backs of our laps.

"Damn! Where did he go?"

"What I expected," Morley said, suddenly morose as he stared down that empty cross street.

"Expected?"

"He's a spook. Or a figment of your imagination."

"No. He's no ghost. He's just lucky."

"I've heard luck called a psychic talent."

"Give me a break, Morley. How can random results have anything to do with talent?"

"Luck was really random it would even out, wouldn't it?"

"I suppose."

"So you ought to have some good luck once in a while, right? Unless you're directing it somehow."

"Wait a minute...." Our squabble wandered far afield. It kept us entertained all the way to the West End. For the heck of it, we set a couple of ambushes along the way. Our tail evaded both through sheer dumb luck. Morley did a lot of smirking.

I told him, "I'm about to come around to your way of thinking."

"You say this Wixon and White place has a flimsy back door?"

"A bad joke. Unless it's a trap." There are spiders that specialize in catching other spiders.

"Show me. We'll treat your friends to chills and thrills."

Right. Morley was along just for the fun.

Wixon and White were open for trade. We lurked, watched a few customers come and go. "We'd better get on with it," I said. "Their local watch is a little too serious for my taste."

Morley grunted. I introduced him to the alley door. He scoped it out, suggested, "Give me ten minutes."

"Ten? You going to take it out frame and all?"

"No, I was considering doing it quietly. You wanted fast you should have brought Saucerhead Tharpe. Finesse, Garrett. Surprise. I don't do Thon-Gore the Learning Disabled."

"Right." I left the artist to his easel.

My old pal was hustling a personal agenda again. I had a good suspicion, too. And I didn't care. I just wanted to get on with my job—the way I had defined it.

I wondered if I had an employer anymore. I hadn't heard.

I waited in the breezeway while Morley did whatever. He did keep the racket down. I never heard a thing. No butternut thugs showed up to inconvenience us, either. I tried to psych myself into a role.

Time. I walked to the shop door and invited myself inside.

42

"Howdy." I grinned. Wasn't nobody there but them and me. I locked the door. I put the CLOSED sign in the window.

One bold corsair demanded, "What *are* you doing?" He wanted to sound tough, but his voice scrambled right up into a high squeak.

The other one didn't say anything. After ten seconds frozen like those mythical birds that stare down snakes, he bolted for the back room. A moment later, he squealed like Morley was whipping him with a naked woman.

I trotted out my cheerful charlie voice. If you do that right, it's really sinister. "Howdy, Robin." It had taken me a moment to sort them out. "We just dropped in to get the real skinny on Emerald Jenn." I pasted on my salesman's smile. Robin squeaked again and decided to catch up with Penny.

Both those fierce buccaneers were taller than Morley. They looked pretty silly being held by their collars from behind, facing me, when I entered their lumber room. They were shaking.

I closed the door. I barred it. I leaned back against it. I asked, "Well? Want to pick a spokesman?" The room was an extreme mess. I'm sure it was a wreck to start but now had the air of a place hastily tossed, perhaps by a dedicated bibliophile in quest of a rare first edition. "Come on, fellows."

Heads shook.

"Let's don't be silly."

Morley forced them to kneel. He hauled out a knife way too long to be legal. He made its blade sing on his whetstone.

"Guys, I want Emerald Jenn. Also known as Justina Jenn. You're going to tell me what you know about her. You'll feel better for it. Start by telling me how you met her."

Wixon and White whimpered and whined and tried to exchange impassioned farewells. Boy, I was good. Oh, the drama. Morley did his bit by testing his edge on Penny's mustache. A big hunk of lip hair tumbled to the floor. Morley went back to work with his whetstone.

"Don't nobody *need* to get killed," I said. "I thought I'd just skin one of you." I toed that glob of hair.

"Immigrants," Morley observed.

"Probably." Karentines don't rattle easily, having survived the Cantard. They would have made us work. "Talk to me, outlanders."

Robin cracked. "It was almost a year ago."

Penny glared.

"What was almost a year ago?"

"The first time the girl came to the shop. Looking lost. Looking for any handle."

"Just wandered in? Wanting to borrow a cup of frog fur?"

"No. She was just looking. In more ways than one."

"Uhm?"

"She was a lost soul, drowning in despair, looking for straws to grasp. There was a young man with her. Kewfer, I believe she called him. He was blond and beautiful and young and that was the only time he came around."

"Sorry he broke your heart. Don't go misty on me."

Penny didn't like Robin's wistful tone, either, but he just kept the glare cooking.

"Kewfer?" I stressed it just as he had.

Thoughtfully, Morley suggested, "Quince Quefour?"

"Quince." Left me thoughtful, too. Quincy Quentin Q. Quintillas was pretty enough to launch a thousand ships filled with fierce pirates. He was a small-time conman of the smallest time, too damned dumb to amount to anything. He was part elvish. Made him look younger than his real years and got him out of army time. A faked spook thing would be right up Quefour's alley.

I barely knew him, didn't want to know him better. I described him.

Robin nodded vigorously, eager to please. I wondered if he was just telling me what he thought I wanted to hear.

"Thank you, Robin. You see? We can get along fine. What was Quefour up to?"

Baffled look. "He wasn't up to anything. He was just with the girl. Wasn't much special about her, either."

Of course not. You were lusting in your heart. "Please explain."

"She wanted an easy answer. She was looking for easy answers."

"I thought she was desperate."

"Desperate after the fashion of her age. Kids want results without work. They believe they *deserve* magical answers. They don't want to hear that real magic is hard work. Your stormwardens and firelords spend twenty years studying and practicing. These kids think you just wiggle your fingers . . ."

Morley's magic fingers darted, slapped Robin's hand. Robin had started wiggling fingers as if by way of demonstration. He might have suckered us had we not been in the back of a shop that supplied witches and warlocks.

"Stick to Emerald Jenn. I develop a taste for social

commentary, I'll head for the front steps of the Chancery." The most marvelous lunatics hold forth there. "Emerald, Robin. Quefour didn't come back but she did. Talk to me."

"You don't need to be brutal. Emmy was a runaway. Came from upcountry. We knew that but not much more till a few weeks ago."

"A runaway," I repeated, trying to put an evil twist on everything I said. Morley rolled his eyes. "On her own here for a year." Scary idea. A girl can live a lifetime in a year on the streets of TunFaire. "What did she run from?"

"Her mother."

Who had been worried because her baby had been missing six days. "Go on."

"She didn't go into detail, but it was obvious the woman was a horror."

"Emerald spend a lot of time here?"

"She helped out. Sometimes she stayed back here." Gesture toward a ratty pallet. I didn't apologize for what I had thought about that. "She was a wounded bird. We gave her a place to feel safe." Hint of defiance.

I could see a girl feeling safer with Penny and Robin than on the street. Trouble was, I had trouble accepting them as philanthropists. Too cynical am I.

Robin was a real chatterbox when he loosened up. I spent a lot of energy guiding him back to the main path.

"Seen her lately?"

"No. She heard her mother had come to town."

"That would make her stay away?"

"She thought her mother would look for her. And she is looking, right? You're here. She doesn't want to be found. People who don't know where she is can't give her away."

Morley and I exchanged glances. "What's she scared of?"

Robin and Penny got into the look-trading business. A growth industry. Only they were puzzled.

"You don't know." My intuition was at work. "She told a tale but you didn't buy it. Think you know her? She the kind to fill you up and leave you to feed the wolves?"

"What?"

"She knows her mother. She'd know what kind of people would be sent."

More looks flashing. The ferocious pirates of this world are paranoid. Given our record, they are justified in expecting evil of the rest of us.

Penny had spent the interview glowering at Robin. He seemed to suffer a sudden pessimistic epiphany. He barked, "Marengo North English."

"What?" Tell me I heard wrong.

"Marengo North English."

I heard right. But why did he have to say that? Things had been crazy enough. I feigned ignorance. "What's that?"

Robin tittered. "That's a who. One of our biggest customers. A very powerful underground adept."

That was disheartening news, but useful if ever I found myself dealing with the lunatic fringe.

Penny said, "He met Emmy here. Invited her into his coven. She went a few times but didn't like the people or what they wanted to do."

Robin said, "We thought she might have run to him."

I stipulated, "He could protect her." Morley looked at me askance. I said, "I've met the man. I didn't know he dabbled in black magic, though." North English mostly concentrated on virulent racism.

Penny and Robin seemed surprised, as though they had not heard of Marengo North English in any but an occult context. Silly boys. The man had a special place in his heart for their sort, too.

Morley moved sudden as heat lightning, startling us

all. He ripped the alley door open, stepped out, stared for a moment, shook his head, and closed up. "Guess who?"

"Some guy who tripped over his own feet getting away."

"You win first prize. Near time to go."

"I have a few more questions."

"That guy is a lightning rod for the law."

Right. And I didn't accomplish much more, though I had hoped to get at their angle for helping Emerald. I did get the names of three people who were on speaking terms with the girl. Not real friends. Not people likely to be useful. Emerald evidently didn't have any friends.

We departed as suddenly as we had arrived. We were gone before those bold buccaneers knew we were going. We were out of the West End moments later. We were long gone before the boys in butternut closed in.

43

Miles from the West End, we ducked into a smoky dive frequented by the lowest classes. The bar was wide planks on sawhorses. The fare consisted of bad red sausages and worse green beer. Nobody paid me any mind, but Morley drew some vaguely hostile looks. Nobody would recognize him if he stayed a year, though. You don't look for Morley Dotes in that kind of place.

Morley settled opposite me at a scarred trestle table and steepled his fingers. "We have some names."

"Five. And none worth the paper it's written on."

"You reacted to one."

"Marengo North English. I don't know why the black magic connection surprised me. The man has the brain of a snake."

"You met him? Tell me about him."

"He's a loony. A racist loony. The Call. Sword of Righteousness. He wouldn't be involved in this. He would have cut Emerald off the second he heard about Maggie and the Rainmaker. Not our kind, you know, old bean."

"Wasn't what I meant. I think."

"He's the Call."

Not many patrons found themselves in circumstances sufficiently insufficient to have to take their custom into that dump, but those that did were curious. Ears pricked up and twitched first time I mentioned the Call. Second time, various faces turned toward us.

This was the sort of place where the Call would find recruits for the Sword of Righteousness, the sort of place infested by folks who'd never once in life had a bad break that was their own fault.

Morley caught the significance of my glare. "I see."

In a softer voice, I said, "He was a founding father of the Call. I met him at Weider's estate. I was doing security. Weider mentioned my military background. He tried to recruit me into the Sword of Righteousness. Sicking him on me was Weider's idea of a joke."

Party police isn't my usual, but Old Man Weider had asked nice and he's had me on retainer so long we're practically business partners. I said, "Be afraid of Marengo North English. He's crazy as hell, but he's the real thing. Had me ready to puke in his pocket two minutes after he started his spiel."

"But you didn't."

"Of course not. That was Weider's place. He was Weider's guest." The brewery retainer keeps me going through the hard times. "Like me, Weider can't help it if he has to do business with crazies."

"You didn't sign on with the Sword?"

"Give me a break. I grunted and nodded and got away from the man. The way you do when you don't want to make a scene. Why're you so interested?"

"Because I know Marengo North English, too. That man is going to be trouble. Why don't you sign up? Give sanity an agent inside."

I hemmed and hawed and cast meaningful looks at the big-eared clientele. I waved for another pint.

Morley got it. "Something to think over. We can talk about it later. Meantime, I think you're right. He might have seen a chance at some sweet young stuff, but he wouldn't keep her around ten seconds after he found out she had a scandal in her background."

I must have had a funny look on. He added, "I get

to meet all kinds." I presume he had done some work for North English. I didn't ask.

"Where are you going from here, Garrett?"

"I was thinking Quefour. Not that he'll know anything."

"I need to get back to the store."

"Got to read that book?"

"Book?" He started out with a hard look, decided on a different tack. "Wasn't a book. It was gone already." He grinned. Beat me to death with honesty.

"I'm heartbroken for you." I tossed coins onto the table. The tavernkeeper made them vanish before they stopped rattling. "Thanks for your help."

"Hey, it was fun. Anytime. I have some advice for you, though."

"I can't wait."

"There's a chance black magic is involved. You should take precautions."

"I'm a certified genius. I was thinking that very thought." Really. Because I was getting uncomfortable about how easy it was for one inept gorilla to keep getting back on my tail.

I knew I would see him as soon as we stepped into the street. And he didn't disappoint me.

44

Handsome's alley was back where it belonged. I examined it as I ambled past, not wanting to lead trouble to the house of a friend. Neither did I want to make a fool of myself by stepping into something unpleasant.

Second time past I turned in, leaving the inept guy trying to blend into a mob of dwarves. What worried me was that my other fans might realize they could stay on me by keeping track of him.

The trash had deepened. It was deeper everywhere. Such was the nature of things.

The shop felt unnaturally quiet—though how that was possible I couldn't say. It never got rowdy. Maybe it was like the breathing of the mice and roaches was absent.

Handsome's ragged cat padded in, sat, fixed me with a rheumy stare. I wondered how bad its eyes were. I didn't move around. I killed time watching from inside while my eyes adjusted. No point finding out how Handsome protected herself.

Then she was there. For one moment, I lapsed into a daydream and suddenly I wasn't alone.

Spooky.

She looked me in the eye. "You grew up with some sense after all."

"Only a fool goes around touching stuff in a place like this."

"Not what I meant, boy. You learned better than

that when you was a pup. I'm talking about you having
sense enough to know you're in over your head."

I did? I was? I nodded. I never shatter illusions.

"Garrett men just bull ahead, confident they can
handle anything."

That was me, sort of. Except the part about the
confidence.

"Explains how you managed to come home when
they didn't."

Mystified, I let her talk. Patience is a sound strategy
when you don't know what is going on. When she did
slacken, I wedged in, "Wixon and White did know the
girl. But it looks like Grange Cleaver faked up the
black magic connection." I related the details of my
adventures as I would have done for the Dead Man.

Handsome let me run dry. She let me stand empty
a while, too. Then, "Why would the Rainmaker want
to find the girl?"

"I don't have a clue. Maybe her mother is dead and
he needs Emerald to control the estate."

"She is valuable or dangerous. One or the other."

"Or both."

"You'll have to find her to know which. Can you?"

"Given time."

"You've made enemies. And you let someone mark
you with a finding spell."

"I was afraid of that. The stumblebum?"

"He's tracking you. He didn't mark you."

"Winger or Maggie, then."

"And the Jenn woman seems to be the Rainmaker
in drag."

"Who wants me sleeping with the fishes."

"And who wouldn't be above using a dollop of sorcery to get his way."

"No way can this klutz be Cleaver's. Whenever I
sit still long enough to draw a crowd, I accumulate
one of Cleaver's own kind. So who could the guy
work for?"

"Am I a mind reader? You want that, go home."

"Why did Cleaver get after me in the first place? I just can't figure that."

"At this point, why don't matter. He is. Deal with that."

I moved slightly. Just a twitch of impatience, really. But the old cat hissed.

"Patience, boy. And caution. These days a hundred evils could jump you before you got a hundred paces from this shop."

"I know." That was why I was there.

She told me, "I'm not going to let you go back out there till you're better prepared."

Who, me argue? "Thank you. That was in the back of my mind."

"I know."

"I'd be eternally grateful for any help."

"Don't heap it on with a manure fork, boy. It's all part of putting the Rainmaker in his place."

She knew the rules. Never let on how much you care. If you care, you're vulnerable.

The cat hissed again.

"What? I didn't do anything."

"Never mind Malkyn. She can smell the trouble on you. She worries about me."

Malkyn. Of course. What the hell else? "I smell the trouble on me, too. It's a curse."

"Or a calling." Her right eyebrow rose. Excellent! There was one talent I hadn't known she commanded.

"No. I just wish I could wash it off. I don't *want* to get into all these crazy things. I'd rather sit around the house drinking beer and—"

"You're bullshitting an old bullshitter, boy. I know more about you than you think."

My cue to hoist a brow.

"That don't slice no ice." She started moving around, fiddling, muttering. I realized she was naming names. "Hey! Wait a minute! What do they have to do with anything?"

"You wouldn't have met one of those ladies if you'd stayed holed up. And you ain't going to meet no more—"

"All right!" Truth is pain. Female remains my great weakness. A flashy smile and saucy wink can lure me away from safety.

Grinning evilly, Handsome cleared nonhuman skulls off a fern stand, started assembling her candidates for weirdest items in the shop. I started to say something but didn't get past opening my mouth.

"Give me that stick, boy."

I surrendered my headknocker, then opened my flycatcher again.

She didn't give me a chance to speak. "We don't got no idea what you're gonna run into, so what I'm gonna do is give you a range of generic defenses."

Oh, that sounded good. If it meant anything. "What are you doing to my stick?"

"Toughening it up, boy. When I get done with it, you're going to be able to whack right through all the common protective spells. You see that red thing there?"

"Looks like a dried-out sow's ear somebody dyed red?"

"The very thing. It looks like a sow's ear on account of once upon a time somebody hacked it off the side of a pig's head. I want you should take it and put it in your right front pocket. And keep it there until you settle up with the Rainmaker."

"Why?" She was getting ahead of me.

"On account of the Rainmaker is the kind who would get a laugh out of fixing you so's you wouldn't have no more reason to leave your house looking for women."

Ouch! I needed only about a quarter-second to mull things over. I accepted the sow's ear, placed it as directed. "You're the expert." Some fates are too horrible to contemplate.

"Remember it." She aligned four more objects, then regrouped them. One was a small wooden box given to fits of angry buzzing. Whatever was in there sounded huge for a bug.

Handsome noted my interest. "It's more wicked than it sounds."

"I wanted to hear that."

"It's not gonna bother you, son. Once I tell it you're its friend."

"Oh, hey, by all means. I'm a bug-lover from way back. I probably met most of its family when I was in the islands. I got intimate with lots of bugs when I was down there."

"You always did have a tongue of nonsense, boy."

What the hell did that mean?

She continued, "You don't want to use the little devil, don't bother. What they call a last resort. When you and your tongue have gotten you into something where there ain't no weaseling out, just pop that lid open."

"Yeah?" Call me dubious. I stopped being a bug booster during my Marine days. "Then what? It bites a hunk out of me and I scare the bad guys away with my screams?"

"Maybe. Or maybe it just comes home and tells me you need help."

Somehow having a bug in a box didn't sound that useful if I was in it deep, but Mom Garrett never raised her boys to backtalk the likes of Handsome. She always said we should keep our yaps shut when we were around somebody who could turn us into table scraps. There were times when Mom was pretty astute. "Uhm," I grunted.

Handsome gave me the fish-eye, then resumed her explanations. I did listen. And found my imagination captivated immediately.

Handsome offered me a doodad that looked like a wood chip stained red on one side and green on the other. She told me, "When you want you should turn invisible to that guy following you, you should rub your thumb three times across the red side here. He shouldn't ought to turn suspicious because the spell he's using isn't all that reliable. You think it would be handy having him tag along, you rub your thumb three times on the green side."

"What? Why would I want him following me?"

"How would I know?" She shrugged. "Reckon that's all I can do for you right now. Time you were getting along, anyway, boy. I've got paying customers backing up."

Where? But I only thought it.

The old cat looked at me like she was thinking about taking a bite out of my ankle before I got away. Or like she thought she would take a bite, if only she had some teeth.

Handsome patted me down, making sure I was carrying everything exactly where she wanted me carrying it.

I kept at it. "What can you tell me about—"

"Go on, boy. Out of here. Shoo. Scoot. How do you kids expect me to get any work done if you pester me all day long?"

Had she gone senile all of a sudden? Or was she trying to make me nostalgic?

I treasured my childhood memories but didn't consider those times the good old days. The good old days never were. These are the good old days, right here, right now.

Won't never get no better than this.

45

I'd told Morley I would see Quefour while doubting there was any point. But brave soldier I, dedicated to my mission, I spent a half hour trying to trace that most useless of beings and learned that when last seen he had been floundering around with an inept homosexual murphy in the Tenderloin, which was a stupid game to play. The wise guys could help him take a swim with a hundred-pound rock strapped to his back.

The beauty of being your own supervisor is you set your own hours. If the spirit moves you, you can procrastinate till hunger boots you into action.

I headed for home thinking life couldn't get any better.

Of course, it could have a Chastity Blaine perched on your front stoop when you came home, so damned radiant all your male neighbors had found some reason to come out and gawk.

She was alone. I broke into a trot, wove through the crowd, felt the deep disapproval radiating from such bastions as Mrs. Cardonlos's rooming house. Chastity was the only woman in the neighborhood smiling when I puffed up. "Where's Saucerhead?" I demanded.

"Saucerhead?" She really seemed puzzled.

"You know. Saucerhead Tharpe. Big goof with snaggle teeth. Your bodyguard. Able to outsmart small rocks if you give him an hour."

She smiled grimly, not in the mood. "I let him go."

"Why'd you do a fool thing like that?" What a sweet tongue.

"I don't have to worry anymore. It seems the episode of the escaping patient who couldn't have been in the first place because there's no record of any admission tore it for me. The Knopfler Bledsoe Imperial Memorial Charity Hospital no longer welcomes my services."

"They canned you. I'm sorry."

"Don't be. It was a learning experience."

"Uhm?" Philosophy straight from the Dead Man.

"I discovered that bitter old cynics like my father are right. No good deed goes unpunished."

"I like his thinking. So how come you're here? Not that I'm complaining. I couldn't have daydreamed a nicer surprise." I was hungry. I couldn't correct that hanging around on the stoop. I went to work with my key.

"I guess because you're the only one who knows what's going on."

"Boy, don't I wish." The door was bolted on the inside. I let out a shriek that got everybody within two blocks looking my way. I pounded away. Nobody responded.

"Is anyone in there? I couldn't get an answer."

"They'd better be dead. If they're not, I'm going to kill them. They're drinking up my beer and eating up my food and now they won't let me into my own house. I'm going to skin them and make myself a suit out of their hides."

"What are you going on about?"

"How many escaped patients have they recovered?"

"Only a few. It's not like they're trying real hard."

"A couple of them turned up here and I let them stay." The Goddamn Parrot was in there hollering so loud I could hear him through the door. I put on eternity's most forced smile. "You said it. No good deed goes unpunished."

"They're here now?"

"Somebody barred the door. If I have to break in, I'm going to carve somebody into rat snacks."

"Aren't you overreacting a little?"

Yes. "No!"

I received a completely unexpected hug. "Guess I'm not the only one who's had a bad day."

"Once we get in, let's butcher one of the clowns and discuss our bad days while we eat him."

"Don't be so gruesome. Who are they?"

"Ivy and Slither."

"Are you sure?"

"That's the names they use. What they want to be called." I pounded on the door and howled some more. "Soon to be past tense." Across the street, Mrs. Cardonlos came to her window and gave me that look. I was going to get another protest from the citizen's committee. How dare I raise hell on my own front stoop?

I sent Mrs. Cardonlos a smile. "Wait till I get my next psychopathic killer, lady. I'll tell him you're desperate to meet a real man."

"You don't have some secret way to get in?"

"You didn't grow up in this neighborhood, did you? If I had a secret entrance, the villains would have used it to clean me out a long time ago."

"You don't expect me to apologize for where I grew up?"

Careful, Garrett. "You didn't pick your parents. Just ignore me. I get testy when I can't get into my own house." I went to work on the door again.

The lady had begun to doubt the wisdom of being with me. I made a special effort to remain calm and reasonable when Ivy finally cracked the door an inch, keeping it on the chain while he checked me out.

"Ivy, it's me. I'm home and I'd really like to visit my kitchen. Think you could speed it up?" I scanned the street quickly. Looked like everybody who'd shown any interest lately was out there watching. Even a guy with an eyepatch and an earring. I couldn't see if he had a pegleg, but I knew where he could pick up a parrot cheap.

The door opened. There to greet me was Slither. "Doc Chaz. Garrett. Sorry. I was in the kitchen whipping something up. I thought Ivy was taking care here." Ivy was at the door to the small front room, looking inside with eyes that had glazed over. "Looks like he's having one of his spells."

"I'm about to have one of mine."

"Bad day?"

"That catches the spirit of it." Slither wasn't listening. He was headed for the kitchen.

Chastity asked, "These men escaped with you?"

"Not with me. But they were both in my ward."

"I know Rick Gram." She indicated Ivy. "The other one is a stranger."

"Slither claims he got in there the same way I did. And the same guy put him there."

"Grange Cleaver?"

"The very one."

"Maybe. I don't recognize him. But there were four hundred men in your ward. And I was expected to concentrate on the female population."

We hit the kitchen. Slither announced, "Not a lot of supplies left here, Garrett. You need to do some shopping."

Scowling, I put an arm around Chastity's shoulder and headed for the back door. I didn't want to be home after all. With the thumb of my free hand I stroked the red side of a wood chip. "I'm ducking out the back way, Slither. The front door ever gets barred again I'm going to cut somebody's heart out. You make sure Ivy understands." Intuition told me that was all Ivy. He been Long Range Recon once upon a time, but he was afraid of his own shadow now. "*My* house, Slither. My rules and my ways."

"Stay cool, Garrett. I got it under control. You and Doc Chaz go somewhere, have a good time."

46

"I hope every villain in town is camped out in front of my place." Chastity and I were enjoying a perfect evening. Nearly perfect. I had one bad moment at a place where I caught a glimpse of Maya Stuub. Once upon a time Maya had thought more of me than I'd thought of myself.

Maya didn't see me. I put her out of mind and had a nice time.

Chastity was all right. I could relax with her. I told her tales of the Garrett that was, suitably edited for modern audiences, and she did the same with Chaz Blaine—though she didn't say much about her family. We lost track of time. Time lost track of us. An apologetic fellow with a grungy towel on his arm advised us that it was time to close. We nodded and apologized back and left too much money and went out to wander streets we didn't see. For both of us the world had come into narrow focus. We were our universe— that teenage feeling. . . .

"My gods you're beautiful," I told her in a place that wasn't mine. And she was. More than I had imagined.

Her insecurities burned through. She protested, "My nose is crooked and one eye is higher than the other and my mouth is tilted and one boob is bigger and higher than the other."

"You got weird toes, too, but I don't give a damn.

You hear me howling about what a prize I am? Lucky you, not even having to find the end of the rainbow."

"We're all overstressed these days, aren't we?"

"Absolutely." Nobody anywhere was comfortable. Conflicts were feeding upon one another. "A moment that loosens us from the cycle of despair is a treasure."

"Was that a compliment? I'm going to take it in that spirit."

Actually, it was a quote from the Dead Man, but why disappoint the lady?

Got to be getting old. I woke up feeling guilty about not having done anything useful about Emerald Jenn. I watched Chaz sleep. I recalled Morley's comment about her quality. I remembered seeing Maya. I felt a twinge of pain.

Chaz opened an eye, saw me looking, smiled, stretched. The sheet slipped off her. I gulped air, astounded all over again.

Next time I knew it was an hour later and I hadn't heard a word from my might-have-beens the whole time.

"So what do you intend to do?" Chaz asked, having heard the details of the case.

"That's my problem. Common sense says walk away. Tell myself some people tried to use me, I made some money, we're even."

"But part of you wants to know what's going on. And part is worried about the girl."

I admitted nothing.

"Waldo told me about the case he helped you with."

Naturally. He wouldn't have missed a chance to play his big It Was All My Fault scene. "Waldo?" They were on a first-name basis?

"Waldo Tharpe."

"Saucerhead. Sometimes I forget he has a real name."

"And your friend Morley told me about a case involving a girl named Maya and something called the Sisters of Doom."

"He did?" That startled me.

"It's pretty obvious, Garrett. You're an idealist and a romantic. With big clay feet, maybe, but one of the last good guys."

"Hey! Wait a minute. I'm turning red here. Anyway, there's never been anybody more pragmatic than Mrs. Garrett's little boy."

"You can't even convince yourself, hard boy. Go. Find Emmy Jenn. Help her if she needs it. I'm getting out of the way. You don't need distractions."

"That's where we disagree."

"Down, boy. When you've wrapped it up, send me a message at my father's house. I'll be knocking on your door before you can say Chastity is a naughty girl."

"Uh-oh." Not again.

"What?"

"Don't get mad. I don't know who your father is."

"You didn't investigate me?"

"I didn't see a need."

"My father is the Firelord Fox Direheart."

Oh, boy. I made a squeaking noise.

"Can you remember?"

Squeak. I don't dally with the daughters of sorcerer nobility. I don't relish the honor of having my hide bind somebody's grimoire.

"Don't let the title intimidate you. He's just old Fred Blaine at home."

Right. What I've been looking for all my life, a girlfriend whose pop is a frontliner but wants me to slap his back and call him Fred.

"You'll get in touch?"

"You know I will, devil woman." I wouldn't be able to resist.

"Then get back to your quest. I can find my way home." Cute little frown. "And then Daddy will get in his 'I told you so' about the hospital job. I hate it when he's right, because he's always right about people being cruel and selfish and wicked."

I collected a farewell kiss and headed for home wondering why one of Karenta's leading sorcerers was here in TunFaire instead of working the cleanup detail down in the Cantard.

47

I slipped in the back door. Slither and Ivy were in the kitchen, one drunk and the other cooking. Slither said, "Yo, Garrett. The cupboard is bare."

"Need a new keg, too," Ivy slurred.

"Sing, Johnny One-Note," I grumbled. If they didn't like it, they ought to do something about it.

Up front, the Goddamn Parrot was squawking about neglect. I wondered if Slither had started eating parrot chow, too.

I wondered what the Dead Man would think if he woke to find himself in this zoo.

I said, "I guess that means it's time you moved on to greener pastures."

"Huh?"

"You done anything to find work? To find your own place? I think I've done my share."

"Uh . . ."

"He's right," Ivy said. His tongue tangled, but otherwise he was more articulate drunk than his sidekick was when he was sober. "We haven't contributed here. It's possible we're not capable. And this is his home."

Damn. The man made me feel guilty when all he was doing was telling the truth.

"I washed the goddamn dishes, Ivy. I did the laundry. I scrubbed woodwork. I even sprayed bugweed juice on the thing in the lib'ary to keep the crawlies off'n it. So don't go saying I didn't do nothing, Ivy.

214

What the hell you keeping a mummy around for, Garrett? And if you got to, how come you got to keep such an ugly bugger?"

"He makes a great conversation piece. The girls all tell me how cute he is."

That didn't wake him up, either.

Slither wasn't listening. "And how about you, Ivy? What've you done? Besides suck down that horse piss till you make me wonder where the hell you put it all? You hungry, Garrett?"

"Yes."

"Sink your fangs into these here biscuits. Gravy coming up." He wheeled on Ivy, but Ivy had gotten going, headed up front. I shut them out, ate hastily, wondered if they'd gotten married. Slither started hollering the length of the house.

"Enough!" I snapped. "Has anyone been around?"

"Shit, Garrett, you got to be the most popular guy in town. Always somebody pounding on your door."

"And?"

"And what? You ignore them, they go away."

"That's always been my philosophy."

Ivy stuck his head in. "There was that cute little girl."

I raised an eyebrow, which was talent wasted on those two.

"Yeah," Slither said. "Ivy answered that one. He's a sucker for a skirt."

Ivy shrugged, looked embarrassed.

"Well, guys?"

"I don't know," Ivy said. "I didn't understand." Hardly the first time, I thought. "She didn't make much sense. Something about could you help her find her book yet."

Find her book? "Linda Lee?"

"Huh?"

"She tell you her name? Was it Linda Lee?"

Ivy shrugged.

No good deed unpunished, Garrett. I downed a last bite, knocked back a mug of weak tea, headed for the front of the house. T.G. Parrot seemed less intolerable by the hour.

Everything is relative.

I used the peephole.

That was Macunado Street all right. Infested with quasi-intelligent life. Not much use studying it through a hole, though. I opened up and stepped onto the stoop.

I spotted nobody but sensed the watching eyes. I settled onto my top step, watched the sweep of commerce. As always, I wondered where everybody was going in such a hurry. I nodded at people I knew, mostly neighbors. Some responded. Some hoisted their noses and wished I would vanish in a puff of smoke. Old Mr. Stuckle, who roomed at the Cardonlos place, was one of the friendly ones. "How you doing, son?"

"Some good days, Pop. Some bad days. But every new day is a blessing."

"I heard that. You got Gert stirred, you know."

"Again? Or still?"

He grinned a grin with only two teeth left to support it. "There you go." Gert Cardonlos always took the other side when my neighbors got upset. I wondered whether she had changed her name to Brittany or Misty, she would have grown old without growing sour.

Probably not.

As I watched Stuckle breast the stream of flesh a neighborhood urchin sidled up. "There's people been watching your place."

"No kidding?" Becky Frierka had illusions about getting involved in my adventures. I don't mind having girls around, but they need to be a little older than eight. "Tell me about it." You never know where you'll learn something useful. And me listening would make Becky feel good.

I don't remember my father much. Mom always said one of his philosophies was each day you should do at least one thing to make somebody feel good. She probably made it up. People like Handsome let me know Mom did a lot of creative revision. But this was a good idea.

"Thank you, Becky. That's quite useful." I offered her a couple of coppers. "Better scoot."

"You took that lady to dinner."

"What?"

"Last night."

"So?"

"I don't want money. I want you to take me out."

Oh. Right. And would I ever hear the end of that? "How come you know what I did last night?"

"I saw you go out the back. I followed you." She put on her devil smile. "I know what you done."

"You a dwarf in disguise? You trying to blackmail me?"

"No. But I could tell you who else followed you."

Whoa! I hadn't noticed any tail. Not even her. "You have my attention, Becky."

"You going to buy me dinner? Same place as the blond lady?"

"You got it." No problem. Her mother would get me out of it. "Soon as I get this job wrapped. Deal?"

She was suspicious. I gave up too fast. But, "Deal. And don't think you're gonna weasel out."

"Talk to me about the somebody who followed me, brat."

"It was a man. A weird man. Not very tall but really huge-mongous anyway." She spread her arms. "He walked funny." She showed me how.

"Mugwump," I guessed aloud. I hadn't seen Mugwump's walk, but that had to be it.

"Mugwump?"

"Man's name. Probably who that was. He have really big hands?"

"I don't know."

Great. "What did he do?"

"Just followed you where you went. After a while he left. He's really weird, Garrett. He talked to himself all the time."

"Probably from living in a neighborhood like mine." I spied Saucerhead Tharpe headed my way. I could think of no reason for him approaching with such a purposeful stride. "Thanks, Becky. Time for you to scoot now."

"Don't forget. You promised."

"Who? Me? Get on with you." I hoped *she* would forget, but I never have that kind of luck. "So who died?" I asked Tharpe. The big goof wasn't even breathing heavy.

"Huh?"

"You were charging this way like a guy loaded with the worst bad news he could imagine."

"Really? I was thinking about Lettitia."

"Lettitia? That off the menu at Morley's?"

"My lady. You haven't met her yet." Saucerhead always has a new girlfriend. I didn't see any bruises so maybe this one was nicer than usual.

"You came for advice to the lovelorn?"

"From you?" His tone wasn't generous.

"From His Nibs in there. The world's foremost authority." On everything. According to him.

"Speaking of him, you give him the latest from down south?"

"Something happen?" The street didn't have the edgy feel it gets when there's big news from the Cantard.

"Ain't out general yet on account of it's supposed to be a big military secret, but I heard from my sister's husband who's got a cousin works for the Stormwarden Burner Skullspite, First Cav Spec Ops raided Glory Mooncalled's headquarters."

"Our guys have found his hideout about five times already, you silly groundpounder." A good-hearted fellow, Saucerhead didn't quite grasp reality. He'd been a plain old foot-slogging infantryman during his service. He suffered from the common army delusion that cavalry were some sort of elite. I mean, come on! They're not even Marines. You add in the fact that they're dimwit enough to voluntarily ride horses . . .

"This was the real headquarters. An old vampire nest."

Something about his tone . . . "Don't tell me."

"The very one."

"Life is weird."

An earlier case had taken me back to the war zone. In the course of events, Morley and I and some others invaded a subterranean vampire nest, a stronghold of horror. We were fortunate. We escaped. We passed word to the Army. The soldiers took time off from the war.

The war with vampires takes precedence.

That was before Glory Mooncalled rebelled. Just.

One of my gang had been a centaur. "There's more?" I asked. Tharpe was antsy. There was something.

"Yeah. The attack was a big ass surprise. They barely figured out what hit them before it was over. They hardly destroyed any documents."

So Mooncalled's deep well of luck was running dry.

"What's the bottom line?"

"Them documents showed he wasn't in the Cantard no more. Our big boys been chasing shadows."

I have my moments. "And the only documents the republicans did destroy were ones that might say where the boss was?"

"How'd you know?"

"I'm a good guesser." This would interest the Dead

Man. His hobby was tracking and anticipating Glory Mooncalled.

"They get anything out of the prisoners?"

"Didn't take no prisoners, Garrett."

"You always take prisoners."

"Not this time. Them guys never had no chance, but they wouldn't give up."

I couldn't believe that. However fanatic a group is there's always a member who doesn't want to die.

"But that ain't why I come here, Garrett."

"Oh?"

"Winger wanted me to—"

"Winger! Where is that oversized . . . ?"

"If you put a clamp on it, I might tell you something."

The best advice I ever got. It repeated suggestions from my mother and the Dead Man. You have a hard time hearing with your mouth open. I shut mine.

"Winger said tell you that you and her ain't pulling the same oar no more but you ought to know them West End pansies was coached to tell you what they told you. You was supposed to head off in a new direction."

He looked at me like he hoped I would explain.

I considered. I thought Robin and Penny had talked straight. They maybe forgot a fact or three but steered a tack close to the truth. Why point me at Marengo North English? Why would Winger turn me away?

Smelled like somebody was dragging a squashed skunk across the trail. Somebody big and blond with too much faith in my naivete. "How would she know?"

"I figure she got it from her boyfriend."

"Her what? Boyfriend? Since when?"

Saucerhead shrugged. "Been around a while, off and on. She never made no announcement. I don't figure she wants us to know. You'd come out of your hole and hang out, you would know, though."

He had a point. Information was the blood of my trade and connections the bone. I wasn't taking proper care of either. I did before I moved in with the Dead Man. "Go on."

"She just wanted to warn you. Didn't want you should step in anything unexpected."

"That's my pal. Always thinking of me. She couldn't drop by herself, eh?"

Saucerhead grinned. "You ask me, she don't want to get close enough you can get your hands on her."

"Surprise, surprise." I glanced over my shoulder. The boys and bird weren't watching. "Think I'll wander over to Morley's. I'll buy, if you want to come along."

48

Morley didn't seem thrilled to see Saucerhead. He gave me a dark scowl. I couldn't understand why. Tharpe was a good customer.

Dotes joined us anyway. It was obvious immediately that he was distracted. He listened with half an ear, kept one eye on the door all the time.

I told him, "I've got most of it figured."

"Uhm?" How did he get so much incredulity into one grunt?

"When Maggie Jenn left town, she was so bitter she never wanted to come back. Her lover had been murdered, his people hated her, but she still had to go through the motions to keep what he gave her, for the kid's sake as well as her own. Her old pal and maybe brother Grange Cleaver played her to get the skinny on the Hill places he robbed, so she got him to play her whenever it was time to make her annual shows. Cleaver was happy to help. It gave him a way to get into and out of TunFaire without getting gobbled up by Chodo Contague. Along the way, he hooked up with the imperials, sold them some con, and got involved with the Bledsoe. Bet you he's been stealing from the hospital and the Hill place both.

"Now get this. One day along come Crask and Sadler with a tale about Chodo and his little girl. Cleaver eats it up. This is what he's been waiting for. This is his big chance to get back into the big time in the big town. But there's a loose end: Emerald Jenn.

She's in the city. A runaway. She knows the truth about Maggie Jenn and Grange Cleaver. And she'll tell it."

Morley and Saucerhead looked like they were having trouble grasping it. Why? It wasn't hard.

"So Cleaver tries to set up an operation here, and nobody signs on because they know about Chodo's old grievance. Except Winger. And she starts wondering what's what. But she smells a chance to score. When Cleaver mentions he wants to look for the girl without it being obvious it's him looking, Winger drops some hints about me, figuring to use me somehow. Cleaver puts on his Maggie Jenn face and hires me, only I mess up by letting it drop that I was warned Maggie was coming. He smells a rat inside his outfit. Who it is doesn't click right away. Being a good actor, he doesn't have any trouble staying in character long enough for me to finish up at the Hill place. Soon as I'm gone, though, he takes off for his headquarters and sets it up to get rid of me. He'll get somebody else to look for the girl.

"Winger hears him sending his men out. She realizes it won't be long before he figures out who told me he was coming. She grabs anything she can carry and takes off. She helps me get away from the Bledsoe.

"She gives me a double ration of bullshit when I ask her what's really going on. She still thinks she can make a big score, so now she's staying away from me."

Sarge brought tea while I theorized. Morley poured, sipped, grimaced. Evidently the tea hadn't been brewed from anything off a tea bush. Big surprise. They serve nothing normal there.

Dotes was distracted. He was listening, but every time the door opened he lost his concentration. Still, he'd remained attentive enough to observe, "Your hypothesis doesn't contradict any of the known facts."

"Hell, I know that. I made it up. But? I can tell— you have a but."

"Couple of them. You don't contradict any known facts, but you don't account for everything that's been happening around you. And you've done a feeble job of examining Cleaver's motives."

"What? Wait. Whoa. You just lost me."

"Chodo's kid shirked any of the duties of a kingpin?"

"Hardly. Ice and iron." I had the gashes and frost-bite to prove it.

"Exactly. So whatever Crask and Sadler might claim, being here is a major risk for Cleaver. I've identified the pro who's dogging you. His name is Cleland Justin Carlyle. He's a specialist assigned to watch you. You get three guesses why. Only the first counts."

I nodded. "And, wonder of wonders, C.J. was never seen in these parts before I mentioned the name Grange Cleaver to my pal Morley Dotes, once said pal failed to meet up with Cleaver his own self."

Morley shrugged, which was as good as a confession.

He had no regrets. He never looked back and seldom apologized. He saw no need to apologize now. He asked, "What's Winger's angle?"

"I don't know. I doubt that it matters. She probably doesn't know what she's doing herself, she just wants to keep the pot boiling till she finds a way to score."

Morley slew a pity smile a-borning.

"You know something I don't?"

"No. You're ahead of me. Though you do seem to be late catching on to an essential point."

"Really? What?"

"That Winger lied about everything. Right from the beginning. That not one word she said can be counted on to be true. That anything that comes from her should be thrown out altogether."

"Oh. Yeah. I knew that."

I knew it now. Now that I looked at it. Forget everything Winger said. Sure.

49

"I conned Puddle into doing you a favor, Garrett," Morley told me. I didn't ask; I just waited for the inevitable wisecrack.

He fooled me again. The crack didn't come. "Uhm?"

"I had a feeling you wouldn't get around to Quefours."

"Puddle scare him up?"

Morley nodded.

"Waste of time, right?"

"Puddle's still sulking."

"What's the story?"

"Quefours hasn't seen the girl for eight months. His choice. He broke it off because she wouldn't play his way. Made her sound prudish."

"And Quefours doesn't have the ghost of a notion where to find her now. Right?"

"Wrong."

"Huh?" I've always had a knack for witty repartee.

"He said dig around among the witchcraft community. The girl is looking for something. His notion was you should start with the blackest black magicians. That was where she was headed when they split." Dotes appended a big nasty smile.

"You saying Cleaver framed her with the truth?"

"Maybe just to get you headed in the right direction." More teeth. He had to have about two hundred.

Looked like he'd been filing them again, too. "Thought you'd get a kick out of that."

"A kick in the butt." It just got more confusing. I started to get up.

"Hey!" Saucerhead growled. "You told me . . ."

"Feed this beast, Morley. Something cheap. Like alfalfa."

"Where are you going?"

I opened my mouth to tell him and realized that I didn't know.

"Like that? Then why not just go home? Lock your doors. Get comfortable. Read. Wait for Dean. Forget Grange Cleaver and Emerald Jenn."

I responded with my most suspicious look.

"You got your advance, didn't you? This Jenn chit sounds like she can take care of herself."

"Answer me one answer, Morley. Why did she run away from home?" Might be important if the whole thing had to do with a missing kid after all.

"There are as many reasons for going as there are children running."

"But they mostly boil down to a perceived need to escape parental control. I don't know enough about Emerald. I don't know enough about her mother. Their relationship is a mystery."

"What did I just recommend? Don't keep gnawing on it, Garrett. You don't have any reason. You don't need any more grief. Turn loose. Spend some money. Spend some time with Chastity."

"What?"

"Gods preserve us," Saucerhead muttered. He stopped attacking his dinner long enough to sneer, "He's got that look, ain't he?"

"Got what look?"

Morley told me, "The dumb stubborn look you get when you're about to jump into something without a reason even you understand."

"About to? I've been in it four days."

"And now you're out because you know it was a game that didn't take. You did your usual stumbling around and knocked over everybody's apple carts. Now it's over. You're out. You're safe as long as you don't go around irritating people. Consider it a phenomenon. You don't go charging around like a lunatic trying to find out why if it happens to rain live frogs for three minutes in the Landing. Do you?"

"But ..." But that was different.

"There's no need to find the girl now. Not for her sake, which is the thing that would bug you."

"Garrett!" I jumped. I hadn't expected Saucerhead to horn in. Everybody in the place stared at him. He told me, "He's making sense. So listen up. Nothing I heared about this makes me think these folks're really worried about the kid."

"He's making sense," I admitted. "Morley always makes sense."

Dotes gave me a hard look. "But?"

"I'm butting no buts. I mean it. You're dead on the mark. There's no percentage messing with this anymore."

Morley eyeballed me like he believed me so surely he wanted to wrap me in another wet blanket. I complained, "I really do mean it. I'm going to go home, get ripped with Eleanor, grab me a night's sleep. Tomorrow I get to work on running my guests off. All of them. Only one thing I'm wondering."

"What's that?" Morley remained unconvinced. I couldn't believe that they really thought I had the white knight infection that bad.

"Could Emerald be another Cleaver disguise? You think he could manage makeup good enough to pass for eighteen?"

Morley and Saucerhead opened their mouths to ask why Cleaver would want to, but neither actually spoke. Neither wanted to feed me any reason to go chasing something potentially lethal.

"I'm just curious. He has a rep as a master of disguises. And Playmate told me he'd always thought that the daughter was dead. I wonder if maybe the plot wasn't more complex than we suspected. Maybe Cleaver didn't just plant clues up on the Hill. Maybe he created a whole character."

Morley snarled, "You're psycho, Garrett."

Saucerhead agreed. "Yeah." He was so serious he put his fork down. "I know I ain't no genius like neither one of you guys, but I do know you got to go with the simplest explanation for something on account of about a thousand times out of nine hundred ninety-nine that's the way the real story goes."

What was the world coming to when Saucerhead got a smart tongue on him? "Am I arguing? I agree. Sometimes I think this brain of mine is a curse. Thank you, Morley. For everything. Even when you didn't mean it." I left enough money to cover Saucerhead's meal, though I could have made it to the street before anyone realized that the tab hadn't been satisfied. I figured Saucerhead deserved it. His luck rolled down a steeper incline than mine. He seldom lived better than hand to mouth.

Me, I, Garrett, was out of the game. Whatever it might be. I was going to go home, get organized, drink some beer, have a bath, scope me out a master plan that included seeing a lot of Chastity Blaine.

But I left Morley's place with my hackles up, like some atavistic part of me expected the same old gang to be out there set to reintroduce me to the pleasures of the Bledsoe. I was on edge all the way home.

The Bledsoe was a sight, they said. Supposedly it was disappearing behind fast-rising scaffolding.

My tension went to waste. Nobody paid me any mind. I didn't even get followed. Made me feel neglected.

I'd never had a case as exciting as this just sputter

and fade away, but some jobs have. Those kind usually see me ending up snacking on my fee. I recalled with pride that this time I'd been clever enough to snag a percentage up front.

I wouldn't win any kudos from the Dead Man, but he would have to admit that I was capable of being businesslike on occasion, even in the face of a lusty redhead.

50

Despite sleeping well I wakened restless. I chalked it up to rising before noon even though Ivy hadn't pestered me. Once again I wondered if the Dead Man wasn't stirring. I looked in but saw no sign that he was. But what could you expect? Awake or asleep, the Dead Man's physical appearance changes only as time gnaws.

Slither and Ivy were unusually subdued. They sensed that I planned to move them out. I had a notion where to send them, too. But old lady Cordonlos wouldn't believe a word I said to make them sound like worthy potential tenants. Darn her.

So after lunch I consulted someone who might actually give a rat's whisker about their welfare.

Wonder of wonders, Playmate had some ideas. Before long, my old campaigning pals had probationary jobs and probationary housing and I found me, O miracle of miracles, with my own place all to my ownself again. Except for the Dead Man and the Goddamn Parrot. That cursed bird had gone into hiding before Ivy could hunt him down and take him along. My generous self-sacrifice wasted.

It would be a while yet before I saw Dean again. I hoped. What with Chaz and all. . . .

I talked it over with Eleanor. She had no objections, so I wrote a letter and hired a neighborhood kid to deliver it to Chastity. He insisted on a bonus for approaching a wizard's house.

I checked and rechecked the street while I gave the little mercenary his instructions. I saw no one even vaguely interested in the Garrett homestead. Even my neighbors were ignoring me. Still, I was uneasy.

I squabbled with the Goddamn Parrot till that got old, then communed with Eleanor. I was lonely. Your social circle isn't much when it consists of a talking bird, a painting, and a character who hasn't only been asleep for weeks and dead for centuries, he hasn't been out of the house since you met him.

My friends were right. This was no way to live.

There was a knock. I would've ignored it had I not been expecting to hear from Chaz.

Even so, I used the peephole.

It was the kid. He held a letter up. I opened the door, tipped him extra, checked the lay of things again, still saw nothing unusual. I like it that way.

I settled behind my desk, read, then shared the news with Eleanor. "Chaz says she's gonna pick *me* up. How about that? One bold wench, eh?"

After a pause, I continued, "All right. Call her a role-breaker, not a bold wench. And she's gonna stay nontraditional. Taking me someplace she likes. And she's bringing her father."

Only a painting, I reminded myself. This chatter was only an affection. No way could Eleanor taunt me with a spectral snicker.

I didn't much want to meet Chaz's pop, him being one of the top twenty double-nasty wizards infesting this end of the world. I hoped he wasn't a real old-fashioned kind of dad. I don't deal well with foamy-mouthed avengers of soiled virtue.

Another ghostly guffaw? "She says he just wants to ask about Maggie Jenn and Grange Cleaver."

Right. That worried me more than if she'd tipped me to expect a daddy smoking with outrage.

No good kicking and screaming now.

Eleanor insisted this was a great opportunity to make contacts among the high and mighty. "Right, babe. You know how I value my contacts among the rich and infamous. Exactly what I've always never wanted."

I went to make myself lunch.

My guests had left me my shoes and half a pitcher of water.

51

I went into that evening with my philosophy of life firmly fixed in mind: expect the worst and you can't possibly be disappointed. Chastity's old man was a boomer. If he took a notion, he could flatten me like a cow patty and skip me across the river.

He surprised me. He was no centenarian gargoyle. He looked like an ordinary guy barely on the lying side of fifty. His black hair had gone half silver. He had a small paunch and stood four inches shorter than me. He was groomed till he gleamed. He glowed with good health. Those were obvious badges of power. But he dressed no better than me. And he had the tanned and roughened skin of a guy who spent a lot of time outdoors. He didn't seem taken with himself, either.

He turned out to be one of those guys who is such a good listener you tell things you didn't know you knew. That skill would have served him well in the war zone. The best leaders are those with ears.

He interrupted only twice, with penetrating questions. Before I finished, I adopted the attitude I take when reporting to the Dead Man or chatting with Eleanor. I talked to me, thinking out loud.

I finished. Chaz looked at her father. He stayed clammed. I asked, "So how come you're interested? Because of Chaz and the hospital?" He called her Chaz, too.

"Our home was looted during the crime spree that paralleled Teodoric's affair with Maggie Jenn."

I gave Chaz a mild fish-eye. She hadn't mentioned that.

"A few items were recovered. They traced back to a Grange Cleaver—who couldn't be found."

"You didn't connect him with the hospital Cleaver?"

"I wasn't here when Chaz decided to work charity. Nor would I have looked for a thief in such a high place."

"No? I think I'd look there. . . ." I got control of my mouth when Chaz kicked me under the table.

The firelord's expression told me I was fooling no one. He was right, really. We look for shady characters in the shade. Unless we're cynics.

"I always thought Jenn was involved, Garrett. That raid took military timing. No outsider knew the family schedule. But you can't accuse the royal mistress of theft."

"I see." Sort of. Chaz offered a smile meant to give me heart. Didn't work. I had a notion where her dad was headed.

I wasn't wrong.

Blaine said, "I'm as vindictive as the next guy. Even now I can't go after Jenn, however much the royals hate her. They take care of their black sheep, too. But Cleaver has no friends that count and no guardian angels. Chaz says she told you we know Colonel Block. I'm pulling strings with the Guard and elsewhere, but I'd really like you to find Cleaver. If Block does it, it ends up on a court docket. I want to deal with Cleaver personally."

Ker-pungk! The daddy of all fat leather wallets hit the table. "Nice workmanship," I noted.

Faint smile. "Chaz gives you glowing reviews, Garrett. Westman Black, though, suspects that you *can't* dance on water." I gave Chaz a look. She reddened. "But I know Block, so I solicited other opinions."

Was I supposed to be impressed? Blaine had begun to sound pompous.

Maybe there was a problem with my hearing.

I gave the Firelord an opportunity to appreciate my raised eyebrow trick. It worked. He told me, "They say you're the best but you're no self-starter." He caressed that wallet like it was a special lady. "Devil snatch you, man! Don't you have a bone to pick with Cleaver? You could've spent your life in a lunatic ward." He edged that wallet half a foot closer.

Chaz smiled, nodded encouragement. Maybe her daddy danced on water, too.

"I did talk to Block, Garrett. There's more than money here." Caress, caress. "There's a letter of introduction over my chop. Use it any way you want. It says you're my agent and anyone who won't help you just might find life unrewarding. There's also a warrant from the good colonel that you can use to commandeer help from city employees. There are letters of credit that should be sufficient to cover your expenses and fees."

Oh? And the damned wallet jingled like it was stuffed with more gold than a troll could hoist.

Chastity's old man had come prepared to do business. He didn't expect to go home disappointed. And I couldn't argue with him.

He wouldn't let me.

He was like all his class—though he did seem inclined to play fair.

Chaz kept right on saying nothing and grinned like she was watching me being inducted into paradise. I stalled. "I'm not sure what you want."

"Find Grange Cleaver for me. Bring him to me or lead me to him. Once we're face-to-face, you're out of it."

Reluctantly, like that wallet was a real troll-buster,

I dragged his bribe toward me. I peeked. I saw pretty calligraphy, nifty official seals, a sweet double handful of shiny gold. And . . . a wishbone? "A killing bone?" I asked.

"What? Oh. That's right. You served in the islands." Where the natives owned their own special nasty magic. To which Karenta and Venageta reacted by exterminating its practitioners wherever they were found.

"Yes." Growl and scowl.

"This isn't that. This is just a gimmick. Should you get into terrible trouble, spit on the bone. You'll go out of focus to anyone concentrating on you. Any disinterested observer will see you fine, but somebody trying to kill you won't be able to fix on you. Clever, eh?"

Maybe. I didn't say so. I didn't say his kind were so clever they fooled themselves most of the time.

"All right. It isn't much. My talents run more toward smashing cities."

And Chaz kept on smiling like she meant to melt me down.

The firelord excused himself. "Got to run. You'd think I could back off and take it easy now we've won the war. You two don't need me getting in the way, anyhow."

This guy couldn't be real. I waved bye-bye. My new boss. Like it or not.

The thrill doesn't last like it used to.

"Isn't it great?" Chaz asked. She was so excited. I wondered if somebody had hit her with a stupid spell.

"What?"

Her smile turned puzzled. "What's the matter?"

"Your daddy." I kept a firm grasp on that wallet.

"I don't understand." She thought I should be pleased.

"I'm concerned about his agenda."

"Was he indirect? Did he blow a lot of smoke?"

"No." I couldn't deny that. "What do you recall about this big ripoff?"

"Nothing. I wasn't here."

"Uhm?" I reached deep into my trick bag and came up with my best eyebrow lift. That drives them wild.

"I was away at school. Being finished. Boys go to the Cantard as subalterns." Her class, she meant. "Debs go to finishing school."

"Let's don't fight." Especially since I'd survived a face-to-face with a father who wasn't overburdened with ordinary paternal prejudices.

"Daddy's people are rustics, hon. He doesn't fake it. Forget his fire talent. *He* calls it a curse." She kept scooting her gorgeous little tail ever closer. I didn't think she wanted to talk about Daddy anymore.

But I had to ask, "Is this like him?"

"What?"

"Would he hire somebody to hunt somebody so he could settle an old grudge?"

"Maybe. We only got robbed one time. I know he's never stopped being mad about it. He'd go burn something down whenever he got thinking about it."

Interesting. Even curious. Not for an instant had he come across as hagridden.

"Come on, Garrett. Forget all that," Chaz cajoled.

"Yeah? Think I should?"

"I think you should think about what the doctor wants to prescribe."

I did my eyebrow thing. "Not another thought in my head." She did an old female trick back that set me to drooling on myself.

In a perfectly cool, rational, businesslike voice she said, "Daddy's paying. Make a pig of yourself."

"Oink, oink. But not here."

"Oooh! Promises, promises. Better be careful. I don't have to work tonight."

That was the best idea I'd heard in a while, but because she was one gorgeous woman, I let her have the last word.

52

A couple of regulars actually lifted welcoming paws when I drifted into Morley's place. The attitude didn't infect management, though. Puddle scowled like he was trying to remember where he put that damned rat poison.

Morley was in a good mood, though. He bounced downstairs as my tea arrived.

I said, "I know that look. You just won big on the water spider races. Or somebody's wife tripped and you ravished her before she could get up."

He showed me a mouth like a shark's. "I gather you're doing some ravishing yourself."

"What?"

"You were seen with a stunning blonde in a place way out of your class."

"Guilty. How'd you know?"

"You won't like the answer."

"Yeah? Hit me with the bad news. I'm overdue."

"A couple came in late last night. Slumming. He was mister Flashy. She was Rose Tate. She'd seen you earlier."

"Bet she had her nasty smile on." Rose Tate was the cousin of my lapsed girlfriend, Tinnie Tate. And Rose had a grudge.

"She did. You're going to star in some interesting girl talk."

"No doubt. But Tinnie knows Rose. Rose mention who else I was with?"

"You running a string?"

"Chaz brought her dad." I told the tale, then asked, "You ever seen Blaine?"

"No. Why?"

"Wondering about ringers again."

"You think Chastity is jobbing you, too?"

"It's paranoia time, Morley. My world has stopped making sense."

"When you're well paid, sense needn't enter the equation. Right?"

"But it helps."

"You're concerned about coincidence."

"What are the chances Chaz would work the same place as a thief that robbed her father?"

"What are the odds you'd get thrown in there where you could meet her? A lot longer, I'd say."

"How come?"

"Where would a female doctor have the best chance of getting started? Where would the imperials set Cleaver up if they wanted to put him into TunFaire?"

"You figure he's into something with them?"

"My guess is they think they are, but he's only using them so he can slide in and out of town without being noticed by people he used to know. You'll recall he meant nothing to Chastity at first."

"And her father?"

"You'll have to do your homework there."

"I've started. His place was cleaned out. It was one of the big jobs of the time. He only got back to town day before yesterday."

"After this started."

"And he's been away for years. Only came home for a few days each winter." Winter is the slack season in the war zone.

Morley looked at me hard, shook his head. "Your real problem is common sense is nagging you."

"What?"

"You can't let this thing alone. You have to keep

picking at it. You set yourself up so you'd find an excuse. Now that you've done that common sense wants to make a comeback. Forget the Rainmaker, Garrett."

I jacked one eyebrow way, way up. "Oh?" Did he have a private line on Cleaver?

"He's on a traveling bullseye now, Garrett. Not mine. You get too close you could get hit by the volley that gets him." He gestured as though to push me away. "Go. I'll find out what I can about your lady's father."

53

Had to be magic. By the time I got home, after visiting a couple war buddies now in the extremist human rights movement, my place was surrounded. Ferocious pirates lounged on convenient corners. The guy from the outfit was back, with friends. The clumsy guy was there, and not alone, though I only glimpsed Winger before she vanished.

I'd even attracted some new folks. How many friends and enemies did the Rainmaker have?

I should have gathered the crowd and suggested we set up a pool, reduce duplication of effort, but I got distracted.

Slither and Ivy were camped on my front stoop.

Ivy had the good grace to blush. "We got thrown out," he told me. "I was trying to explain something to a guy and accidentally said the P word."

"What? What do you mean, the P word?" I checked Slither. The man looked awful.

"You know. Where he goes berserk."

Powziffle. Right. "Just out of curiosity, does he remember what he does after he hears that?"

The answer seemed a little much for Ivy's overtaxed intellect. He shrugged. I had a good idea, though. Might go a ways toward explaining Slither's problems.

Somewhere, sometime years ago, somebody twisted his mind trying to turn him into a human weapon, his trigger a nonsense phrase. Who and why didn't matter anymore, but they botched the job. Slither was out of

control. He went into the Bledsoe improperly, but he
belonged there. Out here he was going to get worse
till somebody killed him.

Half the men roaming TunFaire belong inside somewhere. There aren't that many sane folks around, not
that cross my path.

I went inside. The boys followed. Ivy headed for
the small front room. The Goddamn Parrot started
up. I paused to use the peephole. Morley must have
run through the streets screeching about me being
back on the job.

Interesting to note that the Rainmaker's pals were
out as fast as his enemies. I wondered if some of those
guys worked for Chastity's daddy.

With the boys so thick, it wasn't possible they were
unaware of one another. That suggested possibilities.

If I was working for the outfit and thought somebody nearby worked for Cleaver, I'd snatch him and
forget about Garrett. Were the lot so lazy they wanted
me to do their work for them? Nah. They had to know
about my lack of ambition.

Slither must have lost the landmarks blazing the
trail to the kitchen. He just tagged along after Ivy.
While the boys renewed acquaintances with TGD Parrot, I hit the kitchen fast and got my meager stores
put out of sight.

Some forsaken jerk started pounding on the door.
His knock was so diffident I almost let it go.

The Goddamn Parrot was heaping the Garrett lineage with fulsome praise. "Strangle that jungle
chicken. I'm going to sell the feathers." I returned to
the peephole.

Where did they find these guys? Slight financial
types, they were the kind of guys who fought their
war shuffling papers. The kind of ninety-three-pound
brain cases anybody who ever did any real soldiering
swore he was going to drown in urine if he ever got

the chance.... Curious. Their kind seldom ventured into my part of town.

Macunado Street isn't the Bustee but is in a neighborhood silver spoons are scared to visit.

Maybe they had something to do with the Blaines.

I opened up.

Error.

Maybe I did sense something. I did have one hand on the grip of my headknocker. Useful. Because two men as big as Saucerhead Tharpe materialized from the blind spots beside my door and tried to run me over.

I stumbled back, astonished. I produced my stick. The guy nearest me tried to tackle me. I drifted aside and laid my stick across the back of his skull. These clowns had to be from another dimension. Nobody tries to take me at home.

The Dead Man doesn't suffer disturbances.

Well, not usually. If I hadn't been busy, I would've gone to see what was keeping him. He didn't stir a mental muscle.

That first guy curled up for a nap. His behemoth buddy scoped it out and opted for a less precipitous approach. He remained confident. He had valiant commodities brokers to harry my flanks.

Slither stuck his head out of the small front room. He didn't look like he could be much help, but he *was* behind the crowd. "Hey, Slither. Powziffle pheez."

My pronunciation was good enough.

The screams for help had died away. I didn't hear much groaning or furniture breaking anymore, either. Careful to make no noise, I moved the table away from the kitchen door, took a peek down the hall.

Ivy had Slither up against the wall, shaking a finger under his chin. The Goddamn Parrot was on the little guy's shoulder, singing. Near as I could tell, most of the invaders were breathing.

I stepped into the hallway.

"Why did you have to go and do that?" Ivy whined.

"Because these guys wanted to operate on me without getting patient permission." Even the guy I put down myself had bruises on his bruises. Slither must have been practicing his fancy dance steps. "He all right?"

"He will be. No thanks to you."

"Let's don't squabble. Prisoners of war here. Get it? Interrogation." I opened the Dead Man's door— like I'd be able to see what the hell he thought he was doing, sleeping through all this. I saw what I deserved to see, which was the corpse of a fat Loghyr slouched in a dusty chair.

My pals just needed guidance. When I finished checking on my one-time partner, the invaders were trussed like pigs set for live roasting. The action brought Slither back.

"You guys ever work interrogation?" I asked.

Ivy nodded. Reluctantly, it seemed. Slither looked dumb. He was real good at that. A natural talent.

"My style is to scare them without hurting them—if that can be helped. We have four guys here. One ought to be a weak sister. Right?"

Blank looks.

"We try to figure out which one will tell us what we want to know without we bust them up."

"Can you do that?"

Why do I try to be a nice guy? Even people on the side of the angels, my side, don't understand.

I took my pals into the kitchen. We slapped together a really rough meal while we waited for those guys to wake up.

One by one they came around. They didn't seem thrilled with their circumstances.

54

Cup of tea in hand, accomplices at my sides, the God-damn Parrot cussing like he'd invented the genre, I returned to the hallway. "All right, boys. Let's play a game. Winners get to go home with all their fingers and toes." If they didn't know enough to be wary of the Dead Man, they didn't know I seldom toast off villainous digits.

Slither had his own ideas. He broke a guy's arm. Casual, no big deal, just part of the job, all empathy absent. When his victim stopped squealing, I said, "Mainly, I want to know who you are. And why you busted in, of course."

The clerk type with two good arms volunteered, "We were supposed to discourage you. Warn you off."

"We're gaining ground. Now clue me in. Warn me off what? Why? And who says?"

He looked at me like I was retarded.

Maybe he was right. "I don't have a clue, friend."

"You've got to drop what you're doing...."

"Let's try getting more specific."

That didn't elicit a response. "Lords of Shadow," I muttered, gesturing at Slither. Slither took a step.

"Hold on! Hold on! Mr. Davenport asked us to convince you that you shouldn't waste any more time looking for Miss Jenn."

"Good. Except I don't know any Davenport. I've never heard of any Davenports. Who the hell is he?"

My man got a big "Duh?" look on him. Which

meant he did have brain enough to want to find a connection if he was supposed to pound on a guy who never heard of the guy who wanted him pounded. We were confused, us two. But I had Slither to help clarify. Slither glowered. Slither loomed. I remarked, "He likes hurting folks. You don't want to go home in a litter, you'd better whisper in my ear. And tell me no sweet little lies. What'd I do that got this Davenport clown upset?"

"You're trying to find Miss Jenn."

Miss Jenn, eh? "Give me some details. I'm a detail kind of guy."

The staff type went to talking like he'd contracted diarrhea of the mouth. I squatted beside the flood and panned for nuggets.

He claimed a character named Davenport, good buddy of Marengo North English, didn't much like the idea of me maybe finding Emerald Jenn, so he'd asked some pals to discourage me. His pals had no idea why Davenport gave a damn who did or didn't find Emerald.

I poked in a question whenever he paused for breath. He answered everything. He couldn't shut up now. In time I did understand that I hadn't gotten on the wrong side of Marengo North English himself. This was Davenport's alone. Good. I have no desire to get noticed by the lunatic fringe.

I said, "I know this is going to break your hearts, guys, but I don't give a rat's ass about that kid. I'm not on that case anymore. These days I'm hunting a creep named Grange Cleaver. You help me out there, I'll forget you messed up my hallway. I won't even go break Mr. Davenport's arms."

I harvested a crop of blank looks. None of those guys ever heard of Grange Cleaver.

"All right. Out of personal curiosity, because of all this, I would like to talk to Emerald. Pass that on to her. I want to ask about her mother and Cleaver." I gestured. Ivy and Slither both got my drift without elaborate instructions. Ivy opened the door. Slither herded the gang that way. The Goddamn Parrot got into the game, encouraging their departure.

"Hey! You guys want a talking chicken?"

Sometimes people are just too fast. Those guys got out without answering or even looking back.

You'd think a talking bird would be a real prize—wouldn't you?—if you hadn't been around him long enough to know better.

I watched the watchers watch the flight of the four dismayed human rights activists. Their going didn't generate much excitement.

Could I lay hands on one of those fierce pirates? If he talked, I could get the Firelord what he wanted fast. Maybe. Cleaver had spent a life being light on his feet. He wasn't about to convenience anybody now.

I went back to the kitchen, built another sandwich. I checked on the Dead Man. Out of it still. I went back to the peephole. Evening had started lowering its skirts. Which made no difference. The street was as crowded as ever. My fans hadn't called it a day.

My gaze swept a pair of earringed angels—and I suffered a mighty intuition.

I knew where to find Grange Cleaver. He hadn't hauled his buccaneer behind out of TunFaire. He was still around, laughing at everybody trying to track him down. It was a game for him. A vicious game. If he feared he risked losing, he'd cut and run.

I summoned Ivy and Slither. "I admit I wanted you guys out of my hair. Didn't work, but my misfortune looks lucky now." The Goddamn Parrot didn't like being left alone. He started spouting off in a big way. I stepped over where he could see me, gave him the evil eye. He shut up while he considered the situation. "I need you to hold the fort."

Ivy stared. Slither said, "Huh?"

Great. "I'm going out the back way." I spoke slowly and clearly. "I'm leaving you in charge. Anybody knocks, either ignore them or don't tell them anything." I donned my best scowl, faced the Dead Man's door. Old Bones was way overdue.

Hell, maybe I'd grown too dependent on him. I reminded me that in real life you can't count on anybody but you, yourself, and you.

"All right, Garrett." Ivy's voice was half-strength. Was he fading?

It could be worse. The Dead Man says it can always get worse. Don't ask me how.

I slid out the back way.

55

"What's dis shit?" Sarge bellowed. "I got ta put up wit' you tree times a day now?"

"Bask in the reflection, my man. Morley is my number one boy now. He up there showing some married lady the ins and out of cross stitch? I could maybe tell him something he wants to hear."

"Yeah? Like what?" I wasn't selling Sarge no swamp.

"Like where to find some buried treasure."

Sarge moved out.

We've all endured one another so long we all know when the yak means something and when it's just macho yammer. Sarge figured I had something, so he got intimate with the speaking tube. I didn't hear what he said, but hardly three minutes passed before Morley descended the stairs. A woman of astonishing beauty peeked down for a moment, as though she just *had* to see what improbability could distract Morley Dotes from her. From what I saw of her, I had to consider that an excellent question.

"I'm sorry." The woman retreated, but my imagination went with her. I hated Morley for having found her first. How did he do it? "Who was that?"

He sneered. "Wipe the drool off your chin. Someone might mistake you for a mad dog werewolf."

"Who is she?"

"No, you don't. I was a gentleman about Chaz. I suffered in silence while you wasted Tinnie Tate. I didn't birddog when that went bad because it might get good again. So forget my little Julie, eh?"

"I'll give you half a minute."

"Generous, Garrett. Generous. How come you're down here making my life miserable again?" Oddly, he seemed anxious. He covered by glancing upstairs like he was thinking about maybe spanking somebody for revealing herself to the rabble. Then he eyed me like he really did expect to hear about buried treasure.

"While back I got the impression you wanted to get face-to-face with the Rainmaker."

He glanced at the stairway. Glorious, lovely Julie was very much with us even though she remained unseen. He said, "Tell me about it."

I wondered. I knew Morley's priorities. Seldom did he find a Julie less interesting than revenge. "I think I know where to find him."

Morley cast one more longing glance upstairs. "How did you manage that? You turn psychic? Or psycho? Or did the Dead Man wake up?"

"Through the exercise of reason, my man. Pure reason."

Morley offered me one of his special looks, just to let me know I couldn't fool a stone with a learning disability. "I'll bite, Garrett. Where?"

"On the Hill. Maggie Jenn's place."

He made a show of thinking about it before he smiled nastily. "Damn if I don't think you stumbled into it and came up smelling sweet. I should have thought of that. Let's go."

"What? Me? No way. I did my part. Take your help. Sarge and Puddle need the exercise. I'll stay here and hold the fort."

"Ha. That's ha, like in half a ha-ha, Garrett."

"Some guys got no sense of humor."

"You talking about me? I gave you a parrot, didn't I?"

"My point exactly."

"What can you do? People just won't show any gratitude anymore. All right. Let's go see the man."

I smirked. Behind Morley's back. No sense having him figure out who was manipulating whom. Not just yet.

56

I began to wonder if there wasn't an alert out with my name on it. Three times we tried to go up the Hill and three times patrols got in our way. Unbelievably bad luck.

Morley snapped, "Don't be so cheerful!"

I started to open my mouth.

"And don't give me that dog barf about never being disappointed if you only look for the worst."

"You are in a fine mood, aren't you?" I reflected a moment. "We've known each other too long, you realize?"

"You can say that again."

"All right. We've known each other . . ."

"And you turn into a bigger wiseass every day I know you. The Garrett I used to know . . ." Off he hared on an expedition into reality revision. We live in different worlds. He remembers nothing the way I do. Maybe that's cultural.

The old work ethic paid off. Fourth try we got through. As we gained the high ground, I muttered, "I was beginning to think my magic gizmo was working backwards."

"Your what?"

"Uh . . . I have this amulet thing. Somebody uses a tracing spell on me, I can steer them off."

"Oh?" Morley eyed me suspiciously.

I don't tell him everything. And he keeps things

from me. You just don't share everything, friends or not.

As we neared that grim gray canyon of a Hilltop street we grew cautious. I found myself feeling nervous in a premonitory way. And Morley said, "I have a strange feeling about this."

"It *is* quiet. But it's always quiet up here. These people want it that way."

"You feel it, too."

"I feel something."

But we saw no one, sniffed out no slightest scent of a patrol ambush.

We approached the Jenn place through the alley. And strolled right on past, pretending we were scouts for the ratmen who would come for the trash.

Someone had employed the balcony route to get inside. Someone not very circumspect. We judged the break-in to be recent because there was no evidence of the patrol having taken corrective action.

I told Morley, "I need to go in there."

Dotes didn't argue, but he wasn't enthralled by the notion. He observed, "The roof hatch is unlatched—if nobody cared how we got out before."

We'd left it unlatched because the catch couldn't be worked from outside. "Just what I wanted to do today. Clamber around rooftops."

"You're the one can't leave well enough alone."

"The firelord is paying me very well not to."

"All right. Let's don't bicker." Morley looked around. I looked around. We could've been surrounded by a ghost city. Other than the buildings, there was no evidence of human presence.

"Spooky," I muttered, while Morley scampered up a downspout like some pointy-eared ape. I dragged my bulk after, groaned as he helped me roll onto a flat roof. "I thought I was getting back in shape." Puff puff.

"Tipping a beer stein doesn't stress your leg muscles nearly enough. Come on."

Beer stein? *I* was getting to be a wiseass? Uh-oh.

Starting after Morley, I glanced back into the alley and spotted a housemaid on a balcony down the way, gaping at us. She had come out while we were climbing. "Trouble," I told Morley. "A witness."

"Keep low, then. If she doesn't see where we go, we'll have enough time."

But time for what? I had real strong doubts about the wisdom of my approach, now.

As we neared the roof hatch, I noted that Morley seemed to lack confidence, too. But he was a dark elf, partly. He wouldn't back down without more reason than a growing premonition.

57

We listened intently, heard nothing on the other side of the hatch. Grimly, I prized it open an inch. Morley listened with his better ears, peered into the inner darkness with his better eyes. He sniffed, frowned slightly.

"What?" I whispered.

"I don't know."

"Someone there?"

"Not that. Open it up. We need to hurry."

I lifted. There was no racket in the street yet, but I doubted that that would last. Light poured into the stairwell. Neither villain nor monster rose to greet us.

Morley descended quickly. I followed less swiftly, it having gotten inky dark in there once I shut the hatch again. We entered the top story without incident. Morley kept sniffing the air. So did I. I sucked in enough dust to have to fight sneezing. But there was something . . .

A sound echoed up from below, a moaning wail like the last cry of a lost soul. "Spooks," I said again.

"No."

No. He was right. Somebody was being hurt badly. I'd just have preferred spooks.

We grew more cautious.

Confident that that floor was untenanted, we stole down a level. I murmured, "We're going too slow."

Morley agreed. "But what can we do?" Twice more we heard that cry of agonized despair.

255

What we could do was get out before the goon squad showed.

The next floor down showed evidence of human habitation. Morley and I held silent debate over the numbers, which had to have been more than a half dozen and possibly the whole crowd from that ugly warehouse.

Another cry. From the top of the stair that led down to the second floor we could hear remote voices engaged in argument. Morley held up three fingers, then four. I nodded agreement. Four. Plus whoever was getting hurt.

The Rainmaker had his reputation for torture, I recalled.

That smell in the air was stronger but not yet strong enough to identify.

Morley kept hesitating about going on down. I no longer wanted to risk even a whisper so had to trust his instincts. As he did start down, something made a clunking racket on the floor below. We froze. Surprise, surprise.

Three very large male individuals dripping sharp steel galumphed across our field of view and headed down the stair to the ground floor. Patrol thugs. Come on the scene via the balcony door, I guessed. Moving fast because somebody tripped over his bootlace and gave them all away.

Morley whispered urgently, "Hide!" He jerked a thumb heavenward. I nodded. It did seem likely that younger and more agile guards would take the path we'd used.

Our timing was superb. No sooner had we ducked under the dustcovers shielding adjacent antiques than we heard lots of boots hustling down from above. I worried about sneezes betraying me. Then I worried about footprints in the dust. I couldn't recall if there had been enough prior traffic to disguise our movements.

An uproar broke out downstairs. Sounded like a major battle: lots of metal banging metal, people yelling and screaming, furniture crashing. I guessed patrol types had entered at ground level, too.

A pseudopod of combat scaled the stairs. The expected gang from the roof arrived and jumped in. The hollering and cussing grew ferocious, but I kept squeezing my nose anyway. With my luck, those guys would notice even a little sputter of a sneeze.

It got brisk. For a while, despite their edge in the odds, I thought the patrol guys would lose out. They lacked motivation. They hadn't hired on to get killed protecting property.

I never doubted that people were dying.

The guys on the stairs launched an angry counterattack.

After that the battle lasted only minutes. Soon it left the house for the street. The patrol bunch hollered in angry pursuit of those they had routed.

Came a scratch on the sheet concealing me. I gripped my headknocker, ready for a mighty two-handed swing. Morley whispered, "Let's go. Before they come back to look around."

He was right, of course. They would be back. But at the moment we were invisible—assuming the patrol thought the people downstairs were the guys that maid had seen.

The silence didn't last. I picked out a groan followed by something I hadn't heard for years—the rasp of a man with a punctured lung trying desperately to breath.

Morley and I descended in spurts, always ready to flee. We encountered casualties, all of whom had rolled to the bottom of the stair ending on the second floor. None of the four would brawl again.

I knew that smell—now it was fresh and strong.

Blood.

Three of the fallen wore crude patrol uniforms. The fourth had fought them.

"Know this guy?" I asked Morley, sure he knew pro thugs better than I did. And I had recognized Hammerhand Nicks, middleweight enforcer type for the Outfit.

"Yes." Dotes seemed to grow still more alert.

I told him, "I'm going down." Not that I wanted to.

I made my feet move. I did want to know.

The smell of death grew dense.

Three more patrol types lay dead in the ground floor hall where the stair ended. Blooded steel lay everywhere. I found another syndicate character there, just less than dead. I beckoned Morley. "Gericht Lungsmark?"

He nodded. "Over there. Wenden Tobar."

More Outfit hitters. Lungsmark groaned. I moved away. Didn't want him seeing me if he opened his eyes. "She figured it out before I did."

"Maybe." Dotes eased toward the next room, whence came the sounds of the man with respiratory difficulties. "Or maybe she had help."

"Oh?"

"Lot of ears in my place." He started to say my name, recalled that this was not the best place. "If somebody told somebody and that somebody moved fast. . . ."

Maybe, but I shook my head. Likely the Outfit did have the pull to get the patrols to do a favor, but . . . "They—"

Morley made a silencing gesture.

No. The patrols wouldn't get into it with the Outfit without they didn't know they were up against syndicate guys.

Come to think of it, the hoods probably did the logical thing and snatched themselves a pirate off the street outside my place.

Morley gestured again, slipped through the doorway. I went to the other side, crouching.

We found the fellow with the breathing problem, one Barclay Blue, journeyman bonebreaker. "Going to be some advancement opportunities, looks like," I said.

Morley scowled. His situation was way less comfortable than mine. Further, there was the question of why Contague associates had gotten into a deadly battle high on the Hill. Not politic, that.

Next room boasted the remains of the main encounter. The Outfit guys had come from farther back and met the invaders there. At least one patrol bruno had carried a crossbow. I counted eight corpses. Four were Outfit. Some fine antiques had been rendered kindling. Blood covered everything.

I didn't like the implications. Things had gotten way out of hand.

We entered the dining room I'd shared with Maggie Jenn. I understood why the Outfit guys hadn't been willing to surrender.

The stench of death was heavy. Most of the chairs at the table had dead or probably soon to be dead people tied into them. I recognized the old guys from the warehouse, Zeke, the woman who had served Maggie and me, and others I'd seen on the street. Nobody's breathing was real robust.

I said, "They *were* hiding here."

"There were two battles. Belinda Contague won the first one."

Fourteen people were tied into the chairs. Zeke and Mugwump were among the breathing. Excepting several guys who obviously got themselves killed when the thugs moved in, everyone had been tortured. None of the survivors were conscious.

Morley asked. "You see any Rainmaker? I don't. No Maggie Jenn, either."

"He's famous for not being there when the shit

comes down." I double-checked Mugwump. He was the healthiest of the survivors.

"Yes. He is. What are you doing?"

"Cutting the guy loose. Sometimes I do stuff just because it feels right."

"Think you'll find anything useful here?"

"Probably not." I noted that we were no longer a we. "Probably be a good idea to go." We'd have the victorious patrolmen back soon and the Guard right behind them.

A bloody knife lay on the floor, probably a torture instrument. I placed it in front of Mugwump. "So let's scat."

58

"Freeze, slimeblog!"

Huh?

I was always a rebel. I didn't freeze. I didn't even check to see if I was outnumbered.

Neither did Morley. And he was where the speaker couldn't see him.

I dove, rolled, came to my feet out of view, charged. Morley attacked from the other side of the doorway, low, shrieking.

One lone heavyweight had thought he could bluff me. He didn't pull it off.

Morley smacked and kicked him about nineteen times. I whacked away with a headknocker rendered magically unbreakable. Down the man went, his expression saying it just wasn't fair. Poor baby. I knew what he meant. Just when you think you've got it knocked, along comes some clown with a bigger stick.

Morley and I got no time to congratulate ourselves. More patrol types materialized. After the intellectual form of their subspecies, one demanded, "What's going on here?"

Bippetty-bappetty-bopp!

I was not unaware that real heroes flail around with singing swords while I rated only an enchanted hunk of oak.

Morley whooped and hollered and popped guys all over the place. He was having a great time. He could hustle when he was motivated.

We broke through. We headed upstairs, disdaining the front way because every thug on the Hill had gathered to attend the business of counting bodies, cussing villains, and abusing captives.

My normally abysmal luck failed to assert itself completely, mostly because the patrol guys were making so much racket. They couldn't hear me and Morley getting away.

"Let's try the balcony first," Morley suggested. "And quickly."

I didn't expect an easy getaway. Anybody with half a brain would have posted guards at every potential exit.

You never know, though, when you're dealing with TunFaire's bonebreakers. Most can't think past the next arm they mean to twist. They're efficient and technically polished within their specialty but feeble when it comes to planning and making decisions.

There had been a major engagement on the second floor, back toward the balcony door. There was a lot of blood but no bodies. Blood trails indicated that several bodies had been dragged out of what had been a lumber room last time I looked. My impression was that here was where the Outfit's invasion first met serious resistance. I wondered why. That room was no place to make a stand.

I took time out to look it over.

What the hell?

Seconds later, Morley called from the balcony exit, "What're you doing? Come on! There's nobody out there right now."

I finished scanning the vellum sheet, one of several pages come loose from a book evidently damaged during the fighting. The rest of the book was gone. The loose pages might have gotten lost during a hasty getaway.

"I'm going to leave you here," Morley threatened.

I folded the vellum, slipped it into my shirt. Best to

get going and not pique Morley's suspicion. I'd read the story before, anyway. The whole book, not just one page.

I reached the balcony, saw that Morley had given up on me and dropped into the alleyway. I glanced right and left, spied no trouble moving in. I landed beside Dotes. "We probably ought to split up now."

He eyed me closely. He's sure that any time I know what I want, I'm up to something that won't be to his advantage. I can't fathom why he would think that way. I said, "Do me a big one. Couple hours from now I'm going to lead that clumsy guy down to your neighborhood. Help me grab him."

"Why?"

"I want to talk to Winger. He'll know where to find her."

He gave me another glimpse of his suspicious side, then told me, "Be careful. Right now, they're touchy around here. They'll jump anything that moves."

I nodded, less concerned about me than about him.

59

I wasn't in a real good mood. I didn't turn cartwheels when Colonel Block waved his clowns off and told me, "Cheer up, Garrett. It's all straightened out."

"How can you put these clowns on the street if they can't recognize a pass put out by their own beloved captain?" What, me worry about getting off the Hill? I had passes and paper from a troop of heavyweights.

"The fellow who reads and writes doesn't normally opt for a career in law enforcement. And you'll have to admit that you refused to provide any good reason for being where you were found."

"Where I was found? I was—"

"Detained, then."

"And with way too much enthusiasm. I did try to cooperate. They wouldn't let me talk."

"I will."

"Huh?"

"I'll let you explain. To your heart's content."

A wise guy. I admonished myself to be careful. Quietly. "I was just trying to do what the Firelord hired me to do. I'd heard a rumor the Rainmaker was hiding out on the Hill."

Block offered me a *try again* look. I wasn't snowing him. His agents would have relayed any such rumors. "What happened in that house, Garrett?"

"You have me at a disadvantage, Captain."

"It's Colonel, Garrett. As you know. And that's true. I do have you. If I wanted, I could send you over to the Al-Khar to be held for questioning. It's entirely possible for somebody to fall between the cracks there, same as in the Bledsoe."

The Al-Khar is TunFaire's city jail. "Why you want to be like that?"

"Mainly because I don't like to be jerked around. I have an eyewitness who saw two men climb a drainspout. One of them was dressed exactly like you."

"Without so many rips and tears, I'll bet. Doubtless a daring youth out pretending to swash a few buckles. An amazing coincidence."

"Witness summoned the local patrol. Patrol went looking around and found a house showing multiple signs of forced entries. Inside they found lots of corpses and plenty of people willing to fight. I wouldn't accuse you of stretching any rules, Garrett. Not you. You're not that kind of guy. But I'd bet that if I wanted to spring for a cut-rate diviner, I could place you inside that house. Hm?"

I admitted nothing.

"Give me a hint, Garrett. Who were those people?"

I could discern no obvious profit in keeping my yap shut and sliding farther out of official favor. "Some were the Rainmaker's people."

"Was that so hard?"

Of course it was. Guys like me aren't supposed to cooperate with guys like him, especially if doing so would save some headaches. In my racket, you're supposed to be troll-stubborn. Apparently, dumb is supposed to help, too. "The others answered to the Combine. I've heard that a long time ago Cleaver had some part in the death of Chodo's brother." I doubted Block was hearing much that was news.

"I see. And Chodo pays his debts."

"Always."

Block had stayed seated, fortified behind his desk. Now he picked up a folded document bearing a fancy seal, tapped it against his desk top. "How bad will it get, Garrett? We in for a gang war?" That wouldn't look good on his record.

"I doubt it. You know Chodo's rep. Cleaver had to hire his muscle out of town. After this fiasco, he'll have not friends left. His dearest boyfriend is gonna ask 'Grange Who?' "

Block kept tapping that document. It looked more legal by the minute. He mused, "So many people interested in Grange Cleaver." He waved that paper. "Including mine, now." As if only then realizing what he held, he said, "This just came in. One Grange Cleaver is to be found and brought before the Court of Honor of the Magistry of Manpower Procurement. There's no record of him having performed his obligated service to the realm." You had to be there to get the full effect of Block's seditious sneer and sarcastic tone.

I grunted. Hadn't I thought maybe Cleaver was a dodger?

"I'm not going to strain myself trying to round up dodgers. Get out of here, Garrett."

I patted myself. Yep, I'd gotten back everything that was mine. Block's crew were almost honest. I started to take his advice.

"Wait!"

Damn! I knew he'd change his mind. "What?"

"You still seeing Belinda Contague?"

He knew too much about me. "No."

"Too bad. I thought you might suggest to her that her dad recall that it's to be kept off the Hill."

"Oh." A slightly more than gentle hint that he wanted all that passed along. "I don't think there'll be a problem again." Since all of Belinda's thugs dumb enough to get involved up there were no longer with us.

I got out.

60

It had been a long, hard day. And it was just getting started. Aching all over, looking way too much like a guy who got into one-sided brawls with zealous minions of public safety, I sneaked through the postern door of the Royal Library. Which was a whole lot less of a big deal than you might think.

Old Jake was supposed to keep that door secure, but when he did that his wartime cronies couldn't get in with supplies of liquid refreshments. Old Jake was all the security the library had. He didn't get around so well on his wooden leg, but his heart was in the right place. Linda Lee had a bad habit of saying he was me at twice the age.

Jake was asleep. What the hell. There wasn't a lot in the library your average thief would consider worth stealing.

I slipped past the grizzled old goat. He was snoring. I'd seldom seen him do anything else. Hard to believe he'd been given a job for life because he'd lost his leg becoming one of the all-time heroes of the Royal Marines. Sometimes it's better to have your legends dead.

I went looking for Linda Lee. I hoped I wouldn't scare many of her coworkers before I found her. They were easily spooked.

She found me.

I was peeking around the end of a stand of shelves—stacks, in the approved jargon—when she spoke behind me. "What the hell are you doing in here?"

I caught my breath, got it back where it belonged, made sure my feet were back on the floor, then turned around. "I'm thrilled to see you, too. You're as lovely as ever."

She looked me up and down. Her cute upper lip wrinkled. "You just stay where you are. And answer the question."

I opened my mouth, but she didn't stop. "You really ought to take more trouble with your personal appearance. Good grooming is important. Come on. What are you doing here?"

I opened my mouth.

"You're going to get me into bad trouble—"

I pounced. I clapped a hand over her mouth. She wiggled a little—a not unpleasant experience. "I wanted to talk about the book somebody stole from you. Was it a first edition of *The Raging Blades?*"

She managed to stop wiggling and started listening. She shook her head.

Startled, I growled, "Damn it! I really thought I had it locked." I turned her loose.

"It was a first of *The Steel-Game.* The library has had it since early imperial times." She went on about some ancient emperor having wanted to assemble a set so he could seek Eagle's fabulous horde, about how no outsider could have known the book existed.

I expelled some remarks of my own. "Ha! I *was* right! Wrong book but right idea." I produced the fragment of vellum I'd lifted from Maggie Jenn's place, a solitary page from *The Metal-Storm,* edition uncertain, but people had died trying to protect it from other people who hadn't cared about it at all. The intensity of that encounter had set the tone for the atrocities that followed.

Linda Lee asked, "What about *The Raging Blades*? We've never had a first of that one."

"Because I saw a copy the other day. Somewhere where it shouldn't have been. But I didn't realize that until today. Then I thought I could solve your troubles."

I'd begun developing troubles of my own. Linda Lee wouldn't stay still. I couldn't stay focused. She was too close and too warm and had begun purring like she really appreciated my thinking of her.

"You just come on down here, Jack! I'll show you. You wouldn't believe me, but I'll show you."

A voice muttered, "I wouldn't believe you if you told me the sky was up, old woman."

"You fell asleep. You go ahead and lie, but we all know you fell asleep at your post and let an outsider get in. You're too old."

I hated that woman's voice almost as much as I hated the voice of the Goddamn Parrot despite having heard it only a few times. Those few were a few too many. It was nails on slate, whined through the nose, always complaining.

"Talking about old, you been dead three years but too damned stupid to realize it. Still got people to make miserable, too." Old Jack didn't care if he hurt her feelings, but it wasn't likely he would. She was two-thirds deaf.

"You were sound asleep when I came to get you."

"I was resting my eyes, you impossible hag." Clump! Old Jack collapsed. His fingers weren't too nimble anymore. When he got in a hurry, he sometimes failed to get his wooden leg strapped on right.

I gave Linda Lee a peck on the forehead. "I'd better run."

"Later." She winked fetchingly. I've always had a soft spot for women who wink. "Promise," she breathed, then went to help Old Jack. She ignored the old woman, who didn't miss the attention. She was doing just fine carrying two sides of an argument herself.

I ducked out of sight. The old man hadn't seen me, so he started spouting off about frustrated old maids who imagine men lurking behind every stack.

61

A long, hard day, and not yet done. I had aches where plenty of people don't have places. I'd walked too many miles and had been thumped too many times. Hell, this was like the bad old days when the Dead Man made sure I got no rest at all.

I told myself I would make one last stop, then I would hang it up for the day. Then I groaned. I recalled my arrangement with Morley.

Not Winger on top of everything else. Why had I done that?

Good soldier, I soldiered on.

I wondered what bean-brained civilian had come up with that one. Every soldier I ever knew never moved a muscle unless that was the final option.

I sensed trouble long before I hove in sight of Wixon and White. That end of town was silent with the silence that bubbles around immediate, terrible violence.

The moment passed. The ghouls were gathering when I reached the storefront, panting over the bloody wreckage.

One look and I knew smart money would choose putting one set of toes in front of the other and repeating the process briskly. In my case, while facing in a southeasterly direction. But I just had to take a fast look around the shop.

* * *

271

Colonel Block banished his henchmen with a wave. "Cheer up, Garrett. It's all straightened out now."

"Must be an echo in here." Not to mention way too much sunlight. The stuff flooded in through an open, eastern window casement at gale force. It was way too early for any reasonable man to be upright. Block obviously wasn't reasonable. Tell the truth, I wasn't feeling real reasonable myself. "We've got to stop meeting like this."

"Wasn't my idea, Garrett. You enjoy your accommodations?"

I'd spent a too-short night on a straw pallet in a stinking cell in the Al-Khar, charged with being a possible witness. "The fleas and lice and bedbugs enjoyed my visit." They should feel right at home. Block was a dirty dog.

"This is where you tell me why my men found you right in the middle of another massacre."

"Somebody yelled for help and your gang actually showed up. I was amazed." The old Watch would have headed the other direction, just to make sure nobody got hurt that didn't need hurting. "Thought you said it was all straightened out."

"I meant I know you didn't slice anybody into cold cuts. Witness says you showed after the screaming stopped. I want to know why what happened happened. And how come you were there."

"Grange Cleaver."

"That's it?" He waited for me to say more. I didn't. "I see no connection. Maybe you'll enlighten me. Meantime, you should know it looks like some really nasty black magic did the killing."

I nodded, but I didn't believe it. "That's what doesn't make sense." Someone made it look like magical murder. I was willing to bet Robin and Penny had kept their appointment with doom through the agency of a devil named Cleaver, once again trying to point a false finger at Marengo North English. Made me think Emerald Jenn was holed up with North English and Cleaver wanted to bust her loose.

"Why do I got a feeling you're being too cooperative, Garrett?"

"What? Now what the hell do you want? I answer your questions, you get aggravated. I don't answer them, you get aggravated. If I wanted aggravation, I'd stay home and argue with the Dead Man."

"You're answering questions, but I got a hunch you aren't telling me what I want to know."

I took a deep breath. We were about set for one of those ferocious head-butting sessions so gratifying to men of our respective professions. I exhaled. . . .

An ugly little breed stormed in. He scowled at me like I had no right to be cluttering up Block's office. I nodded. "Relway." He didn't respond.

"It's started," he told Block.

"Damn them." Block lost all interest in bugs as small as me. Must be fatter victims available somewhere else. He glared at me, though. "The Call." He stalked after his secret police chief, who was gone already. "Get out of here. And try not to stumble over any more bodies."

Good advice all. Maybe he wasn't a complete dunce.

What was that about The Call?

Didn't take long to find out. I hit the street. Off east, looking like it might not be rooted far from my place, was a growing tree of smoke. I caught snatches of news from people rushing through the streets.

A bar brawl had turned into major racial trouble. Humans were going after centaurs. Apparently, it hadn't gotten out of hand till somebody in The Call had served up an inflammatory diatribe and people had responded by firing the homes of centaur immigrants. Other species were becoming involved. There had been some kind of deadly guerrilla battle in the scaffolding festooning the Bledsoe. They were losing ground getting the hospital repaired.

The insanity had begun. I hoped Block and Relway could contain it. At least this time.

There would be other times. And they would get worse before they got better.

People were going to get polarized real soon now.

I walked carefully. And went about it visible to anyone who might have a tracking spell laid on me.

62

Slither and Ivy got on me the minute they let me in the house. "Guys. Guys! I want this kind of crap I can get married. I need food. I need sleep. I need a bath. I need that foul-mouth flamingo strangled so I can do the rest without getting so aggravated I have to kill somebody." The bird must have saved up for my homecoming.

I got some money from the Dead Man's room, studied him suspiciously before I left. Was that a restrained amusement I sensed there for just a second?

I sent Slither out for supplies. I told Ivy to let me have three hours of sleep. When he woke me up, I wanted food and bath water ready. Then I dragged me upstairs and splashed me into my bed. The Dead Man could get the bugs out later. I lay there tossing and turning and listening to the Goddamn Parrot cackle for half a sentence, then it was time to get up.

Ivy did his part like that was all he had to live for. I rose on time. I scrubbed up in my ten-gallon copper tub. Downstairs, I found a classic breakfast waiting. Ivy was as drunk as a skunk, the Goddamn Parrot on his shoulder. The bird wasn't talking. It needed its whole attention just to hang on. Its breath was worse than Ivy's. Maybe Slither got him his own bottle. Good old Slither, looking out for everybody.

I stuffed myself, then told the boys, "I was going to run you guys off again today, but I don't think I'm going to have time. Either of you has a good afternoon, I want you to get out and look for a place, find a job. I'm not going to take care of you forever."

Slither nodded. Ivy said, "There's some letters for you."

"Letters?"

"We didn't let nobody see you," Slither explained. "Mainly on account of you wasn't here. So some people wrote you letters. We put them on your desk."

There were three letters. Two showed no indication whence they sprang. The other bore Morley's chop. It was a nag about where the hell was I last night? He couldn't waste all his valuable time playing my games if I wasn't going to show up.

By now he would know why I hadn't. Him and his thugs probably thought it was funny.

I opened a letter that purported to be from Maggie Jenn. She wanted to meet. Oh? Right. "Slither! You remember who brought these?"

The big man leaned through the doorway. "That one was brung by a lady. Cute little bug of a thing with red hair."

Surprise, surprise. Bold little witch. . . . Oh, horrible thought! What if this was the real Maggie Jenn, come in from her island hideout?

No. Because I didn't want that.

"That one you done opened come from your friend with the funny ears."

"Morley Dotes. I know." I picked up the last one. "How about this?"

"One of them fellas that was here when I had my seizure brung that one."

"One of those lunatics from the Call?"

"Them fellas what tried to push you around."

That didn't make sense. I supposed I'd have to open the letter to straighten it out.

It was from Emerald Jenn. She would talk to me if I would meet her at a certain estate south of TunFaire. I didn't know the estate, but I did know the area. I'd met Eleanor out there. Folks down there were a lot like folks from the Hill—only way more reactionary. Their wealth consisted of land rather than treasure or power. A more smugly self-righteous, bigoted bunch would be hard to imagine.

Emerald Jenn's suggested meeting place wasn't far from the main estate of Marengo North English.

Interesting.

"How is your memory, Slither?"

"I'm pretty good today, Garrett."

He didn't sound good, but I had to take his word. "Need you to run over to Morley's. Tell him I'm coming, he wants to get on with what we talked about last night. You manage that?"

He thought about it. "I can do it. You got it. Now?"

"Always a great time to start."

"Pretty rough out there, Garrett. They're killing each other in the streets."

"Take Ivy, makes you feel better."

"I was thinking about you."

"I'll take my chances." Wise ass. Do I carry a sign only I can't see? Garrett's ego. Kick here.

I occupied the stoop in order to field marshal Slither's departure. I checked the street, too. "I know how a horse apple feels," I told Ivy, who was inside the doorway and had to have the allusion explained. "Flies?"

All my fans were back. Except for the fierce pirates. Grange Cleaver friends seemed scarce.

I predicted that, didn't I?

I shrugged, went inside, and scribbled a note to Maggie Jenn. Ivy could give it to whomever came around to get my reply.

63

"Getting predictable in your old age," I told Dotes, settling beside him on the exact set of steps where I'd guessed he would be waiting.

"Me? I'm here because I knew this is where you would come looking. I didn't want you wasting time stumbling around looking for me."

Invisible sign. Absolutely. "Can we take him?"

"He's caught. Nobody is so lucky he gets out of what I have set." He glanced left, at smoke rising in the distance. "Quiet out." The street should have been busier.

All streets should have been busier. Slither was right. They were killing each other out here—though it wasn't as bad as it could have been. Block's heavies were fast on their feet. And they had the army garrison to help discourage disorder.

Trouble never got a chance to grow up.

Too, word was out that Marengo North English didn't approve. He said this wasn't the time. The captains of many sister nut groups agreed. They asked for restraint now, promising license later.

"Interesting times," I told Morley.

"It's always something." Like he hadn't the least concern. "Well, here's our guest."

The clumsy guy smelled a rat. He was moving carefully. Trouble was, his sniffer wasn't sensitive enough. It was too late by the time he got a good whiff.

Morley waved. "Come on over."

The guy looked around. Just the way he moved you could tell he thought his luck was with him still. He was in it up to his chin but knew he always got out. So maybe this time he would fall up and blow away on the breeze. A regular dandelion seed.

Morley's friends and relatives and employees closed a ring. Luck failed its compact with our man. Gravity didn't reverse itself.

I thumbed a wood chip while Morley watched the man get a grip on his disappointment.

"Pull up a step, Ace," I told him.

He did, but he had the fidgets. He kept looking for his lucky exit.

I told him, "I didn't really want you. But I can't get ahold of Winger." Not that I'd tried.

"What? Who?"

"Your girlfriend. Big blond goof with no common sense, always has an angle, never tells the truth if a lie will do. Her."

"Part of that fits everybody in this thing," Morley said. "Even up on the Hill, they turned the truth to quicksilver."

"Untruths, too."

"Quicksilver lies. I like that."

"Deadly quicksilver lies." I spotted friend C.J. Carlyle. "Look who missed the slaughter at Maggie Jenn's place."

Our guest eyed us as though he was sure we were loony. Winger must have mentioned my stint in the Bledsoe. He never noticed C.J. I said, "No telling what story you got from Winger. She comes up with some tall ones. I've known her since she came to town. I don't remember her ever telling the truth if there wasn't a profit in it."

Our man didn't reply, but his skill at hiding his thoughts did not exceed his skill at tailing.

He was inept but loyal. He stayed clammed. I told him, "I want to get ahold of her mainly as a friend."

That hadn't been the case the night before. A few hours had altered my perspective. "I no longer think she could tell me anything I don't know. I am sure I know a few things she doesn't. Things that could get her killed. Maybe right after they get *you* killed."

Not only did I get him thinking, I got his attention.

He didn't plan to die for love. Guys just aren't romantic anymore. He had something going with Winger—and he had a real good idea just what that was worth.

He didn't speak up, though.

"She isn't going to get those books," I told him. "Not a chance. All the guts and luck you can muster won't get that done."

The man stayed clammed. So did Morley, though he looked like he wanted to hear more. I told him, "When you get past all the blown smoke, Winger and Cleaver are after a set of first editions of *When No Ravens Went Hungry*. Winger has the notion she can get them away from the Rainmaker." She had an even sillier notion that she could decipher the clues in them once she had them.

"The woman doesn't suffer from any lack of self-confidence."

"Trouble is, she's digging through the wrong haystack. The Rainmaker doesn't have the firsts. He could have grabbed them all, but he didn't pay attention so the one he did come up with got away."

Morley gave me a big evil dark-elf grin. "Why do I get the feeling you're going to explain everything again? How come I have the notion I ought to bet the deed to the Joy House against you?"

I snarled at our captive, "Tell Winger she's wasting her dreams. Cleaver can't lay hands on more than two books. Go on. Get out of here."

Baffled, the man went, maybe thinking he had found another angle to his luck.

Morley asked, "What was that? I set up a major

operation, then you mutter some cryptic stuff at the guy and let him go."

"You fooling somebody? You know this mess has got to do with Eagle's treasure."

"Maybe. Sort of. I had a passing interest when I thought you'd stumbled onto something there in the West End."

"What you told me then was the key to the whole thing," I exaggerated. That wasn't a lie. Not really. Not exactly.

The truth was I was guessing again, playing with the known information. I had it figured out, but as Dotes hinted, I'd been wrong before. I yelled after Winger's friend, "Tell Winger what I said." To Morley, "She'll ignore me and do something dumb, but this way my conscience will be satisfied."

64

I expected more grief about letting Winger's guy go. But after the one snip, Morley leaned back and, apparently, never gave it a second thought.

I started to nag him. . . .

"Can it, Garrett. Once upon a time I had a notion. But I changed my mind."

I awarded him the grandfather of all raised eyebrows.

"Last night Julie wasn't there to distract me. I got to thinking about Eagle's saga. And guess what I realized? Nowhere does it say that the jerk was really rich—by our standards."

I indulged in a self-satisfied smirk. My good buddy was telling me I'd figured the angles right. "You ever wonder how Eagle murdered those slaves? If he was so blind and feeble he needed them to haul and bury his treasure, how could he get the angle on them slick enough to off them all?"

Obviously, Morley hadn't wondered. "Sometimes I do like the way your mind works, Garrett."

"Let me tell you something you maybe don't know." I hadn't known till I got it from Linda Lee, back when I was reading sagas. "Most of the sagas were composed at the instigation of the guys they're about. The *No Ravens* thing was done by Eagle's sister's grandson, partly in collaboration with the old man himself. And they started long before the business of the mocking women, the treasure, and the murdered slaves."

"I'm sure you'll get to the point eventually."

"You see it. Unless you're slower than you pretend. Say a guy is paying to have puff stories written about him. Not only will he decide what he wants put in and built up, he'll decide what gets played down or left out."

"You mean like maybe Eagle wasn't a big success just because he was treacherous and quick with a blade? Maybe he had a small natural talent as a wizard?"

"Bingo! He was accused by others, but obviously it wasn't anything major, nothing backed by formal training. He wouldn't have stayed quiet about it if he'd had a sheepskin declaring him a heavyweight asskicker. But he had something that helped him slide through the tight places."

"There'll be curses on the treasure, then."

"That's the way these things are done."

"There'll be ill-tempered ghosts in the neighborhood."

"What are murders for?"

The Eagle sort isn't uncommon. Usually he tries to parlay his lucky genetic draw into a big, fast score. Manipulating the fall of dice is a favorite pastime. Hobbling around on crutches after getting found out is another.

"Also, if you ask me, it couldn't be much of a treasure, even if it hasn't been found. They figured wealth different back then."

"Indeed. And here's a thought." Which he didn't bother to relate.

"Well?" I snapped.

"Just checking to see if you've taken up your partner's evil habit of reading minds. Or have started reasoning from the available evidence."

"Not me."

"Silver, Garrett. Silver. You said it. They figured wealth differently in primitive times. Silver wasn't worth much."

It was now, though. Even with the war seemingly settled and the mines solidly in Karentine hands, the silver shortage was severe. The disappearance of silver coinage threatened to strangle business.

Silver fuels most heavyweight sorcery. Lately its value has been on a par with gold. The Royal Mint has been valiant in its efforts to produce alternate means of exchange, some of which are pretty unwieldy.

Silver. An apparent opportunity to unearth an old cache would excite all sorts of greed.

"By the Devil Harry," I swore, rolling out one of my granny's favorites. "Maybe you just tripped over the real core of the thing." That might even explain why a nose-hoister like Marengo North English would take an interest in the daughter of the notorious Maggie Jenn. It might explain why all this insanity had come to a head at this point in time.

The silver shortage wasn't likely to ease soon. Maybe never if the wrong people grabbed control of mine production.

"But what do I do about it?" I muttered.

Morley frowned my way. "Excuse me?"

"I think you're right. We have all sorts interested in Eagle's treasure because of the distorted metals market. People who wouldn't have given it a thought in normal times. Probably including my honey's daddy."

"Here comes that explanation." He stunned me by hoisting an eyebrow.

I got my breath back. "You been practicing."

"Almost forever. What about Chaz's father?"

"Call it intuition, but I'd bet your deed to the Joy House that what he really hated losing to the Rainmaker and Maggie back when was a first edition of the middle volume of *When No Ravens Went Hungry*. Which Emerald took when she ran away from home. Which she gave to Wixon and White for safekeeping, or they got it away somehow. That book is why I was hired. It's why Emerald was framed up with the black magic stuff. Cleaver knew where she was. He couldn't get to her. He thought he'd toss me in there to butt heads with the human rights guys and maybe break her loose."

I rolled right along till I took note of Morley's smug smile. He stared into infinity, listening with half an ear. "What?"

"I was right. It's another explanation. You realize your theories clash?"

"We're not talking mutually exclusive, though. We have a lot of secret motives driving people. You aren't helping me for the same reason I'm helping Chaz's pop."

"I won't argue that, though I wish I was. You made up your mind yet?"

"Huh?"

"About what to do now."

"I'm going to stroll out to this estate. See what Emerald says."

"Flashing more nerve than brains, Garrett. You're jumping into deep doodoo."

I laughed. The professional lifetaker couldn't say one word that flowed easily from naughty six-year-olds. "With my eyes open."

"You're doing a Winger on me, aren't you?"

"What?"

"You've got an angle."

"I'm just not as paranoid as you. And I know how to talk to those people. You stroke their egos and let them think you love the cracks in their pots and they'll act like you're visiting royalty."

Dotes didn't agree but didn't argue. He suggested, "Maybe you'll take Saucerhead along?"

65

I didn't take Saucerhead. I didn't need any help. I was just going to chat with a teenage girl.

I didn't take anybody but me because I sold myself the notion that Marengo North English was committed to an old-fashioned, rigidly fair way of doing things.

So I fooled myself. Eagerness to meet Emerald Jenn didn't take me anywhere near Marengo North English. The estate belonged to the character who had sent his pals to roust me, a fact I could have determined had I bothered to do a little homework before hitting the trail. One Elias Davenport owned The Tops. Elias Davenport thought Marengo North English was a candyass who was just pussyfooting around the human rights thing. Elias was ready to *act*.

I didn't *listen* when Slither told me who brought Emerald's invitation.

Getting onto the grounds of The Tops wasn't a problem. Managing a sit-down with Emerald was a little more trouble.

Silly me. I thought they'd let me see her, get me out of their hair, forget the whole thing. I had no idea they were out of control.

I figured it out, though.

The guys who smiled me through the manor gate shed their senses of humor when the gate chunked shut. Their eyes got mean. They kept on grinning, but the only part of the joke they wanted to share was the punchline. Kidney high.

The guys who'd visited my place ambled out of the shrubbery. Didn't look like their manners had improved.

They made me so nervous I hit them back first, shielded by the spell that put me out of focus to anybody trying to concentrate on me. Damn, that was a neat one! They hopped and flailed and swung and cussed and missed me like a bunch of drunks. Meanwhile, I was hard at work with my mystical headknocker, scattering unconscious bodies. Davenport's gardeners were going to be busy picking up fertilizer for a while.

I amazed myself. But we're all capable of amazing behavior once we're adequately motivated.

The Davenport mansion couldn't be seen from the gate. I undertook an odyssey across vast expanses of manicured lawn, maneuvering between sculpted shrubs and trees. Almost got lost in a maze created from hedges. Gawked my way through an incredible formal flower garden, thinking half the people of the Bustee slum (every one a human) could've supported themselves farming that ground.

The Davenport place was enough to kindle revolutionary fervor in a stone. Something about it shrieked contempt for every race.

I didn't march up to the door and hazard the mercies of another Ichabod. Once I spied the main house I resorted to my old recon training. I sneaked and hustled and lurked and tiptoed till I got to the rear of the house. There were plenty of people around and plenty saw me, but they were cringing characters wearing tattered Venageti military apparel. They were employed at such socially useful tasks as trimming grass with scissors. They pretended blindness. I returned the favor, didn't see their humiliation.

Never had I thought prisoners of war might be re-

duced to this. Not that I had any love for the Venageti. You got people chasing you through the swamps,
trying to kill you, making you eat snakes and bugs to
stay alive, you won't develop much sympathy if they
stumble later. Still, there was an essential wrongness
about their situation. And the core of it, I suspected,
was that Elias Davenport wouldn't distinguish between vanquished foes and the "lower orders" of
Karentines.

Elias must have had him a cushy desk mission far
from the fighting back when he was serving his kingdom. Most ruling-class types get out to the killing
grounds and discover that when they're cut they bleed
the same as any farmboy or kid from the Bustee.
"Sharp steel don't got no respect," one of my ser-
geants used to say, wearing a big-ass grin.

I found a back door that wasn't locked or guarded.
Why bother? Who was going to do a break-in in this
loony nest? Who would dare discomfit Elias
Davenport?

(The name was a cipher to me at that point.)

I don't mind folks being stinking rich. I'd like to get
there someday myself, have me a little hundred-room
shack on a thousand acres well stocked with hot and
cold running redheads and maybe a pipeline direct
from Weider's brewery. But I expect everybody to get
there the same way I would: by busting their butts,
not by burying some ancestor, then raising their noses.

I know. It's a simpleminded outlook. I'm a simple
guy. Work as hard as I need to, look out for my
friends, do a little good here and there. Try not to
hurt anybody needlessly.

That house was a house of pain. You couldn't help
feeling that as soon as you stepped inside. Sorrow and
hurt were in its bones. The house now shaped its in-
habitants as much as they shaped it.

You find houses like that, old places possessed of
their own souls, good or evil, happy or sad.

This was a house possessed by disturbing silence.

It should have had its own heartbeat, like a living thing, echoing comings and goings, creaking and rattling and thumping with the slamming of distant doors. But there were no sounds. The house seemed as empty as a discarded shoe—or Maggie Jenn's place up on the Hill.

Spooky!

I started thinking trap. I mean, those guys had been ready at the gate. A minute stalling around while somebody ran to the house, supposedly for permission, then they were all over me.

Was I expected to get past them? Was I supposed to walk into ... what?

I grinned.

Saucerhead says I think too much. Saucerhead is right. Once you commit, you'd better give up the what-ifs and soul-searchings, do your deed and scoot.

I moved into the silence carefully, wearing a renewed grin. If I ever name my jobs, this one would have to be the Case of the Burglar Who Was the Good Guy. I was sneaking into every place I came to.

Not that I wanted it that way. People made me.

66

I didn't have the strength to lift my eyes in search of the source of the voice that said, "You're a resourceful fellow, Mr. Garrett. And remarkably adept with a truncheon." The speaker had the nasal drawl of an old-line aristocrat, scion of a lineage dangling down from the age of empire.

I barely retained the presence to wonder what had happened. One moment I'm trying to conjure a good rationale for my breaking and entering habit, the next I'm in a cold red place of echoes, tied into a hard chair, limp as a wet towel. No mental effort, however mighty, supplied details of intervening events.

"Pay attention, Mr. Garrett. Otto."

Fingers ungently buried themselves in my hair. The helpful presumptive Otto yanked my head back so I could do my blurry-eyed mouth-breather act in full view of a guy on some kind of elevated seat. He was just a terrible silhouette against a scarlet background.

I was too dizzy to be scared. But I was hard at work trying to get control of my head so I could be. I recognized my surroundings from whispers about it by some less than sane acquaintances connected with the Call. I was in the star chamber of the Holy Vehm, the court of honor of the Call. Not being an active member, I had to assume I stood accused of being a traitor to my race. Only . . .

The way I'd heard, there were supposed to be three

judges. The spook in the high seat should've been the meat in a lunatic sandwich.

I focused my whole being on my tongue. "What the hell is going on?" I don't know why I bothered after the first few words. They all came out in a language even I didn't understand. But I'm an optimist. I kept trying. "I just came here to interview Emerald Jenn." Had I been given the tongue of a dwarf while I was out?

"It takes the spell a while to wear off, lord," a voice announced from behind me.

Can a silhouette glower? This one did. "I am aware of that fact, Otah." Otah? Like in Otto pronounced backward?

I sagged again. A hearty yank on my hair helped me stay focused on the silhouette. A guy started slapping my cheeks. That helped, too.

Oh, heavens. Another guy stepped in to help the first. He was an exact copy of the other. Identical twin thugs? This concept was too bizarre. Time to wake up.

I woke up but only to find identical cretins waling on my face. My tongue had lost its skill at dwarvish. I began to render opinions in only mildly accented Karentine. And my mind raced far ahead of my laggard tongue. "Do you realize to whom you are speaking?" the silhouette demanded. The guy sounded put out.

"I did, I could've said something more specific about angles of approach and velocities of insertion."

The silhouette snapped, "Control your vulgarity, Mr. Garrett. You broke into my home."

"I was invited. To see Emerald Jenn."

"I'm afraid that won't be possible."

"She not around? Then I'd better be going."

Davenport chuckled. He must have done well at crackpot villain school because he brought it up from the pit, full of evil promise. "Nonsense, Mr. Garrett.

Really." He gave me another chuckle just as good as the first. "Where are the books?"

"Huh?"

"Where are the books?"

Uh-oh. "What the hell you talking about?" I never thought anybody would ask *me*.

"Do you think me naive, Mr. Garrett?"

"I think you're a raving lunatic." Pow! Right in the chops. Chaz was going to have to do without a kiss next time we ran into each other. I guess Otto or Otah didn't agree with me.

I also thought Davenport was a damned fool. He'd made the same mistake the Rainmaker's thugs had back in the dawn of time, when they hadn't emptied my pockets. His boys were fools, too, because they hadn't bothered to check. Davenport wouldn't have risked breaking a nail touching me himself.

I had my stuff.

I just needed to get to it. Nothing to that. Once I shed the twelve nautical miles of rope cocooning me.

"Where are the books?"

"Give me a clue, Bonzo. What the hell you talking about?"

"Otto."

Pow!

As the constellations faded I suffered an idea. It wasn't the best I'd ever had. It was going to hurt.

Typical Garrett plan.

"The books, Mr. Garrett. Unaltered first editions of *When No Ravens Went Hungry*. Where are they?"

"Ah. Those books. I don't have the faintest." Could he have been behind the wrecking of Penny and Robin?

"I don't believe you."

"You want to sell me the idea a jerk as stinking rich as you needs to bust people up and kill them and steal old books over a treasure as puny as Eagle's?"

"The record says that treasure consisted entirely of

silver, Mr. Garrett. To accomplish its purpose, the Call needs that silver."

I lost my focus as I intuited the nature of his interest. He meant to become the boss crackdome.

Silver was the fuel of sorcery. Black magic lurked behind the Call. Maybe the silver shortage was holding the Call back more than was any excess of reason, humanity, or common decency. Maybe the guy who brought the silver in would own the Call. And maybe whoever ran the Call would own the kingdom if the lunatics got their racist revolution rolling.

"Marengo North English tell you to find it?"

Elias Davenport said nothing for a moment, which confirmed what I'd guessed. Then, still not speaking, he came after me. He didn't exactly bound my way, though, and when he stepped into a better light I saw why. He was probably around when Eagle sneaked off with his slaves.

He had a bulging, throbbing vein in his left temple. I suggested, "Don't have a stroke, old-timer."

Shucks. He didn't. He just got *really* mad. He made a gesture that must have meant punch Garrett in the face till you turn him inside out because the twins really went to work.

Felt great when they took a break. Gave me a chance to spit the blood out and suck some air.

"Where are the missing pages, Mr. Garrett?" Davenport was shrieking now.

67

Yep, it sure wasn't the cleverest idea I ever had and it sure did hurt. I decided I'd strung them along long enough. "Shirt. Pocket," I gurgled. "Box. Key. To house."

Davenport was right in my face, gagging me with foul breath caused by rotten teeth. He was so eager he didn't wait to hear the story I'd rehearsed. He pawed my shirtfront, found the box I wanted him to find, snatched it, and stumbled toward his high chair. Or whatever he called it.

My ears rang like church gongs, but I still heard the buzz when the whatever in the box woke up. The twins heard it, too. "Please be careful, lord!" one squealed. "There's something wrong. . . ."

Davenport fumbled the box open. I knew when because he screamed to let me know.

If I hadn't hurt so bad I might have felt sorry for him, such was the agony and despair in his shrieking.

One of the twins squeezed my throat. "You better make it stop. . . ." He went to work on his own screams before he made his point. That aggravated his backward named brother, who stepped up to maul me, only just as he reached for me he got a big look of surprise and started howling himself.

I never did see what got them. They'd tied me up real good. I do know the uproar attracted people from elsewhere because I heard new voices rushing around asking what the hell was going on. Then some of those started screaming, too. Their shrieks left the star chamber and dwindled.

Circumstances being what they were, I couldn't do much but sit around plotting my next move. Despite my discomfort I even fell asleep (I'm too tough to pass out) for a while. Probably a long while, though in such situations the whiles tend to stretch longer than they really are. I doubt more than a couple months passed in the outside world.

My big worry was the killer bug coming back, but when sounds disturbed my nap I learned that I had more immediate troubles.

"Got yourself in it real deep this time, Garrett." Winger strolled around me while her boyfriend watched from a distance. This was my fault. I'd made it possible for him to track me again. But I'd had my reasons. They just didn't make much sense now.

Winger wasn't suffering from any overwhelming passion to set me free, so I didn't act like I was as aware as I was. I was confident that Otto and Otah had left me looking well done. I turned loose a moan that didn't take much acting.

"Think he told them anything?" the boyfriend asked.

"What? How? He don't know anything."

The boyfriend grunted but sounded unconvinced. But he'd been on my tail closer than Winger had.

Winger grabbed my hair, lifted my head. "You in there, Garrett? Where did everybody go? Where did you send them?"

"Hon? Wrong question," the boyfriend said. He was over by the judge seats now. "Ask him what he did to them."

Winger went to check what was left of Elias Davenport. "What would do that?" She glanced back at me nervously.

"I don't think I want to find out," the boyfriend

said. "There are more over there. Four, maybe five. All torn up the same way."

"What did you do, Garrett?" Winger actually seemed concerned. Like maybe she was worried I might do it again. Maybe she was getting old.

I noticed that nobody was straining to get me loose yet. Winger asked, "They have all three books, Garrett? Or just the one the girl took from her mother?"

I wondered if I could lure her close enough to bite her.

"Hon!"

I couldn't turn, but I heard them come into the chamber, at least four men. Maybe more. Things froze. Winger was at a loss for what to do. I wondered why.

"Holy hooters! Looka them gazoombies!"

The Goddamned Parrot! What the hell?

Slither moved across my field of vision. For reasons known only to him he was lugging a military entrenching tool. He brandished it at Winger but didn't say anything.

Next thing I knew Morley was lifting my head, looking into what little could be seen of my eyes behind the swelling. "He's alive. Get him untied." A second later, Ivy and Spud went to work on the ropes holding me. They didn't seem to be in any hurry, though. "Saucerhead. Cover that door. Sarge, get that one over there. Looks like they went that way when they ran." He lifted my head again. "What happened?"

"Mimble sif cubby bunka snot!" Oh, damn! I was speaking fluent dwarvish again. Courtesy of my swollen face and tongue. But this time *I* knew what I was trying to say.

The Goddamned Parrot definitely possessed a working man's taste in femininity. And he wasn't going to let Winger get away without hearing about it.

She and her boyfriend were making sure they didn't do anything to get anybody upset.

Ivy and Spud kept fumbling and I kept trying to tell them not to be so thoughtful of the ropes, just haul out a knife and hack away. They didn't understand me, though. They kept doing it the hard way till Morley snapped, "We don't have any call to be careful of property, Narcisio. The owner is over here full of holes. A prosecuter won't worry about a damaged rope."

Saucerhead scolded Winger. Spud and Ivy tried to get me to stand. Morley faked looking like my wellbeing was the only thing of any interest to him. Slither wandered around muttering and waving his shovel. Sarge studied the expanse of his belly, maybe contemplating drawing a map.

Somebody somewhere shrieked in pain, somebody not there in the chamber but not real far away. Then another somebody screamed. Then we heard a furious buzzing, getting louder. My pet was coming back.

That fool Slither chuckled like this was what he'd been waiting for all his life, like he'd finally found his chance to use that killer comeback he'd thought of fourteen years ago. He told Sarge, "Better get outa the way, Ace, 'less you want it coming right through you."

Sarge took a peek at the bodies. He opted for discretion and cleared the doorway fast.

An instant later, something came through that doorway so fast it was barely a blur on a course that curved right toward me.

Slither swung his shovel. He stepped into it, got his arms extended and all his arm and shoulder strength into his swing.

Splang!

He dropped the blade of his tool to the floor and began cleaning it with the edge of his sole. His grin was huge. "There's how you handle them little boogers. They're fast and they're mean, but you can handle them easy if you just don't take your eye off them. I guess nobody around here must've seen them before."

Morley asked me, "Will you be able to walk?" He left Slither's strokes to the others.

I tried to ask the big guy where he'd run into those devil bugs before. Only dwarvish came out. Morley thought I was talking to him. "Good," he said. "You're tougher than you let on. Let's get out of here."

A good idea. After making sure nothing got left that would implicate any of us. Though I couldn't see how it would be possible for some of us not to be connected somehow. There were live people in the house still, and the POWs outside could be forced to reveal whatever they had seen.

Winger and her pal tried to turn sideways and thereby become invisible, but as TG Parrot reminds us occasionally, Winger in profile is hard to miss.

"We can leave you here," Morley told her. "There is ample rope now." He indicated the chrysallis I'd left behind.

"No. No. That's all right." Winger didn't want to stay. It was likely the weather would turn real nasty soon. The Call wouldn't know that Davenport had gone rogue. They would want a blood price paid.

It was all my fault. I admit it. If I'd been able to shuffle my feet faster, we might not have had to play in the rest of the game.

68

We never cleared the star chamber. I mean, I was heeling and toeing as fast as my heels and toes would cooperate, but we just didn't get far.

Morley howled suddenly. That startled the rest of us into freezing. Another bug? I thought. How? . . . Dotes leapt into the air. As he peaked out, a guy stepped into the chamber and presented his chin for kicking. He dropped like his legs had been cut off, but a whole herd of brunos stormed in over him. He was going to have bruises on his bruises and powdered bones if he ever came around.

Everybody but me got into the mix-up. Ivy and Spud propped me against a wall and jumped into it. I stood there so focused on trying not to fall that I had little attention left for rooting for my pals. I did try fishing something useful out of my pockets, but the effort was too much for what meager energy I had left.

I didn't even realize who this bunch were till Mugwump appeared admid the second wave. By then things had grown too serious to be settled amicably. We had dead and bad hurt people everywhere, mostly on the Rainmaker's side, but poor addlepate Ivy made a wrong move and accidentally got himself stabbed in the back about forty-five times. The Goddamned Parrot ripped the scalp off the character responsible, a ratman so weeded up he couldn't stop stabbing long enough to brush the bird off his head.

Slither picked Mugwump up and tossed him about forty yards, then headed for the Rainmaker, who had just made his appearance, had spotted Saucerhead already headed his way, and was concentrating on evading that behemoth. Then Cleaver saw Slither coming, squealed and ducked between the two big men. I wondered where he had managed to find so many brunos stupid enough to work for him, what with everybody in TunFaire out to buy his head. Maybe he put on his girl disguise and let them think they were working for a woman.

His thugs sure were disconcerted when they recognized my friends.

Slither was altogether too determined to pay Cleaver back for Ivy and his own old grievances. He threw pieces of people right and left as he stormed after the Rainmaker, but he never quite caught up and he didn't keep an eye out behind him. I tried to yell, but my yeller was out of action. Just as he grabbed the raving runt somebody stuck a dagger in his spine. I would have cried for him if I could. Instead, I spent my last reserve to bawl, "Pwziffle pheez!"

Slither was a dead man, but he didn't let that slow him down. Nobody he could reach enjoyed the experience. He broke Morley's arm. All Morley was trying to do was get out of his way.

I tried to get my feet moving toward a doorway, but they just wouldn't cooperate. Davenport's headbusters must have given me something more than a beating. I had a bad feeling I wasn't going to make a getaway the way I had at the Bledsoe, even with Slither demolishing the unenthusiastic crowd Cleaver had brought.

I did reflect that everyone who'd ever trailed me seemed to have come to the Tops. I guess everybody thought I was about to glom the mystic trilogy.

About the time Slither wound down, one of the Rainmaker's thugs got a knife into Winger's boyfriend. She had a blood fit, jumped some guys trying to get away. They didn't make it.

I glanced around. It looked like Winger and Grange Cleaver were the only players not hurt. Saucerhead was leaning against a wall, looking pale. Sarge was down, but I couldn't tell how badly he was injured. Spud, with T.G. Parrot on his back, cussing, was on hands and knees not having much luck getting back up. Morley, despite his injury, was making sure none of Cleaver's thugs ever inconvenienced him again.

Looked to me like the whole thing had been a blood sacrifice in aid of nothing. Nobody profited and a lot of people lost big.

I was proud of myself. With a little help from my pal the wall I was making headway toward a door.

Movement took all my concentration. I had to stop to catch up on the struggle.

Things had not gone well. The floor was littered with bad guys, but the good guys had vanished. Unless you counted the Goddamned Parrot, who swooped around exercising the slime end of his vocabulary. I wanted to yell for Morley or Winger or somebody, but my yeller was out of commission.

Cleaver was still upright. So was Mugwump, mainly because he was so wide he rolled back upright whenever somebody knocked him over. Slither had had the right idea: just hurl him through the wall.

Where were my pals?

Ducking somebody else's pals?

I was moving again when Cleaver and Mugwump got to me, just as yet another gang of players plunged into this pool of insanity.

I recognized one, Belinda's specialist, Cleland Justin Carlyle. I assumed his companions were Outfit heavyweights, too.

Now I knew why my friends had disappeared.

Carlyle and his buddies had blood in their eyes. Events at the Jenn house had to be avenged. Somebody messes with syndicate guys, somebody has to pay. Didn't matter than much who.

Mugwump grabbed me by the shirtfront. He snagged Cleaver with his other hand. He hauled us both to a door. I don't know what he was thinking. I guess he was a little distressed. He chucked Cleaver through, held me a second, rasped, "Even, fella," and chucked me, too.

Into some damned hidey-hole behind the ever-loving thrones of the lunatic judges of the Call. Not through an exit.

Mugwump made a whole lot of noise negotiating with the boys from the Outfit. Then the debate ended. Utter silence filled the universe . . . unless you counted the sonofabitching Goddamned Parrot, who wouldn't shut up if you drowned him.

Everybody else had left him behind. Maybe I could work it that way, too.

Not bloody likely. Not with my luck. The gods probably had me whipped up on like this just so I couldn't shed that talking feather duster.

It was real tight in that closet. It hadn't been intended to take two people. It hadn't been intended to take two people of the sorts we were.

Well, Mugwump *had* put me close enough to Cleaver to choke him, which is where I'd wanted to be for a while. But I didn't have the strength.

The squabble between the parrot and sanity continued as I blurted, "Get your hands off me!" I suppose prowlers nearby, possessed of sharp ears, might have heard. Might have understood, too. My diction was improving. "I don't play your game."

Cleaver giggled.

And I blushed red enough to glow in the dark. Because Cleaver's movements had nothing to do with me. Sometimes the man did dumb stuff, but only a total damnfool would make a pass with slavering cut-throats stalking around looking to chop him into beagle chow.

"Garrett, you're a wonder." That was the voice of Maggie Jenn, sizzling like a red hot poker. "Maybe I will lay hands on. If we get out of here."

"Back off!" I barked.

He backed. But his Maggie voice chuckled wickedly. Evil, evil person. A moment later, he became all business. "You have your strength back?"

"They gave me something. I'm not going to be any good for anything for a long time."

"We have to step out of here sometime. And I don't have so much as a nail file."

I said "Fooey!" which is dwarvish for "Oh, shit!" Getting out was a significant goal. Out of the closet—out of *that* closet, damn it!—out of the Tops, maybe even out of the province for a while, all seemed attractive goals. The mess here was beyond any cover-up now.

The closet door whipped open.

Light poured in. It nearly blinded me. I could barely make out the silhouette of somebody short and impatient. The Goddamn Parrot swooped past, cussing.

69

"Get out of there!" a hard voice snapped. I shuddered—then recognized the voice.

"Relway?"

"Yes." The little halfbreed secret policeman was curt always, impatient forever. "Move it."

"I wondered if you or the firelord's men would turn up."

"Direheart's guy was the first one here: you. And I find you in a closet with some bimbo in yet another place where we're gonna need wagons to haul the stiffs off."

Relway's men helped us out of the closet. They were particularly solicitous of the bimbo.

I covered my surprise. They said Cleaver was a master of disguise. Here was proof. That bit of wiggling in the dark had been him rearranging his clothing and donning a black wig. He looked like the devil woman lurking around many a man's fantasies.

Relway said, "I wouldn't be here if it wasn't for who owns this place. Block kowtows to the panjas, but I . . ." He stopped before he wasted half an hour on a favorite gripe.

"Panjas. I haven't heard them called that since I was a kid."

"Call me old-fashioned. What's your story, Garrett?"

"The girl I'm looking for was supposed to be here. I got a letter supposedly from her. Wanted me to come talk. I came. Some thugs grabbed me, I woke up here drugged to the gills, tied into a chair. They started asking questions that made no sense. Then a bunch of people busted in, there was a fight, somebody cut me loose maybe figuring I was one of their guys. I headed for cover since I wasn't in any shape to help myself."

He seemed somewhat less than convinced that I was telling the whole story. Can't figure why. He showed no interest in Cleaver and didn't ask questions about known associates of one Garrett who might have been seen lurking.

I asked, "Why is Elias Davenport of interest?"

"He's a lunatic panja who makes the rest of the Call look like a social club. He's behind most of the rioting. What kind of magic did they use?"

"Magic?"

"Something made a lot of corpses. Put holes right through them. No weapon will do that."

"Didn't play no favorites, neither, Lieutenant," one of Relway's men observed. Relway grunted.

I said, "I never got a good look, but I thought it was a giant bug. Some guy took it out by whacking it with a shovel." Said guy and his guilty tool weren't lying all that far away. Relway stepped over for a moment, scowled down.

He asked, "You get what you came for?"

"Hell, no! Never saw her. I came straight here. Wherever here is—I never saw the in-between."

Again Relway's look said he lacked conviction in his acceptance of my tale. People just don't take your word anymore. "That so? I'll be busy picking up the pieces here now. I'll want to talk later. Meantime, you might report to the firelord. I have a feeling he's uncomfortable with the bloodshed that follows you."

"I can go?"

"Just don't go so far I can't find you."

"Perish the thought." I tried to recall old war buddies who lived outcountry and might put me up.

"Garrett."

I stopped oozing toward the doorway. "Yeah?"

"Unusual mix of stiffs. You happen to notice who brought them in here?" His tone and expression suggested his thoughts were on a plane not even vaguely connected to my own.

"Not really. Not that I recognized."

"Any centaurs? Anyone with an unusual accent?"

"Huh?" He really was somewhere else.

"You see anybody might have been a refugee from the Cantard?"

"Not that I knew was. Why? What's up?"

"There's cause to think the refugees have organized for their own protection. Directed by fugitive Mooncalled officers."

"Oh." Now wouldn't that be the bloom on the rose? TunFaire hiding Glory Mooncalled's survivors. "Interesting notion." Relway would give it up as soon as he identified a few bodies.

I resumed traveling. I made sure I kept a deathgrip on my bimbo. And a close watch on her free hand, lest it dart into her bosom in search of some equalizer.

Cleaver always had a fallback.

70

Looked like Relway had brought the secret police cavalry brigade. Must have been ten thousand horses outside the manor house. Every damned one gave up tearing up property to glare malice my way. I limped and lumbered in between police equipment carts and made my getaway before they could get organized.

They aren't so bright. If you catch them by surprise, you can get the best of them.

A guy had passed me while I was creaking up the stair from Davenport's cellar. He must have given the word I was free to go. Hardly anyone even bothered to notice me, except a few vaguely familiar guys who nodded.

Cleaver kept his lip buttoned till we were far from anybody who might listen in. "That was nice, Garrett. You could've ratted me out."

"I didn't do you any favor."

"I didn't think so, but I wanted to check." He made a feeble attempt to get away. You could almost hear him sorting options.

I glanced back. Those horses had decided to let me go. This time. They seemed nervous, preoccupied. Weird, considering this was a chance to hoof me some major grief.

Cleaver sensed my unease. "What's up?"

"Something weird here."

"You just noticed?" That in a Maggie voice.

"Besides our weirdness. Walk faster." I smelled politics. Relway was around. Relway's world didn't encompass good guys and bad. Heads there didn't get busted for profit but for the power to make people do what they were told rather than what they wanted.

I let myself become distracted. Cleaver tried to yank my arm out by the roots. He got loose. I chugged after him, running weakly. The front gate came in sight. The little villain was gaining when he went through. I kept on plugging. I could outlast him. I was used to running.

Galoop, galoop, I turned into the lane. And, behold, there was my pal Grange Cleaver, passing the time of day, ducking around and betwixt Morley, Sarge, and Spud, who were trying to surround him. Sarge and Spud seemed to be in moods as dark as mine. Morley, though, was grinning like a croc about to pounce on a not very bright wild pig.

Cleaver chopped him on the bum wing. He yelped. Cleaver pranced past and darted away.

"Hi," I puffed.

Morley said a few things. Surprised me. Spoke quite fluent profanity when he wanted. Then he added, "Your luck with girls never improves, does it! Even that kind runs away."

"He bet he could beat me back to town. I was gaining on him." There was no hope of catching Cleaver now.

"Of course you were."

"Where's Mr. Big, Mr. Garrett?" Spud rasped. The kid was putting on a show of boldly standing up to his pain.

"Damn! It's silver lining time." I glanced back at the gate. "If we're lucky, by now Relway has taken all the beak he can stand and he's twisted its fowl head off."

The kid glared daggers.

I asked Morley, "You going to be all right?"

"I'm giving up cartwheels. Listen. Somebody coming."

Turned out to be a lot of somebodies.

We faded into the woods opposite the Tops before another troop of Guards arrived, their mounts acting spooky. "Those look like regular cavalry," Morley whispered.

Did to me, too. "Relway is putting on a big show." I wondered if maybe there wasn't something to his paranoia.

"We better scat," Sarge suggested. " 'Fore they get so thick we cain't move."

Good idea.

"Not yet," Morley said.

Baffled, Sarge asked, "How come you want to hang out?"

Good question. We couldn't do ourselves any good.

"I'm waiting for Tharpe."

"He all right?" I asked.

"Was."

"How long we gonna ... ?"

"I'll let you know, Sarge. Garrett!"

I'd begun shaking, had lost focus. I had passed beyond the immediacy of the moment and had time to reflect on what I'd lived through. And on the fact that a couple of mentally handicapped guys hadn't made it. . . . "What?"

"You're the healthiest. Go watch for Saucerhead."

I sighed. I wanted to go home. I wanted to put myself to bed and sleep a week, till the pain and guilt were gone. Then I could get shut of this life. I could see Weider, tell him I was ready to take that full-time security job. They don't drug you and torture you and kill your friends at the brewery—and you're never far from a beer.

I found me a nice spot and settled to watch the manor gate.

I'd been there just seconds when buzzing flies and

an odd odor grabbed my attention. Well. Fresh horse
apples. And horsehair in the bark of a nearby tree. I
looked around. Leaves on the ground had been
turned. I found the impression of a shod hoof smaller
than that of any riding horse. The shoe style would be
recognized by anyone who had served in the Cantard.

It was a centaur's shoe.

The impression wasn't clear enough to tell me which
tribe, but that didn't matter. What did matter was that
a centaur had been watching the manor gate from this
same spot until very recently.

The ugly angles grew heavier by the minute. I
wanted away. None of this stuff out here had anything
to do with me and my troubles.

71

That misbegotten Saucerhead. He didn't bother using the gate even though there was nobody there to contest it. He came over the wall, down the lane. I noticed when a major tree branch suddenly dipped its chin in the dust. It popped when Tharpe let loose.

He was carrying somebody.

How does the man do these things? He isn't human. I limped over. "What you got?" Like I hadn't figured it out at first glance.

Her mother had told me that she looked like her only with less wear. I promise you, Maggie Jenn turned them to stone in her day. The kid made it plain why Teddy went goofy back when.

"Spotted her when we was sneaking out. I figured it wasn't right we went to all that trouble, so many folks got hurt, you didn't get a crack at what started it all."

His shirt wiggled, heaved. Something made an ugly noise. I had a bad feeling.

Saucerhead worsened it immediately. "Oh. Yeah. I brung your bird. I stuffed him in my shirt on account of he wouldn't shut up."

I brandished a fist at the sky.

The breeze in the boughs sounded like divine snickers.

Saucerhead asked, "You want the bird or the girl?"

"Looks like I got the bird already."

"To carry." He did understand, though. "The chit, she don't really want to come."

"No. And you with your sweet tongue."

She hadn't said anything yet. She didn't now but did flash me a cold look that made me glad she couldn't do what she was thinking.

"Give me the talking feather duster. I can't manage anything bigger."

"Suit yourself." Saucerhead had kept the girl on his shoulder, sack of grain style. He asked her, "You want to walk? Or do I got to keep carrying you?"

She didn't answer. Saucerhead shrugged. He hardly noticed her weight.

The others joined us, drawn by our voices. Spud fussed over the bird. Morley had rigged himself some crude splints. I gestured at the parrot. "My pal had to do me a favor."

Morley tried to chuckle. Pain got in the way. I asked, "Can you manage?"

"Just won't play bowls this week."

"Poor Julie."

"We'll work something out." He offered a glimpse of his wicked grin. "Let's roll. Before Relway realizes he's played it wrong and wants us to explain."

"What happened to Winger? Anybody see?"

Nobody had but Morley opined, "She got away. She has her own guardian angels."

"She gets Relway after her she'll need them." We walked as fast as we could with wounds and burdens, the Goddamn Parrot denouncing the whole bleeding world for all the indignities he'd suffered. Even Spud's patience became strained.

Sarge sneered, "Least it ain't blamin' everythin' on you no more, Garrett."

Morley eyed that jungle chicken like he was considering abandoning the vegetarian life-style. I told him, "Thank Saucerhead. *I* left it for Relway. They're perfect for each other."

Nobody laughed. Sourpusses.

"Was that the Rainmaker you was chasing back there?" Saucerhead asked. He spat a wad of sourgrass he'd been chewing. He remained indifferent to Emerald's weight.

"Yeah."

"That runt? Hey!" The girl was wiggling. "Knock it off." He swatted her bottom. "I always thought the Rainmaker had to be nine feet tall."

"With hooves and horns. I know. I was disappointed, too."

Morley snickered. "He sure was." I gave him a dirty look. He never let up, pain or no pain.

72

I lost the election. My place got picked for the human reassembly party. Morley hinted that he didn't want word of his injury getting out right away. He didn't want the wolves smelling blood before he was ready.

I bought it. He has his enemies.

I had trouble getting comfortable. My home contained too many reminders of Slither and Ivy.

"It wasn't right," I told Eleanor. "They didn't deserve it." I listened momentarily. My kitchen had become an infirmary. Saucerhead had recruited a defrocked doctor who imagined himself a crusty town character. He reeked of alcohol and hadn't stumbled against soap or a razor for weeks so I guess he qualified.

"Yeah, I know," I told Eleanor. "Life don't make sense, it ain't fair and don't ever ask the gods for dramatic unity. But I don't have to like it. Got any idea what I should do with the girl?"

Emerald was confined in Dean's room. She hadn't delivered a word yet. She wouldn't believe me when I said I wasn't on her mom's payroll.

Could be she didn't care if I wasn't. You snatch some people, they never do warm up.

Eleanor had no suggestions. I said, "I'd cut her loose if there weren't people out there who'd jump all over her." Eleanor did not disapprove. "Speaking of whom, I wonder how long it'll be before Winger turns up with one of her outstanding stories?"

I was looking forward to that.

Morley howled. There was a crash. I headed for the kitchen. Dotes began threatening bloodshed. "Not in my kitchen!" I yelled. I stopped to check on the Dead Man.

A bug darted across his cheek, hid behind his proboscis. If Dean didn't get home soon, I was going to have to clean him up myself. Maybe I'd bring him some flowers. He used to like bouquets.

The Goddamn Parrot started yelling louder than Morley. I told the Dead Man, "You're not earning your keep."

It wasn't pretty in the kitchen. All that whimpering and whining. The doc had finished, though. He was under an inverted wine bottle, using a half pint to clear his palate. I made a face. Even ratmen shunned the stuff he was swilling. "You all going to live?"

"No thanks to that butcher," Morley snarled.

Saucerhead asked, "You ever see him act like such a baby?"

"You oversized ... If brains were fire you couldn't burn your own house down." He jumped up on a chair and started ranting like some Holy Roller soul-scavenger.

I asked Sarge, "The doc give him something?"

Sarge shrugged. "Come on, boss. Give Doc a break. He fixed your arm. And he ain't been getting much work since they cut him loose from the Bledsoe."

No wonder he was drinking bottom of the barrel. He *was* bottom stuff himself. ... I glanced at Saucerhead. Doc must be some relative of his new lady.

Surly but silent, Morley paid his fees. Spud didn't look much happier. I decided to get the old boy out while Dotes was feeling generous. I got hold of Doc's arm and pulled.

"You really get the boot at the Bledsoe?" Hard to imagine that as possible, yet I'd met two such in just a few days.

"I drink a bit, son."

"No."

"Steadied my hands when I was young, chopping off arms and legs down in the Cantard, couple lifetimes ago. Don't work anymore, though. Barley kills the pain now."

He stepped outside, cloaked himself in what dignity he retained, started down to the street, stumbled, fell the last two steps. On her stoop, Mrs. Cardonlos paused to glare and nod to herself. I blew her a kiss. I studied the street.

It was hard to tell, but I thought I saw a few folks who didn't ring right.

Again? Or still? I eyed Mrs. Cardonlos again. Her being out on point might mean she expected further proof that Garrett was a peril to the neighborhood.

I shut the door, thoughtful.

I had an idea.

I headed for the kitchen. "Saucerhead, want to run an errand?" I showed him some shiny copper.

"Talked me into it, you smoothie. What?"

"Give me a minute. I need to write a letter."

73

At last the house was quiet. The mob was away. The Goddamn Parrot had a full crop and was sleeping. I was in my office sharing the silence with Eleanor.

Naturally, somebody came to the door.

"My answer from Chaz." Or maybe Winger, if her creative side was hot.

I was hoping she had a block.

I used the peephole.

Got it right first guess. Mr. W. Tharpe with mail.

I leaned into the gloom of the Dead Man's room. Vermin scurried. I told him, "I'm off. And she's the most beautiful blonde you never saw. Don't wait up."

He didn't wish me luck.

I left the house without so much as a passing thought about the gorgeous redhead stashed upstairs.

It was the best table in the place but still only the Joy House. You do business with a world-class sorcerer, you can be a little more comfortable doing it on familiar ground.

Conscious of their bid to go upscale, Morley and his thugs were on their best behavior. Puddle even donned a clean shirt and tucked it in.

The Firelord had dressed down. Excellent. I didn't want casual acquaintances getting nervous because of my contact with him.

He looked like a big old dock walloper.

With him dressed down and Chaz dressed up, nobody paid him much attention. Even I had trouble concentrating. "Excuse me?"

"I said I'm serving my own interests."

I recalled now. I'd thanked him for not making a show. "Oh."

"Believe it or not, there are people who might do me an injury if they caught me off my usual range."

"Really?" My gaze swerved back to Chaz. The woman had dressed to kill and was armed with her best assassin's smile.

"Hard to believe, right? Big old cuddle bear like me?" He turned to Morley, who hovered at the head of a platoon of ready servers. "I'm not real hungry tonight. I'll take half pound of roast beef rare, sides of mutton, and pork. No fruits or vegetables."

Morley went paler than a blanching vampire. He nodded sharply, once, some postmortum spasm. He fish-eyed me and my grin. His eyes were the lamps of hell. I decided not to rub it in.

I ordered one of the more palatable house specialties. Chaz followed my lead.

Morley stamped toward the kitchen, dragging Puddle, muttering orders. I wondered which neighboring establishment would subcontract Direheart's order.

I fought the chuckles as I brought the firelord up to date.

"You let him get away?"

"I didn't let. Let wasn't part of the equation. He got. You want, I'll take you to see him after supper."

Good Old Fred raised both eyebrows. But then he came after me about the centaur sign outside The Tops. His intensity confirmed my suspicions. He'd had definite reasons for coming home from the Cantard early.

In time, I led him back to the Rainmaker. He frowned, told me, "I'm generous to a fault, Garrett. Anyone will tell you that. Especially where my little girl is concerned. But I won't let you milk this forever."

"That's good to hear. 'Cause I'm sick of the whole damned thing. I've got one bruise too many, for nothing."

Morley returned to hover in time to overhear. He lifted an eyebrow.

I continued, "I'm closing this down soon as we eat."

Morley stifled his surprise, but Chaz and her pop both blurted, "What?"

"We eat, I take you to Cleaver, my part's done. You all settle up. I'm home having a beer before I hit the sack."

Direheart started to get up. He was ready.

Morley started slide-stepping toward the kitchen. Maybe he was headed for cover.

Chaz smiled like her brain had gone north. I'd begun to wonder about her. When her dad was around, she worked at cute and dumb.

"Sit down," I said. "Morley went to a lot of trouble with your order. And Cleaver will be there when we get there." Dinner hadn't yet arrived.

Morley could've been going to check its progress, but I wouldn't have bet two dead flies on that.

Nice of him to be so predictable.

After the Tops, I didn't have a trick left. What I hadn't used I'd lost or had taken. Might have been smart to see Handsome before dinner.

Too late now.

Dinner did come. I drooled over Direheart's while I choked down mine, a kind of souffle thingee I'd had before and hadn't found myself vomiting. . . . But this time somebody clever had chopped green peppers into the mix.

Morley looked so innocent I would've strangled him if I hadn't needed him.

I told Direheart, "There's no way you're going to get your book back. It's long gone."

The man was resilient. He displayed one scant instant of surprise. "Oh?"

"Near as I can tell, Maggie Jenn's daughter swiped it from Cleaver about a year ago, brought it to TunFaire, showed it to the wrong people, had it snatched by the human rights nuts." Which was true, to that point.

The Firelord smiled, in control. "I rather doubted I'd see it again, especially considering the bloodletting following it."

"Just wanted you to understand."

"Could you recover it if I hired you to?"

"I don't want the job. There're too many people ready to kill people over it."

Direheart didn't like what he heard. It wasn't Good Old Fred who laid that evil eye on me while he wondered what I was doing.

I saw him decide that I was too damned lazy to glom the book for myself.

The Firelord ate like a little dog trying to get his fill before the big dogs come. I ate at a leisurely pace, mostly staring at Chaz, who matched me bite for bite and stared right back, all but hollering her wicked intentions.

74

My stride faltered a few steps into the street. There should have been more people out. Some hint must have escaped the Joy House.

If the Firelord noticed he didn't let on. Maybe he didn't. He'd been in the Cantard forever. He'd be street naive.

Chaz was uncomfortable, though. She knew an off odor when she smelled one. The dumb blonde disappeared fast.

Considering my recent experiences, I didn't think it unreasonable to be alert to the point of frayed nerves. So, naturally, nothing happened. Except . . .

Wings beat the cool evening air. I braced for the advent of some batwinged demon belched from the hell of one of TunFaire's thousand and one cults.

The mythological is manageable.

Reality can be uglier.

The Goddamn Parrot plopped onto my shoulder.

I batted at it. "That goddamn Dean! Comes home in the middle of the night, lets that monster get loose." How did the damned thing find me?

The bird remained silent as it fluttered to Chaz's shoulder. It was unnatural.

"What the matter with you, bird? Chaz, he'll probably mess on you." This adventure wasn't going the way I'd hoped.

I didn't try to confuse anybody. I took the direct

route. We weren't halfway there when Chaz chirped,
"The Bledsoe?"

For Morley's sake—he had to be out in the darkness
somewhere—I replied, "Where else? He's used up his
other hideouts. And they don't know the real him
there."

Maybe. I'd begun to doubt my intuition already.

And I'd begun to doubt my good sense. Head into
danger with a sorcerer? I had no cause to trust Direheart. His sort were notoriously treacherous. And my
only insurance was a dark-elf with a broken wing who
might not remain devoted to my well-being once he
sighted the Rainmaker.

People say I think too much. No doubt. . . . Why on
earth did I think Cleaver would hang around TunFaire
after his latest misadventure? Why, of all places,
would he hide out at the Bledsoe?

I was one rattled guy when I pushed into the
Bledsoe receiving lobby. But I got my confidence back
fast.

Two steps in I spotted the female half of the elderly
couple I'd held captive at that ugly warehouse. She
spotted me, too, and headed out at her fastest shuffle.
She made her break for the stairwell I'd used to make
my getaway a couple of ages ago.

I won the race. "Hello again."

Direheart joined me. "Somebody you know?"

I offered a brief synopsis.

The Firelord surveyed the area. Our arrival hadn't
gone unremarked. Staff were gathering. I saw familiar,
unfriendly faces. "These guys can't take a joke, Fred."
He'd heard a bare bones version of my incarceration.
Those guys made the mistake of thinking it was pay-
back time.

The Firelord did one of those things that make regular folks uncomfortable when his sort are around. It
involved muttering and finger-wiggling and a sudden
darkness as black as a lawyer's heart. An instant after

that there were pillars of fire everywhere. Each contained a staffer who objected loudly. One unfortunate goose-stepped toward us. Direheart fixed it so we needn't hear his shrieks, but the guy kept on trying. He became a human torch to light our climb.

Chaz wasn't shocked. Her daddy hadn't disillusioned her.

The old woman broke away and tried to outclimb us. She failed. We passed the ward where I'd done my damage. The fixing up had hardly begun. I wasted a tear for Ivy and Slither.

The old woman suddenly wheeled like she had some mad idea about holding us off. She was a horrible vision, illuminated by the burning man. Her terror was absolute, but so was her determination. Death was in her eyes. She was a sow bear between hunter and cub. . . .

Bingo. I knew her now, nose to nose and her eyes on fire. Take away a few decades of pain and poverty and you'd have another Maggie Jenn.

Maggie hadn't said anything about her mother's fate.

75

The topmost floor of the Bledsoe was reserved for those who had no truck with poverty except by way of charity. It sustained an environment those folks would deem minimally adequate while they decided the fates of TunFaire's Waldo Tharpes.

We didn't need the burning man up there. Good Old Fred let him go. He collapsed, burnt meat and charred bone. Direheart ignored the old woman. We didn't need her. I tried to shoo her away. She wouldn't go.

Chaz wasn't frayed but didn't seem to be in close touch with reality anymore, either. During my own occasional brushes with sanity I'd begun wondering if she really was the girl for me. Her good points were obvious, but something was missing. When Good Old Fred was around she could turn into a zombie.

That green-and-yellow-and-red feather duster on her shoulder didn't betray any character, either.

Weird.

It got weirder.

First, Ichabod rematerialized. Pardon me. Make that Zeke. Maybe he came back from the grave. I'd thought he'd got plenty dead on the Hill. But here he was, all skin, bones, and white hair, trying to heft a big black sword that was beyond his strength. Good Old Fred did some evil things. That sword turned on Zeke. The old boy didn't even get out a good scream.

Mugwump emerged from the shadows. That human

stump was not in a good mood. (He had to be immune to disaster.) I was glad Fred was in between us.

Direheart wasn't ready for a Mugwump. Mugwump like to broke him into kindling before he conjured a bucket of eldritch fire. Mugwump ended up blind and burning. Direheart came away dragging a foot. He couldn't use his left arm.

Chaz showed no distress. She drifted along, gorgeous and empty and handy. Her dullness worried me more and more.

The Goddamn Parrot's silence didn't help.

Then we found a sleep-fuddled Grange Cleaver trying to pull himself together. Twenty feet separated us from him. Fred went out of control. He snarled, cursed, pulled a knife, and charged. Cleaver got loose from his cot and discarded his surprise. He pulled *two* knives. Lucky he wasn't one of those gods with a bunch of arms. He threw both blades. One knicked Direheart's right shoulder.

The blow wasn't crippling, but it did put the firelord's good arm out of commission. Sorcerers don't do well when they can't talk with their hands.

I closed in on Cleaver. Cleaver had another blade. He assumed a knifefighter's crouch, edged sideways. His eyes were hard, narrow, and serious. He didn't seem frightened.

Chaz said something. I told her, "Take care of your father. After you lock the door." The Bledsoe was crawling with guys who begrudged me my fine escape.

Direheart shook Chaz off. Calmly, he explained to the Rainmaker how he was going to feed his scumsucking corpse to the rats. Direheart had him an awful big anger about that old burglary.

Cleaver kept his knife weaving between him and me. He edged toward an outside wall. His caution seemed to be taking him back into a corner.

I got it way too late.

Direheart tried to let me become Cleaver's focus while he got ready to sneak in some deadly spell. . . .

Cleaver lunged at me. I stumbled back. Quick as a conjurer, the Rainmaker spun and flipped his blade. It sank into Direheart's throat.

I froze. Chaz screamed. Cleaver cackled, whirled, jumped out a window. Chaz grabbed me with one hand and her father with the other, pulled like I could do something.

A born gentleman, I grabbed blond hair and pried her loose. "You're a physician. Do what you trained for."

I threw one angry glance at the old woman, let her get on with her shuffling getaway. Oh, she was ready to go now. I went after Cleaver.

I'm not fond of heights—especially if Mrs. Garrett's boy might conceivably fall therefrom. I paused to eyeball the scaffolding below me.

Sneering laughter electrified me. I dropped the eight feet to the highest level the workmen had reached. I made a lucky grab and didn't plunge sixty feet to the cobblestones, where shadows darted. I was too far up to recognize anybody—not to mention I didn't consider trying.

The Goddamn Parrot swooped past, dove through the scaffolding. He zig-zagged like a bat, let out one serious squawk as he ripped past Cleaver. The Rainmaker cursed. Softly.

I concentrated on not achieving the unexpected experience of flight. All my hands grabbed anything convenient. All my feet assiduously maintained contact with whatever lay beneath them. I stormed slowly toward the Goddamn Parrot's noxious racket.

Cleaver cursed again. He'd looked down into a dark future. Big trouble was waiting.

I checked the street, too. Its shadows harbored folks who wanted to talk to the Rainmaker up close and personal. They must have picked up a clue or two via denizens of the Joy House.

Instead of heading down, Cleaver fled around the

Bledsoe. Through one open window I spied Outfit hardcases on the prowl. Belinda must have had a crew on standby.

I don't quite get Morley's relationship with those people. He's no made man himself. He does them more favors than seems right.

The Goddamn Parrot kept beaking news of Cleaver's progress. I really wondered about that bird. This was out of character. His natural style would be to betray me, instead.

The thugs below couldn't see us. They tried to track the bird, too.

That hunk of spoiled hawk bait blew the big one. Cleaver set an ambush. He let me slink right into it.

I was twice Cleaver's weight and twice Cleaver's strength and that saved me a three-story decline in fortunes. He threw himself at me. I grabbed some scaffold and absorbed the impact. I tried to glom onto him while I was at it but didn't do real well.

He ricocheted off me, banged into an upright, bounced back toward the stone face of the Bledsoe, let loose one whimper of outrage, dropped into the gap between scaffolding and building. He scratched and grabbed and banged around as he fell but didn't verbalize at all.

I followed more cautiously. The Goddamn Parrot flapped around me but managed to keep his big damned beak shut. I caught up.

Cleaver had broken his fall and dragged himself onto planking maybe ten feet off the ground. His breathing was shallow and rapid. He wasn't in good shape. But he bit down on his pain.

The vinegar was out of him, but I moved carefully anyway. A guy has the Rainmaker's rep, you're careful with him even after he's dead.

76

I dropped to one knee. A hand seized mine. I jerked away for an instant, startled. That hand was warm and soft.

"We could have had ... something. But you're ... too damned dumb ... Garrett. And stubborn."

I don't know about stubborn, but I was doing dumb pretty good. I didn't get it right away.

Cleaver was fading. Didn't seem right, considering his record. A long, agonizing cancer was more in order, not this just kind of drifting off into oblivion.

My hands were trapped. I didn't try hard to pull away. I had empathy enough to guess what was happening in Cleaver's mind. Though broken, he pulled himself toward me, closer, closer ...

Realization came slowly, sort of sideways, without generating much shock. This creature desperately grasping at one final moment of human contact wasn't male at all.

I held her. I murmured, "Yes, love," when she returned to her notion that we might have had something remarkable.

I'd been wrong from the beginning. But so had all TunFaire. Past and present, high and low, we'd all seen only what society had conditioned us to see. And in her madness, she had exploited that blindness.

There never was any nasty little villain named Grange Cleaver. Not ever. Never.

I shed a tear myself.

You had to if you encompassed any humanity, recognizing the enduring hell necessary to create a Grange Cleaver.

You could weep for the pain of the child while knowing you had to destroy the monster it had become.

77

I lost Chaz at the Bledsoe. I don't know why. Maybe, emotionally, she chose to blame me for what had happened to her father.

Her medical skills hadn't been adequate.

Whatever the reason, the magic failed that night.

It was not one of my better nights. I blew the rest of it retailing explanations. Seemed anyone who'd ever heard of me or Grange Cleaver wanted all the dope. I was actually pleased when Relway materialized.

He was a magic man was Relway. People vanished in droves.

"It's all straightened out now, Garrett," Colonel Block told me. I was visiting him again. After having been allowed another ten hours of cell time to ripen. I'd had to do my time with the Goddamn Parrot, too. "Weren't nearly so many bodies this time." He looked at me expectantly.

I tried not to disappoint him but kept it short and got out. He wasn't much interested. Didn't even ask much about the Tops. He was preoccupied with the racial strife.

I headed for home. I didn't manage to leave the bird of doom behind. For no obvious reason, that breathing feather duster didn't have much to say. Even while we'd been locked up he'd held it down most of the time.

Maybe he was sick. Maybe he had some terminal bird disease.

I couldn't be that lucky.

Dean didn't respond when I pounded on my front door. Irked, I used my key, went in and stomped around hollering and cussing till I was convinced the old boy wasn't there after all. There was no sign he'd come back.

Huh? How'd the bird get loose?

Add another puzzle. Why hadn't Emerald taken advantage of my extended absence? The kitchen suggested that she had visited several times and was less than fanatical about order and cleanliness. But she hadn't tried to bust out.

Strange.

Stranger still, T.G. Parrot went to his perch without a squawk.

That was more than strange. It was suspicious.

"Justina? I need to tell you something." It wasn't going to be easy.

She was seated on Dean's bed. She looked at me without emotion but with what seemed too-knowing eyes.

Straight ahead seemed the best way. I told her.

She continued to look at me, apparently unsurprised.

But she did love her mother—despite knowing the truth about Maggie Jenn and Grange Cleaver. She broke.

I held her while the tears flowed. She accepted that but nothing more and never said a word, even while I led her to the front door and told her she was free to go.

"Chip off the old blockhead," I muttered, a little put out, as I watched her fade into the crowds. "Oh, but she was beautiful, though."

I was in no way pleased with the case. I don't like unhappy endings even though they're the most common kind. And I wasn't certain that much had been settled or wrapped up.

78

I locked myself in. I didn't answer the door. I just used the peephole whenever some sociopath compulsively exercised his knuckles. I argued with the Goddamn Parrot. That squawking squab was slower than normal but nailed me with the occasional zinger.

Suspiciouser and suspiciouser.

Ever bold in the face of despair, I sent a letter up the Hill. Never got so much as a "Drop dead!" back.

And I'd just about decided Chaz was the lady for me. Oh, well. Live and learn.

I asked Eleanor, "Don't know what she's missing, does she?" That killed the ache, boy.

I swear Eleanor sneered. I could about hear her whisper, "Maybe she does."

I got the distinct feeling Eleanor thought it was time I stopped being stubborn about not apologizing to Tinnie Tate for whatever it was I didn't know I did, or maybe never did.

"Or I could look Maya up. She looked good the other night. And she's got her head on straight." Eleanor's smile threatened to become a grin.

I broke training once, allowed one special visitor inside. You couldn't refuse the kingpin of crime. Belinda Contague spent an enigmatic half hour at my kitchen table. I didn't disabuse her of her notion that, with the invaluable assistance of my acquaintance Morley Dotes, I'd engineered the fall of Grange Cleaver just for her. I guess for old time's sake.

She's one spooky black widow of a gal, bones of ice. Probably a real good idea she decided we should stay "just friends." Anything else could turn fatal.

Belinda expressed herself the one way she knew well, learned at daddy Chodo's knee. She gave me a little sack of gold. I passed it quickly into the Dead Man's care.

The Rainmaker business had been profitable, anyway.

Days slipped away. I sneaked out on several little errands, each time discovering that I still had one watcher on me. Becky Frierka was determined to collect her dinner. I saw no evidence her mother discouraged her from dating older men.

Mostly I kept it up with the bird and Eleanor, then went to reading with a frown that threatened permanent headache. I began to think Dean wasn't coming home and Winger might actually have the sense to stay away from me. Or maybe her luck had run out.

"It's gotten awful damned quiet," I told Eleanor. "Kind of like in those stories where some dope says, 'It's *too* quiet. . . .'"

Someone knocked.

Starved for real conversation, I scurried toward the door. Hell, a night out with Becky didn't sound that bad anymore.

I peeked. "Well!" Things were looking up. I yanked the door open. "Linda Lee Luther. You lovely thing. I was just thinking about you."

She smiled uncertainly.

I grinned. "I've got something for you."

"I'll bet you do."

"You're way too young and beautiful to be so cynical."

"Whose fault is that?"

"Can't possibly be mine. Come on in here. Got a story to tell you."

Linda Lee came in but made sure that I saw she still had her cynical face on. And that after she'd come all the way down to see me.

The Goddamn Parrot let out a whoop. "Hey, mama! Shake it up!"

"Stifle it, catfood." I closed the door to the small front room. "You interested in a new pet?" So happened I knew she had a cat.

"If I wanted one that talks, I'd pick up a sailor."

"Marines are way more interesting." I set us up in the kitchen, which was clean. Life had been that slow. I poured Linda Lee a brandy. She nursed that while I talked about the Rainmaker business.

One of Linda Lee's less blatant charms is her ability to listen. She doesn't interrupt and she does pay attention. She didn't comment until I paused to freshen my beer and pour her a dribble more brandy. Then she cut right to it. "What did you find when you went back?"

"Wreckage. The Guard tore the Tops up. Sending a message to the Call. Most of the Venageti were still there. They didn't know where to run. Guys like them could turn out to be another big headache. Come on to my office."

She gave me a kind of puzzled look, like my office was the last place she expected to be lured. She stretched like a cat as she left her chair. Woo!

I got my breathing under control. "Plop it into that chair." I squeezed around and into mine, dropped a hand down under my desk, dragged out one of those masterpieces that had been giving me wrinkles. "Look at this."

"Oh, Garrett!" She squealed. She bounced up and down. She squealed some more, jiggling deliciously all the while. "You found it!" She dashed around the desk and hopped into my lap. "You great big wonderful hero."

Who am I to complain? I had an idiot bird in the

next room covering that. He went to carrying on like he was being murdered. I smirked and surrendered to Linda Lee's excitement.

When she paused to catch her breath, I leaned down and coaxed another book out of hiding. "Apparently nobody who knew those were there survived the excitement at the Tops. None of the interested parties thought to check, either." At least they hadn't before the notion came to me.

"This is a true first, too! I've never seen a *Raging Blades* before. Where did they find it?"

"It's the book Emerald stole from her mother. Her mother stole it from Firelord Direheart. No telling who he stole it from. The boys at Wixon and White got it away from Emerald somehow, but she complained to her pals in the Call. That wasn't real bright, but how many kids her age, spoiled the way she was, have a full ration of sense?"

Linda Lee snuggled down and opened the book.

"Wish you'd treat me that tenderly," I observed.

"Oh, no. I'm not going to be tender at all." She purred and turned a page.

I stretched down and retrieved the third book of the trilogy.

"*The Battle-Storm!* Garrett! Nobody's had a complete set for three hundred years." She let *Raging Blades* fall into her lap and grabbed *Battle-storm*. I leaned back, relaxed, felt smug.

I got so relaxed I almost dozed off while Linda Lee sighed over her treasures.

A squeal of fury ripped me out of a reverie wherein I stood idly by while my old pal Winger enjoyed her just deserts. "What?" Silly me, for a second I thought she'd stumbled onto the secret of Eagle's treasure.

"This is a forgery! Garrett, look at this page. It shows a watermark that didn't appear till two centuries after Eagle's sagas were recorded." She seemed totally deflated.

"You were floating a yard off the floor when you only thought you had your *Steel-game* back. Now you've got two originals and a copy. . . ."

"Grrr! Yeah, you're right. But it really makes me mad. It isn't really all a copy or forgery. Part is original. You see what they did? They took out some pages and replaced them with forgeries."

I showed more interest then. I leaned over. She was examining the book I'd seen at Wixon and White, not, as I'd expected, *The Battle-storm*. "Emerald's book. Any idea how long ago it was altered?"

"The paper is old. It's just not as old as it ought to be. And if you look really close at the ink, you can see it isn't nearly as faded as it should be."

"Never mind the paper, love. I wanted old paper I'd steal an old book somewhere and scrape some pages down." Which is what master forgers do when a document has to look old.

"Oh. You're right." She studied the book some more. "I'd guess it was done quite recently. Somebody dismantled it, then put it back together with the new pages but couldn't match the original thread. This looks like a standard bindery thread like what we use at the library." She got after the other two books. "Damn! This *Battle-storm* isn't even a first. It's early, though. Maybe a student's copy of the Weisdal Illumination. And look! Somebody's tampered with *Steel-Game*, too. This whole signature is a replacement. They're going to hang me out, Garrett. This book was all right before it was stolen."

Interesting. It occurred to me to wonder if Emerald Jenn wasn't just as clever and conniving as the woman who'd borne her. "You do have a copy, though. Don't you? Squirreled away, just in case?"

Linda Lee scowled. "Maybe."

"Of course you do. It might be interesting to compare texts."

Up front the Goddamn Parrot started having a fit. Sounded like he was laughing.

Linda Lee hugged a book to her chest with one hand, gulped the rest of her brandy. "I need you to walk me back to the library."

"Right now?" Boy, don't whimper.

"There's nobody there." She took a big key out of a pocket in her skirt. "They're gone for the weekend."

My white knight side took over. "Of course I'll go with you. People kill people because of these books."

I locked my door, pranced down to the street. I waved to Mrs. Cardonlos. She hoisted her nose so fast she threw her neck out of joint. Then I stuck my tongue out at my own house.

I was sure the gesture wasn't wasted.

79

Two days passed. I was distinctly distracted when I headed home. I entertained only one non-nostalgic thought during the walk home. Was I the only sucker who hadn't known about the tampering with the books? Was that why nobody raced to the Tops after the Guard cleared out?

My door opened as I dug for my key. An old guy about as impressive as Ivy glared out at me. "About time you made an appearance. You turned this place into a shambles. The cupboards are bare. You didn't leave me a groat to shop with."

Beyond him, the Goddamn Parrot went to work on me, too.

"I had a feeling my luck wouldn't last."

"What?"

"You didn't stay lost." He'd aged, it seemed. Must have been rough work, keeping reality from setting in on the young couple. "You know where the money is."

He didn't like getting close to the Dead Man so he'd moped around hoping to con me. He didn't say so, though. "And you let someone use my bed."

"Couple of someones. And a good thing you took your time getting back. Your heart couldn't have taken being around the last one. You going to let me get into my own house? It's too early to be out here." My master plan included half a dozen hours in my own bed. I'd had to vacate the library at that worm-catcher time of day when only abnormals like Dean are awake.

"Mr. Tharpe is here."

"Saucerhead? Now?" Tharpe's attitude is more flexible than mine, but he isn't fond of getting out while there's still dew in the shade.

"He arrived moments ago. Inasmuch as you were expected shortly, I settled him in the kitchen with a cup of tea." Not to mention with most of the meager supplies I'd laid in recently, I discovered.

Saucerhead seldom lets a polite refusal get between him and a free meal.

I settled myself. Dean poured tea. I asked Tharpe, "What gives?"

"Message from Winger."

"Really?"

"She needs some help." He had trouble keeping a straight face.

"I can't argue with that. What's her problem? And why should I give a rat's whisker?"

Tharpe snickered. "Her problem is she needs somebody to bail her out of the Al-Khar. Seems she got caught digging around inside a certain country home and couldn't con the Guard into believing that she lived there. In fact, they were on the lookout for a big blonde who might be able to tell them something about what had happened there."

"I love it. But how did you find out? You sound like Colonel Block."

"Block came around to Morley's place on account of he couldn't find you here."

"Why'd he want me?" I could guess. Some little question about events at the Tops.

"He said on account of Winger claimed you as her next of kin when they asked who to notify she was inside so she could make bail or get bribe money for the turnkeys or whatever."

"I see." Boy did I believe that.

"And I went up and seen her. She already got into it with some screw thought he ought to collect special favors. Broke his arm."

"They charged her with anything?"

Tharpe shook his head. "Relway's just trying to squeeze her about what went down. But you know Winger. She's gonna be stubborn."

"I know Winger. She's lucky Relway's in a good mood these days. Things are going his way." Bad weather and ferocious behavior by the Guard and secret police had calmed the riots. For now.

There would be more. There had been no good news from the Cantard, like a resumption of the fighting.

"Yeah, I told her. Probably won't even beat her much."

"Then let her rot. No. Wait. Here. Run a message for me. Ask Block if he'll warn me before he turns her loose."

Saucerhead took my money. "How come?"

"So I can meet her coming out and tell her what a hard time I had getting her cut loose."

"You're wicked, Garrett."

"It's the company I keep. Been learning from a master." I jerked a thumb toward the Dead Man's room.

80

I shut the door behind Tharpe, locked up, strode to the Dead Man's door. I leaned inside. He looked the same: big and ugly. "I did all right for a guy whose help is so bone lazy. . . ."

I kept close watch. You were less at risk than you imagine. He puts thoughts directly into your head.

"After you started siccing the bird on me, maybe. By then I'd been through the hairiest part."

You understand that the Winger creature knew the Jenn woman and Cleaver were one, right from the start?

"Sure. And she knew you were snoring or she'd never have came in here to set her hook. She still has an angle. She thinks. Only Emerald was ahead of everybody, probably from before she ever left home."

Indeed. The female of your species, if at all presentable, is capable of manipulating the brightest of you.

"If that's her scheme. The Belindas and Maggies and Emeralds aren't that common, though. Luckily."

Far be it from me to note your eagerness to be suborned by such females.

"Yeah. But not far enough." In the other room the Goddamn Parrot started preaching what the Dead Man was thinking with one of his other minds. "Got to do something about that thing."

Somebody knocked. *Once more you have the opportunity to keep your word.*

Becky Frierka. And her mother, of course.

"Why should I be the unique truth-telling character in this part of town?"

As I went to the door the Dead Man sent, *The quest for Eagle's hoard is vain. The burial cairn lay on a slope overlooking Pjesemberdal fjord. That entire mountainside collapsed into the fjord during an earthquake three centuries before my mishap.*

"Really?" If anyone around today would know, he would. "Might have been handy to know that before. When you were watching so close."

Any adventurer who deciphers the sagas discovers the truth eventually. But so much blood gets spilled that the guilty dare not give warning to the world. He loaded that thought up with a cargo of amusement at human antics. But something unrelated leaked through, too. He was worried about the political climate. He had a stake in a tolerant TunFaire.

Details plucked from my mind didn't reassure him.

I pasted on my boyish grin and got to work. It took an effort to keep smiling. Becky's mother doesn't have a husband. She's actively screening candidates.

Couldn't have been a better time for my parrot to go berserk, for my houseman to show his mean streak, for my partner to be himself. Naturally, nobody cooperated.

I am nothing if not valiant in my efforts to do the right thing. Becky got her date, exactly according to terms.

81

Playmate was with me, trying to look fierce as a favor. So were Saucerhead and Winger, whom we'd collected from jail. Two weeks inside hadn't taught her a thing, which is why I had recruited my friends. I needed help getting Winger to go in the direction I wanted.

A couple weeks can make a big difference in the Safety Zone. Morley's place had a new name: the Palms. Scraggly palms in pots stood out front, already wilting in TunFaire's chunky city air. Street lamps had appeared. Elf-breed lads decked out like Venageti colonels stood by to handle horses and coaches, despite the time of day.

Playmate observed, "I don't think I'll feel comfortable around here anymore."

"That's the point," Tharpe said. "Dotes has got him some high-tone ambitions all of a sudden. No place here for the likes of us now."

I glanced at Winger. Still sulking, she didn't offer an opinion.

The interior of the Joy House had been redecorated to fake the inside of a lunatic's idea of some tropical shack. I've been to the islands. It didn't work. After Morley bustled us upstairs, so we wouldn't frighten the customers if any turned up, I told him, "There aren't enough bugs, old buddy."

"What? Bugs?"

"Tropical places got bugs. Bugs big enough you got to fight them for table scraps. Flies and mosquitos that'll hang you up in a tree for later. And lots of them."

"You can overdo atmosphere, Garrett."

"Bugs don't sell to the Hill," Saucerhead guessed.

Dotes scowled. Our presence made him uncomfortable. I hate it when people social climb. He asked, "What do you want?"

"Just a couple wraps on the Rainmaker thing. Winger's out, which you probably noticed. And all the trilogy books are accounted for, only somebody mutilated them. Which won't do them any good." And I briefed him on what the Dead Man had told me. Given their natures and acquaintances, these four would get the word spread. And people would stop following me around.

I'd begun to accumulate watchers again. I guessed the Venageti at the Tops had mentioned my visit to someone who cared.

Pained, Morley asked, "Seen the girl?"

"Vanished without a trace. Gone treasure hunting, I presume." I hadn't tried to find her.

"That's it?" He was puzzled. He didn't see my angle.

I didn't clue him in. "That's it."

"Then I have to rush you. I have a million things that need doing before our reopening tonight. One thing before you go, though. A favor I need desperately."

"You're starting to talk like those ferocious pirates. What?"

He faked hurt. "Friends are always welcome at the Palms. But we have to present a refined image. If you could dress a little more . . ."

I got no chance to respond because Winger unloaded first. "You guys ever stick a foot in a fatter load of camel shit? Can you believe this seeping sack of slime? You half-breed runt, I know who you are."

The lady is articulate in her own special way.

*   *   *

Winger and I came to a meeting of the minds, more or less. Playmate and Tharpe took off. I straggled homeward. Winger tagged along. She didn't seem eager to put distance between us anymore. "Garrett, it true, what you said about Eagle's treasure?"

"Absolutely. Came straight from the Dead Man."

She didn't want to believe me but decided she had no choice. I was too damned dumb straight-arrow. "That thing awake again?"

"*And* Dean came home. I'm back to being errand boy in my own house."

She snapped her fingers. "Shucks. Been a long dry spell, too."

I shook my head. This is where we started. "You never fail to surprise me, Winger."

"Huh?" She grabbed my arm, pulled me out of the way as a flight of pixies, buzzing like angry hornets, harried several centaur kids they'd caught stealing. Idly, I noted what looked like one of Relway's spooks trailing the action.

"Last time you told me that, I found out you had a boyfriend you never mentioned to anybody and he can follow me around like he's got me on a leash."

She didn't lie straight up. "Hightower? Wouldn't exactly call him a boyfriend. . . ."

"No. More like a sucker who thought he was. And got dead for his trouble."

"Hey! Don't you go climbing on your high horse with me! I seen you with your pants down."

"I'm just reminding you that people you care about get hurt, too, Winger. Lies can kill. If you have to lie to your friends and lovers to get where you want to go, maybe you'd better stop and give a good hard think about whether this is the road you have to follow."

"Stick it in your do-good ear, Garrett. I got to live with me. You don't." Which was about as close to an admission of error or offer of apology as anyone was likely to get out of Winger.

"When you came down here fishing me in, you knew Maggie Jenn was the Rainmaker. You figured you could work an angle, you being the only one outside her crowd that knew. I won't forget you trying to do that to me."

Winger never apologizes in any of the customary ways. "I found out by accident. Pure dumb luck. And nobody but her kid really knew for sure. Her old lady and Mugwump and a few others maybe had all the facts right there in their faces, but they didn't want to believe it. . . . What the hell am I doing? It's over. Done. We got to move on. All the crap that's going on around town now, this racist bullshit, there's got to be lots of opportunities. But I'll check it out later. Why don't you come on over to my place?"

A temptation, if only to find out where she lived. But I shook my head. "Not this time, Winger." The Dead Man wanted me to bring him up to date on Glory Mooncalled, events in the Cantard, and recent events in general, real soon now. I knew because he had the Goddamn Parrot following me around, telling me all about whatever notions happened to be bubbling through his feeble minds.

My worst nightmare had come true. I couldn't get away from him even when I was away from him.

Also, I needed to consult Eleanor on potential career changes. I had some ideas. At their root were the willies I got every time I thought about being caught inside the Bledsoe cuckoo ward.

If I had planned this thing out right, I would have been born rich and would have lived out a useless life as a wastrel playboy.

Doing that life somewhere besides TunFaire probably would have been a good idea, too.

Still, life won't be completely awful as long as I'm somewhere where they keep brewing beer.

FANTASTICAL LANDS

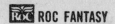

If you and/or a friend would like to receive the *ROC Advance*, a bimonthly newsletter featuring all the newest and hottest ROC books and authors, on a complimentary basis, please fill out this form and return it to:

ROC Books/Penguin USA
375 Hudson Street
New York, NY 10014

Your Address

Name _____

Street _____ Apt. # _____

City _____ State _____ Zip _____

Friend's Address

Name _____

Street _____ Apt. # _____

City _____ State _____ Zip _____